Forever Cursed

The Forever Series

2

Amber Paige

To those who never felt worthy, I see you.

And if no one tells you, I will: you are worthy.

Trigger Warnings

Absent parent, abandonment, burnout, emotional abuse, alcohol abuse, narcissistic tendencies, manipulation, and sexual content.

Chrissy's Playlist

Genie in a Bottle—Christina Aguilera
Sparks Fly (Taylor's Version)— Taylor Swift
Lovesick—Jenna Raine
Forever Drunk—Peach PRC
Friends—emma lov, Loote, JORDY
8 billion people—Kiran + Nivi
Perfect For You—Peach PRC
Creep—Kina Grannis
So High School—Taylor Swift
Pretty Bird—Miles Hardt
Too Good At Goodbyes—Sam Smith
The Way I Loved You (Taylor's Version)—Taylor Swift
Touch My Body—Mariah Carey
The Alchemy—Taylor Swift

Rome's Playlist

The Grudge—Olivia Rodrigo
Jungle—X Ambassadors, Jamie N Commons
Tear in My Heart—Twenty One Pilots
You're On Your Own, Kid—Taylor Swift
Daylight—David Kushner
Tarantino—PLVTINUM
The Man—The Killers
Movement—Hozier
Bloodshot—Here At Last
I Feel Good About This—The Mowgli's
Like I Can—Sam Smith
8 Letters—Why Don't We
Bang!—AJR
STUPID IN LOVE (feat. HUH YUNJIN of LE SERAFIM)
—MAX, HUH YUNJIN

Spotify Playlist Link

While the book takes place in 2016, I included current day music because it fits the characters' personalities and tastes. I write my stories based on vibes, and this playlist is a perfect mix of where I was when I wrote this book. So, have fun and enjoy!

Chapter One

Chrissy

"I'm cursed to be single forever," I groan as I lie on a beach towel beside Gwen.

I dig my left hand in the sand, warmed by the sun, and the ocean's waves crash like a harmony. I've always loved the beach. When we were kids, Mom and Dad would pack the car with food and beach toys, and we would spend the entire day lounging in the sand.

"You? Cursed? That's not possible," Gwen states as a fact.

I glance over at her. She sits under the umbrella, wearing a linen swimsuit cover-up and sunglasses, engrossed in a newly released book by her favorite author. I asked her what it was about, and she got all giddy. Her day was made, and she went on and on, talking about romance and magic. I don't read many books, but I may have to borrow that one when she's done.

Pursing my lips, I say, "I'm cursed and lonely—two things you know nothing about."

Right on cue, Ash jogs over, falls to his knees, and kisses Gwen as if his life depends on it.

"I take it back. I'm cursed to be lonely forever and constantly on the verge of throwing up."

I adore Gwen and Ash—I really do—but I would be lying if I said I didn't get a pang of jealousy now and then. I would kill to have someone look at me the way Ash looks at her. After everything they've been through, they deserve all the happiness in the world. That doesn't mean I can't loathe them for it every now and then. I know I'll never have what they have. I'll never find love that deep and real. My parents and them have something rare and almost unobtainable. I hope they know that.

"Whatcha girls talking about?" Ash asks with a hint of a smile.

"Chrissy thinks she's cursed," Gwen offers.

"Chrissy? Cursed? That's not possible."

"Watch it, Waylen." I point up at him from my spot in the sand. "I'm cursed and doomed. And I'll drag you both into the abyss with me."

"Dude, you ditched me!" His voice arrives before he does. Not long after, Zack—my twin—peers down at me with a grin of amusement.

"Hey, Chrissy. Are you okay? You look like you've been cursed."

I lunge upward to unleash my building attitude on him, but he runs away, barking out a laugh.

"I know where you live!" I shout after him, and he chuckles in response.

"Who cursed you?" Ash asks in that damn sweet tone of his.

I hunch over, my pout obvious as I stare at the endless ocean horizon.

"I did." I can't hide the whine in my tone.

"Why?"

"I let Miles go . . . again, and now I'm all alone." I peer over at Gwen, and she offers me a reassuring smile.

"You did the right thing; you know that."

And she's right. Miles and I weren't meant to be long term. I couldn't see myself walking down the aisle to him, marrying him, having his children. Miles is a great guy, and he deserves someone who will love him until the end of time.

"I know . . ." I mumble to myself.

Ash's phone rings, drawing our attention as he retrieves it from Gwen's bag.

"Hey, are you here?" Ash asks, standing up.

Gwen and I look at one another, confusion warping our expressions. "Who is he talking to?" we mouth at the same time.

Not long after Ash answers his phone, he whirls around with a bright smile.

"I'll be right back. Rome is here."

I'm so glad I'm wearing sunglasses because my eyes grow to the size of Florida oranges. Ash jogs down the beach, slipping in the sand.

Gwen smirks knowingly, her tongue poking the inside of her cheek. "Oh, this is about to be the best birthday ever," she chirps.

I can't pick my jaw up from the beach towel I'm sitting on. Rome and I are *friends*.

Friends who have cute nicknames for one another, like Bubbles and Sir Eats A Lot. I admitted my complex feelings toward him to Gwen last winter. Five months later, nothing has changed.

Since summer break started, I haven't seen much of Rome because he's always training or working out. Being one of the best wide receivers in the region is a tough title to keep up with, but he does it with a smile on his face and abs made of steel.

Anticipation churns my stomach into a nervous frenzy at the thought of seeing him. Rome has been my longest-lasting crush, which is an unusual occurrence for me. I think I have undiagnosed ADHD because my interest flips from one guy to another like there's no tomorrow. The fact that Rome has secured himself in the depths of my mind is both impressive and terrifying.

"Is it possible he got more jacked since the last time we saw him?" Gwen asks, and my head snaps to the right.

"What? Where? I don't see him," I whisper as I crawl closer to Gwen for a better look.

"Gotcha," she snickers.

"Gwen Roman, you daughter of a bitch!" Our combined laughter fills the air as our hands collide. "You're going to pay for that, missy."

"No way, bubbles!" Gwen chuckles as she topples on her back, still holding me back with her hands.

With my knees deep in the sand, a wide smile stretches across my face, causing my cheeks to ache.

"I was only gone for five minutes." Ash's voice brings me to a sudden stop. Gwen's eyes widen just as mine do. If Ash is here, that means that Rome is—

"Happy birthday!" Rome cheers.

"Okay, Chrissy, get off the birthday girl." Zack wraps his arms around my waist and pulls me off Gwen.

"She started it!" I tattle as he places me back on my beach towel; quickly discovering that Rome got Gwen a gift, and my heart melts.

"Thank you, Rome." Gwen's heart must also be a puddle because her tone is sweet and starstruck.

My eyes linger on Rome as she opens her gift. The first thing I notice is that he cut his hair. The last time I saw him, it was pulled back in a ponytail, nearly the same length as Gwen's shoulder-length waves. Now, it's short and neatly slicked back with a bit of height. He's wearing a white muscle tee with tropical green swim trunks. The sun casts a warm glow over him, accentuating the contours of his body.

Gwen's squeal frees me from my trance. When I look at her, she's flipping through a book. "How did you know?!"

"I'm an excellent gift giver." Rome beams.

"He's stealing my thunder. I told him that book has been on your TBR for months," Zack admits.

"But who told *you* that?" Ash fires back.

The boys go back and forth, not allowing anyone to steal the other's spotlight. Gwen and I glance at one another. This has been our life since Ash sat next to her in biochem. It's new, but at the same time, it's normal. Ash and Rome fit into our circle so easily. It's like they were always meant to be there.

"Well, no one beats what I got her." Ash grins as he pulls on his invisible suspenders.

Gwen's eyes bug out in response. As Ash opens his mouth, she tosses a beach towel over his head.

"Shut up, Waylen!"

"I don't want to know. La, la, la, la! I can't hear you!" Zack covers his ears as Ash struggles to untangle the towel from his face.

"I don't know why you boys are bothering. I won the gift exchange this year," I say with all the pride I can muster.

"What?! What did you get her?" Ash asks as he frees himself from the beach towel.

"The special edition of that princess book she enjoys so much."

I don't have many great qualities, but I'm proud of my gift-giving ability. The copy Gwen has is worn, tattered, and old. I know she'll never part with it, but she deserved a new, pretty edition. Even if all she does is look at it.

"She's right. Chrissy won long before you guys ever stood a chance."

"So, last night was—"

Gwen leaps off her towel and launches herself at Ash, shutting him up instantly.

"I'm going to throw up," Zack mutters as I fight back the reflex to gag.

"I think it's sweet." Rome grins as he watches the two of them smiling and laughing. "We all know Ash has been through a lot. He deserves this." Rome gestures toward them. "It's nice to see him smiling again."

I thought my heart melted when Rome gave Gwen his present. It's completely disintegrated now. I can't fight the grin that spreads across my face.

"Hey, Chrissy." Rome's tone is soft, eliciting chills along my skin.

When I meet his gaze, a lump forms in my throat. He offers a half smile, his lips gently curved. His green eyes gleam with natural warmth. I don't allow my eyes to trail over his sculpted body. I'll lose all of my motor functions if that happens.

"Hi, Rome." And there goes my ability to talk.

My voice lodges in my throat, and nothing I can do frees it. Rome has me in the palm of his hand, and he doesn't even know it.

"Hi Zack, how are you? I'm great, thanks for asking," Zack asks himself, but his words go in one ear and out the other.

It's not until Rome breaks eye contact that I remember to fill my lungs with air.

"Zack? When did you get here?" Rome teases, and I can't help but snicker.

Rome's eyes flicker in my direction, my cheeks reddening in milliseconds.

"Stay away from her." Zack's tone drops, and I swear, Rome gulps. "She's cursed."

Leaping off my towel, I run at Zack, who screams like a five-year-old girl.

"You're dead!" I shout, hurling myself on his back and rubbing my fist in his messy black hair.

"Get her off me! She might be contagious!"

Another set of hands wraps around my bare waist. Rome's deep, husky chuckle sets my body on fire.

"Chrissy can't be cursed; just look at her face."

His muscles are pressed against my back, and I'd give anything to feel his chest against mine, to feel his lips, to see his eyes darken in lust.

"Drop her. She's dangerous," Zack orders playfully.

"Rome would never drop—" I land back on my beach towel with an *oomph*.

"Ash, are you coming?" Zack calls out.

Ash and Gwen return, and after giving Gwen a loving kiss, he heads down the beach with Rome and Zack.

"Are you okay?" Gwen asks with a hint of laughter.

Watching Rome strip off his tee, I shake my head. "Definitely not."

Chapter Two

Rome

I need a break.

Wait, let me fix that.

I've *needed* a break since the end of last football season. While keeping up with my workout routine is easy, I need a break from the drills, memorizing plays, and all the hits on the field. My brain is exhausted, too; classes last semester were rough. I don't have any concerns about not being drafted into the NFL before I graduate. Still, any smart player has a backup plan, and mine is history.

I've always been fascinated by history, particularly the American Revolution. My fifth-grade teacher, Mr. P, made learning interactive and fun. We ran missions like the colonials and pretended to sneak past the English army. I love football, so I'll play until my body demands I quit. After that, I'll teach history and aim to be a great teacher like Mr. P.

When Ash asked if I wanted to join the crew at the beach for Gwen's birthday, I was all in. I adore Gwen Roman. She carried Ash out of the darkness of his mind. She showed him what love is and cared for him even when he lost faith in himself. If I could find someone like her, my life would be complete.

With a sigh, I drop all my dark thoughts and focus on the sign straight ahead.

Finding parking is easy. The beach that Ash praised up and down is supposedly always deserted, and I'm thankful he was right. I park next to him and pick up my phone to call him.

"Hey, are you here?" Ash asks, answering the phone within the first ring.

"Yeah, but I'm gonna need you to find me. I see your car, but not you," I say while gathering my things.

"We walked a bit farther down. Walk past the ice cream stand, and I'll be right there."

"Sounds good."

We hang up at the same time. Ash and I were close in high school. We've gotten close again since Zack brought him to the pavilion last September. Zack and I have always been friends. Our friendship is effortless. He's the kind of guy who will defend you until his dying breath.

Zack and I bonded in high school. We were partnered up during a science experiment. Mistake number one: We were complete goofballs and failed not only that project but the class. Ever since then, we've been best friends. He knows what happened with my mom, but I don't think he sees how it affects me to this day.

I was happy when I found out we were attending the same university, but over the years, we drifted apart. We didn't see much of one another until last year, and we snapped back together.

After locking up my car, I step onto the pier and walk down the withered planks. I hear her before I see her. Chrissy has a signature giggle—high-pitched and always filled with excitement. She's a literal ray of sunshine, a bubble of explosive energy. Her smile could light up a room that's only ever known darkness.

She's always been beautiful, but I didn't notice until last November. She was hunched over a psychology textbook, her nose wrinkled in deep thought. Her pen flickered away as she pondered over whatever thought ran wild in her head. I sat across from her in the library, but she didn't notice me until I spoke up.

"What's up, bubbles?" Since I met her, she's reminded me of Bubbles from *The Powerpuff Girls*. Always so kind, energetic, and sweet.

"What do you think of Piaget's theory?" she asked.

"I can't handle big words," I said with a small chuckle.

She grinned back, blushing, and she giggled.

I was done for. We exchanged numbers shortly after, and I've walked around with Chrissy in my heart for months, but nothing can happen.

So, when she appears in my line of sight, I push down any butterflies that attempt to emerge from the depths of my stomach. I put on my game face and meet Ash a few more feet down the beach. When he loses his footing, I can't help but laugh.

"I think Gwen's clumsiness is rubbing off on you." I smirk as I slip my sandals off and step into the hot sand.

"It could be worse," he says with a shrug. "Look at your hair!" He messes my hair with his hand, wearing the widest smile I've ever seen from him.

"Had to look more *pro*," I say with air quotes. That, and I was tired of combing through the tangles and sweat after every game.

"Remember me when you make it big. I kept and still keep you fed."

"I also get the feeling Max may sue me for eating his fancy yogurt."

Shrill laughter and squeals pierce the air as we near Gwen and Chrissy. I can't help but grin when we find Chrissy and Gwen swatting at one another.

"I was only gone for five minutes," Ash sighs while running his hand through his hair.

They freeze at the sound of his voice, and Zack barrels in to save Gwen from Chrissy's antics. She fights against him, trying to hide her amusement.

I didn't think it was possible, but Chrissy is more beautiful than the last time I saw her. Her blonde hair is long with tight curls, her lips are lathered in pink chapstick, and even though her eyes are covered with dark sunglasses, I can imagine the sparkle behind her lenses.

I shake my head and avert my attention to Gwen. "Happy birthday!"

She smiles up at me and takes the purple gift bag from my hands.

I don't know what she says next. My gaze and ability to listen are drawn to Chrissy. I feel her eyes on me, trailing from my hair to my pecs, leaving me hotter than I was a second before. I get the feeling she shares the same feelings as me because she's never quiet. Whenever I'm around, she gets shy, and it's fucking adorable. I'd give anything to hold her against me, to feel her body pressed to mine.

Fuck, I'm doing it again. *Game face, Rome, game face.*

Gwen's shriek brings me back to reality. "How did you know?!"

"I'm an excellent gift giver." I'm lying. I'm a terrible gift giver, but I don't want to burst her moment of happiness.

"He's stealing my thunder. I told him that book has been on your TBR for months." Zack says, completely stealing *my* thunder.

"But who told you that?" Ash chimes in, and before you know it, we're all going back and forth.

Chrissy pops in, and my voice cuts out. She's talking, but I can't hear what she's saying. Her beauty has stunned me.

Next thing I know, Gwen throws a towel at Ash's face, and they start to play fight.

"Hey, Chrissy." I can't hold it back anymore. I need to have her attention on me again.

"Hi, Rome."

And there goes my game face.

We don't pack up until the sun sets. Ash offers to treat everyone to ice cream before the trek back, and who am I to deny free food? It's practically against my DNA to refuse.

As I look out at the beach, I zip my hoodie and rest my elbows on the wooden rail. Night has settled in, giving the view an enchanting ambiance. The sky has become a vast canvas adorned with countless twinkling stars, and the moon casts a silvery glow upon the gentle waves lapping at the shore. The cool breezes carry the scent of salt and seaweed.

I perk up at the sound of my friends' laughter, prompting a weak smile. It's been so long since I felt truly at home, but in this moment, surrounded by laughter, I'm reminded of what it feels like. The salty sea air comforts me. My muscles relax the moment the scent hits me. When I was younger, my parents loved taking spontaneous beach trips. That all ended when my mom left. Ever since then, I seldom feel comfortable or safe.

Maybe that's the reason I don't date. I tend to keep girls I'm interested in more than an arm's length away. Perhaps it's best I leave the romance side of my life to casual hookups.

"Whatcha doing over here?" Chrissy jolts me from my thoughts.

"Just thinking."

With a wide smile, she hands me a waffle cone with chocolate soft serve and sprinkles.

"I don't think too often. It's not worth the headache," she teases before placing her spoon in her mouth. "Want to talk about it?"

"I just don't get out much. This is nice." I lick around the cone, snagging the melting areas before they reach my hand.

Turning around, I rest my back against the rail, and Chrissy does the same. I observe Gwen and Ash as they smile at one another. Zack is there too, but he's always grinning at something.

"They really are lucky," Chrissy mumbles.

"Why do you say that?" I know why *I* think Gwen and Ash are lucky, but I want to hear why Chrissy shares the same thought.

"They have each other. Can you imagine having someone to rely on day in and day out? Knowing there's someone out there who loves you as much as, if not more than, you love them? I watched that girl crush hard on him for years. I used to tease her about it, harboring a crush for so long. It's like she knew they were meant to be, and she waited until the time was right. But man, their journey was an adventure. A very fun, heartbreaking, and romantic adventure." Chrissy sighs before dropping her bowl in a trash can.

"I thought you and Miles were close to having what they have. Was I wrong?"

"We might have been close last summer, but it didn't click. I admire that man. I really do. He deserves someone who will look at him, well, like that." Chrissy gestures toward Ash.

He smiles softly at Gwen even though she's not looking. She's too busy bopping in place, eating her vanilla soft serve.

"I'm starting to think I can't do that for anyone." She turns, and her eyes meet mine.

A slight hitch of air passes through her lips, and I realize I've been looking at her the entire time. If only she knew the effect she had on people, the effect she has on me.

"Ready, guys?" Zack calls as he dunks his wrapper into the trash.

"You better not be driving," Chrissy groans before smiling at me one final time.

"Never again!" Ash threatens, eliciting a laugh from the entire group.

"I make one wrong turn, one time!"

"Down a one-way street." Chrissy pretends to cough to cover her words.

"Says the girl who didn't know the difference between the gas and brake pedal."

Chrissy lunges forward but stops when a gust of chilly air blows past us. With a harsh shiver, her teeth start to chatter violently.

"Chrissy, wait." I drop my ice cream wrapper and unzip my hoodie. I'm removing my arms from my sleeves when she turns around. "Here."

Chapter Three

Chrissy

What is happening? Why is Rome offering me his hoodie?

With an outstretched hand, his lips form a kind smile, but I can't move. "Chrissy?" he chuckles, and the noise spears through me like Cupid's arrow. "Take it. I can't have you shivering all night."

Forcing my legs to move, I wrap my fingers around the red jacket.

"What's the holdup?" Zack calls, making my face scrunch.

"We're coming!" Rome smiles down at me as I put his hoodie on.

His natural musk and ocean cologne surrounds me, and I inhale the scent. Turning around, Rome rests his hand on my lower back, and my cheeks react feverishly.

Was I just cold? I don't remember feeling cold.

When we catch up to the group, Gwen looks knowingly at me. Of course, she would notice Rome offered me his jacket. This girl has a knack for noticing things like that. Rome jogs ahead toward Ash and Zack.

I can't wipe the smile off my face when she wraps her arms around me. She squeals quietly, and I let my excitement bubble over.

"He's all I can smell right now." I take in an obnoxious breath, and Gwen snorts in response.

"Rome Carter, who would have thought?"

The two of us giggle and dance along the boardwalk the rest of the way. Thank goodness the guys don't find it suspicious. Ash looks back every so often and just smiles. Zack rolls his eyes, but I can see the hint of a grin. And Rome . . . Rome blushes when he sees me grinning ear to ear.

Maybe I'm not cursed after all. Maybe, just maybe, Rome has feelings for me, and there's a chance something could spark between us.

When we reach the cars, everyone piles the supplies in the trunks. Rome didn't bring much, so he starts his car's ignition and leaves the door open so the interior can cool off.

With outstretched arms, he pulls Gwen into a hug and spins her around. "Happy birthday! I hope you had a blast."

"I did, thank you," she chuckles.

Her feet meet the floor, and she wobbles from the sudden dizzy spell.

"I gotcha. In the car you go." Ash ushers her into the passenger seat. "See you, buddy!" Ash and Rome pat each other's backs as they hug one another.

"I'm going to miss you!" Zack says while wrapping his arms around Rome's waist.

"I'm gonna miss you too!" Rome nuzzles his head on top of Zack's and starts to fake cry.

"We have the pool party next week. Chill it with the bromance!" Gwen sighs from the car.

"Wait, I'm going to miss you too!" Ash runs into Zack and Rome and hugs them.

Gwen covers her forehead with the palm of her hand and shakes her head. It's a solid couple of minutes before the boys pull apart. Zack hops in the backseat, and Ash gets comfortable for the drive back home.

My eyes wander over Rome, and a spark of mad genius hits.

"Do you want company?" I ask while shoving my hands in my new jacket pockets.

Rome's brows raise, and he flicks his eyes over to Zack.

"Zack!" He jumps at the sound of my raised voice. "I'm going to accompany Rome on the drive back. See you at Ash's?"

"Whatever, woman. Just stop screaming at me." Zack groans and waves me off.

With a wide smile, I glance back at Rome. "Only if you want the company, that is." *Please want the company. Please want the company.*

With a soft smirk, Rome nods toward the passenger seat. "Get in."

Chapter Four

Chrissy

The windows are rolled down as we drive down the road, leaving the shore. I soak in the sea air, letting the breeze take my hair and toss it however it wishes. I would live on the beach if I could. When I was younger, I used to pretend I was a mermaid. Gwen and I would spend hours in the pool at home, splashing around and trying to do the iconic hair flip.

The road is dark; there are no streetlights on this long road. The faint lights from the car's dashboard and headlights create an eerie atmosphere, but with Rome, I feel safe, especially in his hoodie. I'm trying to memorize his scent, soaking it in.

My phone buzzes violently in my back pocket. I try to ignore it, but the relentless vibration shakes my bones. Shifting in my seat, I pull out my phone and see two messages from Gwen.

How's it going? ;)

Chrissy! Answer me, woman!

Are you alive? Say "pineapple" if you need help!

It's quiet.

There you are!

It's quiet? With you in the car? I have a hard time believing that.

Shut up, lol.

"Are you feeling okay?" Rome asks.

Peering up from my phone, I notice his eyes are still on the road. One hand is on the steering wheel, and the other rests on his lap.

Gotta go.

Wait, wha—

I put my phone in my shorts pocket before I can finish reading the text. Looking over at Rome, I work on summoning all my courage.

"I'm fine. Why do you ask?"

"You're quiet." His tone is soft and gentle.

"I'm just thinking." That makes him smirk and snicker. "What's so funny?" I ask with a hint of laughter.

"I thought you said you try not to think often," he says, and I purse my lips.

"This is one of those rare occurrences," I fire back, crossing my arms over my chest.

"You're adorable." His eyes scan over to me, lingering for a moment.

Adorable. My grandma calls me adorable. Normally, I wouldn't take such a compliment to heart. Although, the way

Rome says it, how he seems to admire me, I can't help the warm butterflies that whirl in my chest.

"How are you? The last time I saw you, your hair was down to your shoulders." I lean over to ruffle his hair, earning myself a chuckle.

"I'm doing okay. Football is intense. I feel like all I do is eat, work out, and sleep most days."

He does sound tired. I saw him two weeks after Christmas, and he was fine. What happened between then and now? Is football weighing on his shoulders? Or is it something else? A girl, maybe?

"I really needed this today. It was nice." He glances over at me and smiles. "I missed you, bubbles."

And there goes my heart, right out the fucking window.

"I missed you too." I try to hide the hint of longing in my tone. "You didn't have to cut your hair though."

"Do you know how hard it was to manage the tangles after practice? All the detanglers in the world couldn't help me!"

"You think you have an issue with tangles? Look at me! I'm a walking bird's nest." I shake my head and show off my tight curls. "Do you know how many combs I've broken over the years?"

Rome's laughter fills the car, and a rush of happiness makes me smile widely.

"Your hair *is* something else," he teases.

"I know. I'm a walking, talking mess," I joke, but deep down, I know it's true.

What kind of girl lets go of a decent guy because he didn't do something as simple as offer her his jacket on a chilly night? What kind of girl my age hasn't had one decent relationship? What kind of girl stares at her best friend and her boyfriend and wishes she had what they had? The answer is simple. This girl.

"You're not a mess, Chrissy," Rome states, pulling me from my thoughts. "You're a *hot* mess."

"Shut up!" I giggle while punching his bicep, but he's like a brick wall, and my knuckles almost crack. "Ow! I should have known better." I wince while shaking my hand.

"Sorry, Willows." He lets out an airy laugh and looks over at me.

"Don't be sorry. Ladies love muscles." Looking down at the hoodie I'm wearing, I wonder how many other girls have worn it. Rome is a sexy football player, so of course he would have fangirls. I don't know why I didn't think of it sooner.

"I don't care about that," he states, and my brow wrinkles.

"Really?"

"Really."

"Interesting," I say without thinking. I'm trying not to go all psych major on him, but my thoughts are running rampant. "And why don't you care?" I ask, trying not to sound like a therapist.

"I need to focus on football," he says with a casual shrug.

"Hmm," I muse as I try to pull the truth out of him because he's clearly lying to me. "You don't date? At all?"

"Nope."

"Casual hookups?"

"Not as often as I used to."

"Huh." I click my tongue in wonder.

"What do you mean, *huh?*" he asks with a laugh. "Wait . . . are you going all psychology major on me, Chrissy Willows?" he asks in disbelief.

"I can't help it! What twenty—wait, how old are you?"

"Twenty-one."

"What twenty-one-year-old guy doesn't have an interest in girls? Oh, wait." Is Rome gay? Fuck, this is embarrassing. Here I am, trying to capture his attention, and I'm not even his type.

"Hold on, missy. I never said I wasn't interested in girls. I said I needed to focus on football." He raises his finger and wags it.

"Huh," I repeat myself, and his smirk widens.

"Don't *huh* me. I am perfectly content with how things are going right now. Football, casual flings, classes, workouts, meal prep. I've got it down to a science."

"Sounds dull."

His light-hearted expression falters, and silence fills the car.

"I'm sorry. I didn't mean—"

"It's hard sometimes. Most days, I struggle because it feels like I'm running in circles," he admits. "But it's getting better now that I'm friends with Ash and you guys."

"I'm here for you, Rome. Whatever you need. You're always welcome to our outings." Reaching out, I squeeze his hand that's on his lap.

"I appreciate that, Wildflower."

"Wildflower?" I ask with an arched brow.

"It's a cuter nickname than hot mess. You're wild and pretty like a flower." He smirks before wrapping his hand around mine.

With a faint smile, I lean back into my seat and run my thumb over the backside of his hand.

Chapter Five

Rome

I dropped her hand after a few minutes, and the moment I did, I missed how her skin felt against mine. That was a terrible idea because now I want *more*.

I want to see where things may lead with us, but I can't for several reasons. The first reason is my deep-rooted fear that she'll up and leave me when I'm falling too deep. The second reason is football. I need to focus this year, especially with the NFL draft. The third, and possibly most important reason, is Zack. That guy is my best friend. What would he think of me if I went behind his back and went after his sister? How would he react? He'd probably kick my ass. It doesn't matter that I'm twice his size. Zack Willows would pummel me senseless, and I would let him. Friends don't do that to friends, no matter how deep the feelings may run.

I pull into the Waylens' driveway and leave the car running, stealing a glimpse at the woman in my hoodie. Even in the dark, she radiates pure light. She's playing with her thumbs and chewing on her lower lip. I'd give anything to weave my hands in her curls and pull her close. The desire to have her lips on mine starts to cloud my judgment.

With a soft sigh, Chrissy unzips the hoodie and frees her arms. "Thanks again," she says with a sweet yet sad smile.

"No problem." I take the jacket, and another moment of silence passes.

"See you on Saturday?" she asks as she opens the car door, preparing to hop out.

Stay, don't go, not yet. The words build in my throat, but I swallow them down. Instead, I give her a simple reply. "Absolutely."

And then she's gone. She walks up to Ash's home while I silently beg her to look over her shoulder. When the door opens, she enters with her head down. Zack pops his head out to wave goodbye. I raise my hand and put the car in reverse, wishing I had the guts to go after what I desperately want but can never have.

I don't turn the radio on during the drive back. I listen to the wind until I pull into the parking lot of my apartment complex. After grabbing my bag, I lock up my car and head inside. Taking the stairs, I climb four flights before I reach my door. When I open it, the smell of home greets me, and I can't help but feel relaxed.

I don't have a roommate, so I walk into silence daily, which isn't terrible. Most nights, I come home after practice and pass out. Today, though, I wish I had someone to keep me company. Someone who would talk my ear off, and I would return the favor. Someone who would laugh at my jokes and hold me in their arms as we lie in bed. Someone who would love me for me.

Walking across the gray carpet, I make the right into my bedroom. I turn on the box fan by the door for white noise and plop into bed face-first. Focusing on the fan's blades, I tune out my surroundings and fall deep into my subconscious.

"Where are you going?" I ask, trailing after Mom as she carries an oversized bag to the front door.

"Don't worry. I'll be back soon." She kneels before me and swipes my hair away from my forehead.

"But where are you going?" I sniffle as tears stream from my eyes.

Mom smiles and wipes my face dry. "I just need a little vacation. Dad will take good care of you while I'm gone."

"But he doesn't know our routine," I whine.

"Teach him."

"But, Mom—"

She interrupts me by kissing my head and wrapping her arms around me. "I love you, my little troublemaker." Her voice breaks, and when she pulls back, her eyes are watery. "Be good for Dad."

"But, Mom—"

My body jolts like it's falling, and I gasp for air. *Fuck, when did I fall asleep?* With a groan, I check my phone, squinting at the blinding light. 5:43. I have to be up in seventeen minutes for my morning run.

Sitting up, I run my fingers through my hair. Eyeing the fan, I suddenly feel like it's my enemy instead of a calming white noise machine. My skin starts to itch, and the walls begin to expand, reminding me I'm all alone. What would it be like waking up at Ash's this morning?

Knowing Ash, he would sleep in until noon. So, Gwen, Chrissy, and Max would be cooking breakfast in the kitchen. They would pull Ash out of bed so that they could all eat together.

"You're always welcome to our outings." Chrissy's words slice through my dark thoughts.

My lips quirk into a half-witted grin as an idea surfaces.

Fuck the run, I have a different set of plans for today.

Chapter Six

Chrissy

A polite knock on the front door startles me awake. I can feel my hair going in all sorts of directions. The tapping continues, and I shove my face into my pillow. I made myself at home on the couch last night and kicked Zack to the loveseat across the way. It's not my fault he has long legs. I like to stretch, dang it. He can suck it up.

The noise echoing from the front door continues, and I groan.

"Zack, get the door." I hurl a spare pillow across the room, hoping it hits my target.

An obnoxious snore is the only response, which only means that asshole won't be waking up anytime soon.

Flipping over on my back, I reach for my phone on the table and check the time. With a grumble, I sit up and stomp toward the door. "Who the fuck has the audacity to knock on someone's front door at seven in the morning?" I ask as I swing the front door open, quickly regretting my actions and choice of words.

"Morning, Wildflower," Rome says, beaming his flawless smile at me.

With wide eyes, I start to close the door, but he grabs the edge of it and chuckles. "Not happy to see me? I thought you were a morning person." He steps inside and drops his voice once he sees Zack is still asleep on the couch.

"I normally am, but I was out past my bedtime."

Spinning around, Rome takes note of my appearance and crinkles his eyes. "Love the hair." He tousles it and chuckles.

"I'm going to murder you," I try to threaten him, but my lips betray me.

"You would never." He grasps at his chest, playing inno-cent. "You'd be bored without me."

Well, he isn't wrong . . .

"Did you need Ash? He and Gwen are still passed out, along with the rest of the neighborhood."

"No," he replies.

I can't help but tilt my head. Why is he here at seven a.m. on a Sunday if he doesn't want Ash?

"Did you need Zack?" I ask, and he shakes his head in response. "Gwen, Max?"

"Nope." He rocks back and forth on his feet while shoving his hands in his dark blue jeans pockets. If he doesn't want them, does that mean . . .

"Me?"

"No."

What the fuck?

"I'm confused." I sigh. "If you don't want anyone in this house, why are you here?" His eyes flick over to the kitchen, and I get the hint. "You're hungry."

"Bingo, Sherlock." Rome strolls into the kitchen.

When he's out of sight, I jog up the stairs as quietly as possible. When I pop into the bathroom, I cringe when I catch my reflection. My hair is indeed going in different directions, and my eyes have dark bags under them. I work a comb through my curls to try and tame them, even though I won't be able to get them perfect until I shower. They need to be less, well, all over the place.

Once I manage my hair, I splash cold water on my face and jump up and down to wake myself up. Looking into my blue eyes, I repeat the affirmations Mom cemented in my brain from middle school.

"You are strong, kind, and beautiful. I love my hair, my eyes, and my nose. You are a badass." I might've added that last bit myself, but Mom would approve.

Stepping out of the bathroom, I remember I'm not wearing a bra. Gritting my teeth, I look around for something, *anything*, to cover my breasts that I'm sure anyone can see through my white shirt. My eyes land on Ash's door, and my lips turn upward.

I sneak toward his door and open it, praying those two love birds are decent. The last thing I need to see is my best friend and her boyfriend going at it. They're both hot, but I'm not into that kind of stuff.

With a quiet sigh, I peer around the room and thank the universe that Ash isn't as tidy as Max is. I grab a stray crewneck hoodie and give it a quick sniff test before putting it on. I can't help but smile at the two of them as they sleep peacefully.

After closing the door with a muffled click, I take the steps back downstairs and walk into the kitchen. I snicker when I spot Rome head first in the refrigerator.

"Don't touch that fancy yogurt. Max swore he'll end your football career if you do that again," I warn him.

Rome turns around, and I snort at the sight of the opened yogurt and spoon in his mouth.

"Too late," he says as he licks the spoon clean.

"Oh, Rome," I laugh.

"Don't tell him?" he asks with a mischievous smile.

I pretend to zip my lips with my fingers.

"That's my girl." He clicks his tongue and swings back around to face the fridge.

My girl.

Did he just call me that? Do I need to get my ears checked out? There's no way Rome Carter just called me *his girl.* Excuse me while I go faint.

Rome puts the yogurt back, closes the refrigerator door, and then looks through the cabinets. Sucking on the spoon that's in his mouth, he reaches for the chocolate chip cookies. My eyes fall right on his toned ass before they linger over the skin that is exposed under his shirt. His forearm muscles bulge under the sleeves of his simple forest-green T-shirt. His hips sway back and forth as he starts to snack mindlessly on cookies.

A goofy grin spreads across my lips as naughty thoughts circulate in my brain.

What would his skin feel like against mine? How would he feel between my legs? I bet Rome is the type of guy who ensures you finish first. And fuck, do I need that right now. Rome has been haunting my dreams. I find myself daydreaming about him, losing myself in these lustful thoughts. Maybe I'll get over him if I can get him into bed . . .

"Earth to Chrissy." Rome pulls me back to reality. His cheeks redden as he beams.

"Yes?"

"I think your blood sugar is low. You just blacked out. Here —" He leans across the kitchen island and offers me a cookie.

I take it from him, trying to ignore the heat that spreads into my fingertips from brushing against him. Taking a bite out of the soft cookie, I realize that fucking Rome won't be enough.

That man stitched his way into my heart like no one has ever done before.

It started in the library when he first called me Bubbles. After that, it was our back-and-forth texting. He would check in on me and make me smile without knowing that I needed it at that precise moment. We would send one another pictures and laugh for hours.

The thing is, I don't know anything about him, and it's infuriating. I'm an open book, and then there's Rome, shoving cookies in his face and housing his secrets in a vault. I don't know his favorite food, color, or subject. I saw very little of him in high school. Even then, he was always surrounded by other jocks.

"Take another one. I don't like that look you're giving me." Rome raises his brows as he offers me another cookie.

"What look?" I take the snack from his hand and bite into it. "I'm not giving you a look."

"You were squinting your eyes at me, and your nose wrinkled upward. It does that when you're in deep thought."

"And how would you know that?"

Rome lowers his gaze with a small grin.

"I didn't mean to give you a look," I say to try and ease his worries. "I have resting bitch face."

Rome's eyes flick back up. His cheeks are flushed, and his hair starts to fall over his forehead. I resist the urge to rake my fingers through his gorgeous blond hair, stand up, and walk to the cabinet.

"How do pancakes sound?" I ask, knowing for a fact he's still hungry.

"That sounds great. Thanks, Wildflower."

Wildflower. Just take my heart, Rome. For my sake, be still with the flirtatious remarks. I can't take much more of it.

Chapter Seven

Rome

I need to stop. The moment the nickname left my lips, Chrissy's face lit up and fell at the same time. I didn't think the motion was possible until she did it, but there it was as clear as day. Her lips tilted into an invisible smile, and her eyes glossed over in a daze. Yet, her posture stiffened, almost like she was waiting for someone to walk in and catch us in the act.

I should know better. Zack is in the other room. Ash and Gwen are upstairs. What would they have thought if they caught me calling Chrissy Wildflower?

Looking over at her, I'm mesmerized by her. She embodies everything good in this world, even as she curses under her breath because she keeps dropping random ingredients.

"Are you just going to look at me, or are you going to help?" she bites out while wagging a wooden spoon at me.

"Tell me what to do, boss." I stand at attention and salute her, earning myself an amused smile.

"Heat a pan on the stove for me and drop a tablespoon of butter in it."

"Yes, ma'am!"

Marching over to the refrigerator, I pull on the silver handle and grab a stick of butter. Fighting the desire to take the yogurt again, I close the door and glance around the kitchen for the pans.

"In the lower cabinet to the left of the stove." Chrissy directs without looking.

Dropping to my knees, I grab a medium-sized pan. Following her instructions, I place it on the stovetop, drop a slab of butter on it, and turn the heat on.

"What's next?" I ask while spinning around to face her again.

"Do you want *fancy* pancakes or boring pancakes?" Chrissy asks as she starts to dance to the music in her head.

"What are *fancy* pancakes?" I ask with a slight chuckle.

"You don't know what *fancy* pancakes are? Oh, this is going to be great." Chrissy jumps up and down as she approaches the fridge. "I'm about to blow your mind!"

"Chrissy, stop squealing!" Zack groans from the other room.

"Fuck off!" she hollers back, not caring about the level of her voice.

She beams when she looks back over at me. "Okay, mister." Standing on the edge of her toes, she spins me around, grabs me by my shoulders, and escorts me to a stool on the other side of the kitchen island. "You're going to sit right here."

I plop on the stool while she goes back to the stove.

"And watch the master at work."

I observe Chrissy as she chops up bananas to add to the pancake mix. My disappointment becomes evident because banana pancakes are not *fancy*. It's only when she dumps half a bag of chocolate chips in the mix that I perk up. Watching Chrissy cook is comforting. She hums a familiar tune and sways to the rhythm as she flips the pancakes effortlessly. It's not long before she has an entire stack set to the side, resting on a plate.

"Ready to have your mind blown?" she asks as she slides a dish across the counter with a neat stack of pancakes toward me.

The scent is heavenly—browned butter, melted milk chocolate, and ripe bananas. My mouth salivates as I patiently wait while she gathers a plate, utensils, and maple syrup.

Sitting next to me, she does a little shimmy, the kind of tiny dance a girl does when she gets food. "Go ahead," she says with a sweet grin.

Drizzling syrup over my food, I cut a rather large piece and cram it into my mouth. My eyes flutter closed, and my head rolls back.

"Fuck," I moan. "These are *fancy* pancakes."

She must have some special ingredient hidden up her sleeves. There's no way she only put bananas and chocolate chips in the mix. There's also a hint of cinnamon, vanilla, and something I can't identify, but it's on the tip of my tongue. Swallowing the piece in my mouth, I quickly go for another bite, not caring about the syrup leaving the corners of my mouth.

"So, you like them?" she giggles.

Nodding my head, I let out a "Mhm." Because that's all I can do at the moment.

"You're adorable," Chrissy mumbles with a sweet smirk.

Pointing at myself, I feign shock, and she laughs. "Me?" I ask while finishing the food in my mouth.

"Yes, you." She snickers while punching my arm. "Oh, god dammit." She shakes her hand off, and I chuckle. "I fucking forgot already. Apparently, I didn't learn my lesson last night."

"Sorry, not sorry," I tease.

Chrissy takes a bite from her food and continues to dance

in her stool. How can she make such a simple gesture look so cute?

"I have a question for you."

Yes, thank god. Please distract me from these thoughts.

"My mom used to make these when Zack and I were kids. Did your mom or dad have a special recipe they shared with you?"

I take it back. Can we go back to the distractions that were racing through my mind?

"No," I mutter, my gaze automatically shifting away from her.

"I'm sorry. I didn't mean—"

"It's okay. I just prefer not to talk about my parents."

The room falls silent, so quiet you could hear Pickles scratching at someone's door upstairs.

"Zack and I got lucky with our mom and dad. Gwen's parents don't pay much attention to her. Ash and Max's parents are toxic and secretive. I sometimes forget that not everyone grew up around rays of sunshine and rainbows." Chrissy reaches over and squeezes my thigh. "I didn't mean to upset you."

"It's okay." I force a smile and meet her gaze.

The light in her eyes dims, and the natural blush on her cheeks becomes more vibrant.

"It wasn't always bad," I start without thinking. "My mom used to make homemade pizzas. The dough and sauce were always from scratch. We would pick out our toppings and eat until our stomachs hurt." Why am I telling her this? How is she pulling these memories out of me? A strange sensation of safety wraps around me.

Chrissy reaches for my hand and traces her thumb over mine.

She would never judge me, and I know so much about her.

She can have this tidbit of information. Maybe then she'll understand why I opt to stay alone and single. "It was only after she—"

"Do I smell fancy pancakes?" Zack asks from the other room.

"Go back to sleep," Chrissy yells, but he's already on his way over.

"Don't tell me what to do, woman." Zack walks straight to the stack and moans when he places one in his mouth. Leaning his back against the counter, he perks up at the sight of me. "Hey, man. When did you get here?"

Chrissy removes her hand from my thigh. My muscles twitch from the sudden loss of contact. She runs her hands through her hair and rests her elbows on the counter.

"About an hour ago. You would have noticed if you weren't snoring," Chrissy answers for me.

"I don't snore." Zack defends himself before taking another bite.

"Yes, you do!" Gwen's voice sounds from upstairs.

"Where did you come from?!" Zack shouts so she can hear him.

"Your nightmares!" She cackles like a villain.

"Do you see what I have to deal with?" Zack asks me.

I throw my hands up, look down at my plate, and then pick up my fork.

"I'm going to plead the fifth and eat these fancy pancakes." My tone lightens, like the dark conversation Chrissy and I were just in the middle of didn't happen.

"See, Rome is smart. Take a few lessons from him," Chrissy lectures while pointing her fork at her brother.

Another pair of feet slap on the floor, and it's not long before Gwen strolls in wearing one of Ash's hoodies.

"Oh, pancakes," she says while pushing Zack out of the way.

"Hey!" he grunts.

"Fuck off, Willows," Gwen threatens while picking up a pancake and eating it dry.

"I was here first." Zack tries to grab the plate, but Gwen dodges his hands.

"I said fuck *off*. You're so selfish." Gwen bumps her shoulder into Zack, and it's not long before they're both fighting over the stack.

A smile spreads across my face as I watch the two of them. It must be nice to have a sibling, or in their case, someone who is like a sibling. It was only me growing up; being an only child isn't what it's all cracked up to be.

"I'm here if you ever want to talk," Chrissy whispers as the two knuckleheads across the way bicker.

With a grim smile, I nod at her. "I appreciate that."

I wish I could take her up on that offer, but I'll only bother her if I do. Sometimes, the past is meant to stay in the past. And my secrets are meant to remain secret.

Chapter Eight

Chrissy

The best thing about summer break is doing absolutely nothing. The last couple of days, I've been crashing the Waylens' pool. I was able to keep my dorm back at Castle Brook because I'll be participating in a psychology mentorship next week, but it gets boring when I'm there alone.

I managed to talk Max into letting us have a mini pool party today. He said that as long as no one fucks in the pool or trashes his house, he's cool with it. The only problem is a certain cat can't help but be the center of attention and create chaos in the midst of it.

"Here comes trouble," I warn Gwen as she opens the sliding glass door from the kitchen to the backyard.

With a brief squeal, she hurries outside and closes the door before Pickles can make a run for it. Pickles almost runs face-first into the door, and I can't help but chuckle at his attempt to join the party before it even starts.

"Shall I grab your floaties, Your Majesty?" I tease.

Pickles turns around and squints his lime-green eyes at me, like he's responding to my comment.

"Oh no, did I walk in on a Pickles versus Chrissy standoff?" Ash halts when he catches the two of us in the act.

"He started it," I say without looking away from this maniac.

The door slides open, but Pickles doesn't dare break our eye contact.

"Not again," Gwen sighs. "Come here, crazy boy." She picks him up, and he literally melts in her arms. "I'm going to put him in our room so he doesn't try to run away."

"Mama's boy," I snark while Gwen passes by, and that asshole tries to swat his paw at me.

I purse my lips together, and Ash chuckles when he catches the face I'm making.

"It shouldn't surprise me that the cat is your nemesis, but somehow, it does." He grabs a carrot stick and munches on it. "How many people should we expect today?"

"Yeah, about that." I throw a charming smile his way, hoping it'll ease the blow.

"Chrissy . . ." he chastises. "How many people did you invite?"

"Not that many, I swear!"

"How many?" He drops his tone to convey his seriousness.

"The usual suspects. Zack, Rome, *most of the football team*, and *twenty-some* of my friends," I mumble, hoping he doesn't hear me, but this is Ash we're talking about. This man hears everything.

"You better hope Max doesn't find out. And you better pray this house doesn't get trashed."

"I will take full responsibility. I can keep everyone in line, trust me."

Ash's eyes wrinkle behind his glasses, and as he finishes the carrot, he grabs the tray to bring it outside.

"I'm watching you, Willows."

"Don't worry, Waylen!" I throw him a thumbs-up when he manages to slide the door closed.

"Don't worry about what?" Gwen asks when she returns.

Smiling as innocently as I can, Gwen sighs in defeat, already knowing I'm about to recruit her for something crazy.

"All right, tell me what I have to do."

Convincing Gwen was easy. Implementing the plan? Not so much. I'm starting to second-guess my idea of inviting nearly the entire football team, but Rome wanted to get to know some of his new teammates before practice starts next week. And we all know I'm a sucker when it comes to Rome. When Zack strolls through the front door, the backyard is booming with music and chatter. His deep ocean eyes gloss over in confusion when he walks into the kitchen.

"I thought this was supposed to be a small gathering." My brother's accusatory tone makes an entrance.

"It was, but Chrissy pulled a Chrissy," Gwen says while peeking outside and pointing. "That doesn't surprise me one bit."

With a bottle of water in hand, I peer over her shoulder and scoff at Ash.

"That dick gave me shit for inviting all these people. Look at him now." I throw my hands up in the air.

Gwen rests her hand over her forehead as we observe *the* Ash Waylen in action. A group of guys and a few random girls huddle around him. He's talking with his hands and grinning ear to ear as he tells whatever crazy tale he's sharing.

Gwen's cheeks flush red as she fixes her bathing suit strap. She's growing self-conscious, and that one nervous tick is too familiar.

I drape my arm over her shoulder and rest my head on hers. "Do you want me to get him for you?" I whisper so Zack doesn't hear me.

With a gentle shake of her head, I nod and kiss her temple.

"Zack, will you go out there and make sure no one fucks in the pool or trashes Mr. Lawyer Man's property?" I ask while secretly gesturing to a nervous Gwen.

Zack recognizes my protective stance over Gwen and agrees.

"Anything for my two favorite people in the world." Zack offers Gwen a smile before going outside.

We watch as he charges Ash, pulling him into one of his famous bear hugs. Gwen doesn't have anything to worry about regarding Ash. This is her anxiety over crowds creeping in. She wants to be with Ash, but her fear is stopping her.

"You can go outside and have fun. I'll manage the fort from here." She pulls away and puts on a strong front.

"I promised Rome I would wait for him. He should be here any minute. Speaking of which. . ."

"Oh no," Gwen mutters.

"What do you mean, *oh no?*"

"What master plan do you have up your sleeve today?" She chuckles, and I grin.

I remove my black tank top, adjust my bright red bikini top, and then ruffle my hair to give it volume.

"No trick today, my Gwen." I wink at my best friend as her jaw drops to the floor.

"Zack is going to murder you," she chuckles breathlessly.

"Zack can suck on a donkey's tail. I have a blond football player who needs wooing."

I haven't seen Rome since the fancy pancakes incident; it's been nothing but casual texts. I almost got him to spill a tidbit from his past, but Zack ruined the moment, and Rome shut down. He wore a brave face and acted like his usual, light-hearted self. Which only makes me wonder, how much of his pain is he hiding? And how often does he hide that trauma with a charming grin?

My feelings toward Rome are becoming overwhelming. I think about him nonstop, waiting for my phone to buzz, hoping he'll text or call me. Or that he'll show up at Ash's while I'm there. Being around him fills a void in my chest that I didn't know was there, and I'm tired of waiting for him to make the first move.

"How do I look?" I do a tiny twirl, and when I face her, her eyes are still wide.

"Like your boobs are going to fall out."

"Perfect."

Unlike Gwen, I don't have gorgeous curves or a nice set of tits. My body curves to a point, and my breasts aren't small, but they're not big either. I was made fun of a lot in middle school for having small boobs and no ass. I grew since then, and with a lot of self-affirmations, I learned to love my body. But that doesn't mean I don't have my bad days.

"Hey, Gwen!" A familiar voice sounds behind me, but it's not from the man I'm looking for.

"Hey! How are you?" she asks as Miles pulls her in for a hug.

Patting his back, Gwen keeps her eyes on me, unsure how this scenario will play out. I haven't seen Miles since we ended things last winter. As far as I know, we left on good terms.

"I'm good. How are you?" Gwen asks as they pull apart.

"Great. I haven't seen you or Ash in a while. Let me guess— he's outside?" Miles looks outside and nods his head. "Yep, that makes total sense." He turns around, finally noticing me, and he smiles at me.

"Hey, Chrissy. How are you?" His caramel eyes shine as he looks at me.

"Fine, thank you for asking. I thought you were headed back home after graduation."

"I'm leaving on Monday, just wanted to stop by and see everyone one last time."

"I'm glad you could make it," I tell him with a soft smile, and he matches it before grinning ear to ear.

"Look who it is!" Rome's hypnotic voice enthralls me.

Walking right past me, he and Miles hug one another and pat each other's backs rather aggressively.

"Where have you been, man?" Rome asks while beaming his flawless smile.

"I've been around. Last semester was busy." Miles goes on about his classes, quickly sucking Rome into a black hole.

Blowing a stray curl away from my face, I glance over at Gwen and catch the moment Ash opens the door. He notices Miles and Rome, but his eyes land on a rather antsy-looking Gwen.

"There you are," Ash says.

Gwen turns around, and relief washes over her expression. Pressing her face into his chest, he runs his fingers up and down her spine and kisses the crown of her head. Ash catches my gaze, and I offer him a sweet grin.

They've been together for almost a year now, and they seem to know when each other needs them the most. It must be nice to have someone like that.

"Hey, guys." Ash speaks up, quickly earning the attention of his friends.

Ash keeps Gwen close as he and Miles start to catch up, but Rome tilts his head in my direction.

"Hey, blondie." Rome's voice is deep yet soft.

His cheeks flush as his lips tug into a smile. He's wearing black swim trunks and a red Castle Brook Knights football tee. His blond hair is a tad messy today, like he just got out of bed and drove here without looking in the mirror. And it's painfully hot.

"Hi, Rome." I stutter, and I want to smack my forehead.

When the hell did I start acting shy? It's like I absorbed Gwen's personality, and it's confusing my brain.

His eyes linger over me, but they don't inch down my body like I was hoping they would. He's observing my face, and my blushed cheeks.

He opens his mouth to say something, but Miles interrupts him.

"Come on, Rome! We've got places to be and girls to see." Miles guides Rome outside.

My attention doesn't waver from the football player who manages to confuse me on a daily basis. With a brief glance over his shoulder, he jogs toward his teammates, who are congregated around the drink cooler.

"Coming, ladies?" Ash asks while opening the door again.

"Just give us a moment," Gwen says in a sweet tone.

With a nod, Ash heads outside, leaving Gwen and me alone in the kitchen.

"What the hell was that?" she whispers.

"I don't know," I mutter back.

"You totally fumbled over your words. And you blushed! You never blush!"

"I know!" I groan while raking my hands through my curls. "That boy's got me under some spell. And did you see him? He didn't even look at my boobs. I wore my skimpiest swimsuit for nothing." I slump against the kitchen island in defeat.

"Listen, if Rome likes you, I know a surefire way to get him to react. He's a stupid boy, and you know what stupid boys respond to?"

Lifting my head, I smirk at Gwen. "You're a genius."

Chapter Nine

Rome

"Damn, she's hot." one of the rookies says while gawking.

"Do you know who she is?" another new player asks, and my jaw clicks.

It took everything I had not to let my eyes travel down her body. Chrissy is a bombshell, and the entire party sees it. I observe her as she takes a shot, and Gwen chuckles as she sips on a wine cooler. Jumping up and down, Chrissy shakes her head from the sting of the alcohol.

"Rome, do you know who that is?"

"Chrissy Willows," I bite out as a vein nearly bursts in my forehead.

"Is that her boyfriend?"

I catch the moment another familiar face approaches the two girls across from the pool.

Blake sweeps Gwen in his arms and rubs his knuckles on Chrissy's head.

"Do you seriously not remember who that is?" I ask rookie number one. Levi Faulkner has black hair and dark brown eyes, is our new quarterback alternate.

"I can't remember what I ate for breakfast," he jokes.

I shake my head and take a swig from my water bottle.

Blake pushes up his glasses and walks over to us.

"That's Blake. He's the running back we met a few days ago," rookie number two reminds Levi.

Rookie number two, Chris Williams, has dark chocolate eyes and neat yet wavy trimmed brown hair, and he's our new wide receiver alternate.

"Oh, right." Levi nods as he remembers. "Hey, Blake!"

"There you guys are. How's everyone doing?" Blake asks while grabbing a beer bottle from the cooler.

"Pretty decent," Chris responds.

They start to go back and forth, but I don't hear what they're saying. My eyes and attention are glued on the bubble of energy across the yard. A guy I've never seen before approaches her, and my muscles tense in response. I'm about ready to walk over there and save her from the strange guy, but he walks away just as quickly as he appears. Chrissy's gaze meets mine, and her lips quirk into a lopsided grin.

Dropping my eyes, I try to focus on the crew in front of me.

"Everyone ready to start practice next week?" I ask without trying to sound distant.

"No," Blake chuckles. "I need a fucking break. My body is getting too old for this shit."

"You're twenty-one," I state with a smile, and he sighs.

"Twenty-one is the new sixty." He stretches his arm, and I hear it crack.

The rookies look at one another, sharing a quick *what the fuck did we get ourselves into* look.

"Don't get old, kids."

"Don't listen to him," I reassure them. "Maybe if you stretched instead of jumping straight into practice, your body wouldn't be at war with itself."

"Whatever, Carter." Blake snorts and punches me in the arm.

"I'm back, and look who I found." Miles returns from the pool with Zack in tow.

"I was on a secret mission, but I can take a break." Zack stretches like he wasn't just lounging on a pool floaty, drinking a fruity cocktail out of a crazy straw.

Whatever secret mission he was on, I don't think he was succeeding at it.

"Secret mission?" Miles dares to ask.

"Yeah, I'm kind of a big deal. Don't worry, your cute little head over it," Zack says while scanning the perimeter.

"Mr. FBI, have you seen your sister?" I ask, knowing damn well his demeanor is about to take a nose dive.

"I refuse to look." Zack found a random pair of black aviator sunglasses and avoids looking across the pool. "But if I find out *anyone* was googly eyeing her, I will end you." He does the *I'm watching you* motion to the two rookies, and they drop their pervy gazes instantly.

"I would run if I were you because she's coming." Miles chuckles.

Everyone but Zack looks over as Chrissy saunters toward us.

"Rome, do me a solid." Zack grabs me by my shoulder, earning my attention. "Don't let any of these drooling mouthpieces make a move on my sister."

"You got it." I give him a thumbs-up, and he nods.

Zack jumps back into the pool and swims for his post to resume his "secret mission."

"Hey, boys. Is he okay?" Chrissy asks and nods toward Zack.

Noting her concern, I turn around with a wide grin. "He

just needs to cool off," I say, darting toward Levi, whose eyes are glued to Chrissy's chest.

Clearing my throat, I wrap my arm around his shoulder to shake him out of whatever trance he's in.

"Have you met the new guys? This is Levi, and that's Chris." Fucking freshmen, you put a pretty girl in front of them, and they go numb.

"I love freshmen. They're so adorable," Chrissy coos as she squeezes Chris's cheeks.

"Will we see you at any of the games?" Levi chokes out.

I hold back my eye roll, and Chrissy smirks. "Absolutely. I've got to cheer on the team's all-star." She nudges my arm.

"Since when do you care about football?" I ask.

"Since my new friend is a football player," she says as a matter of fact. "I know nothing about the sport, though. I'll need some tutoring before the first game."

"I can help!" Levi volunteers.

"Aw, thank you," Chrissy coos while ruffling his hair. "Now, if you'll excuse me. I have to go to the little girls' room." Chrissy skips away, either fully aware or completely ignorant of all the eyes on her.

"Rome, is she your—"

I storm off before Chris can finish his question.

When she passes him, Malik tries to follow her, but I place my hand on his shoulder and firmly squeeze it.

"Fuck off, Malik," I hiss.

Normally, I wouldn't talk to my QB like that, but my rage is fuming, and he's on my warpath. Chrissy is gorgeous, and she has every man here under her thumb. I won't let them near her, though, even if it means I become an asshole in the process.

Chapter Ten

Chrissy

Gwen is a fucking genius. I avoided him during the party because absence makes the heart grow fonder and all that jazz. I went up to him because I felt him watching me, and I got selfish. I would have stayed longer, but the wine coolers and bottles of water I've been drinking are expanding my bladder to an uncomfortable level.

Scurrying inside, I'm surprised to find that everyone is outside. At least that means the house is safe and clean. I head up the stairs and run into the bathroom in the hall, locking the door behind me. I moan when I sit on the toilet, and my bladder is more than happy to free itself of all the liquid I've been downing. When I'm finished, I wash my hands and examine myself in the mirror. Now that I'm done messing with Rome, it's time to relax and have some fun. Gwen and I plan on huddling in a corner with some wine coolers and eavesdropping on random conversations. If we can't hear anyone, we'll make them up. Either way, we'll be laughing our asses off.

I open the door but am immediately ushered back into the bathroom.

"What the fuck?!" I shout as Rome closes the door and locks it. "What do you think you're doing?"

"Put this on." Rome strips out of his shirt and tosses it at me.

Not catching it in time, I unravel it from my face and grunt. "And why would I do that?"

"Because I'm tired of fighting all these guys off for you," he growls.

"Who said I wanted you to?" I bite back, and his jaw clenches. Oh yeah, Gwen's plan worked way better than I expected it to. "Are you jealous, Rome Carter?" I click my tongue in amusement.

"No." His cheeks are flushed. His eyes are glossed over and dilated.

This man is the definition of bottled rage, and for some reason, it's hot.

Taking a step closer, I drop his shirt. Rome steps back, and his spine lines up with the door.

"You're lying." I poke his chest and look up at him. "Why are you lying, Rome?"

My breasts press against his bare chest. My stomach brushes along his, and the feeling makes my heart stutter.

"Chrissy, please take a step back." His eyes bore into mine. His throat bobs as he swallows, and he licks his lips.

"Why?" I whisper, knowing damn well how seductive my tone sounds.

"This is something neither of us can do."

"Why not?" I repeat while standing on the edge of my toes to bring myself closer.

"There are many reasons," he mumbles, sounding out of breath.

"Name one." I feather my nose against his, and my gaze shoots down to his full lips.

"Zack."

"I don't care what Zack thinks."

I only want him. I want Rome to throw himself at me, to kiss me, and never let go. I want to feel his body against mine. To feel the weight of his muscles bearing down on me.

"If you didn't care what he thinks, you would have told him about Miles."

Ouch . . . he's got a point there. There's a reason I didn't tell Zack about Miles. I was nervous about how he would react. He's super protective over me and Gwen. I mean, he nearly combusted when he found out Gwen slept over at Ash's last fall. Everything he does is to protect the ones he loves. He and Rome are close. It would shatter him if he found out we went behind his back. He wouldn't trust me or Rome ever again. Hell, he and Rome would stop being friends. And that's something I can't take from Zack. He's been through too much. He deserves the best, and I won't ruin that for him.

"You're right," I murmur as I take a step back. "I'll chill out. I'm sorry I upset you. I'll wear the shirt and mind my business for the rest of the party." Putting on his shirt, I try to ignore the scent that envelopes me. The same smell I drowned myself in on the drive home from the beach.

"Chrissy, that's not what—"

"It's okay," I say with a weak smile. "How do I look?"

He trails his eyes over my body and meets my gaze, and my heart stutters.

"Gorgeous," he responds.

My brows furrow, but I don't ask questions. "Let's go, Mr. All-Star." I gesture for him to open the door.

Rome takes a minute before unlocking the door and opening it. Stepping out into the hallway, I aim for the stairs but stop when he wraps his hand in mine.

"I'm sorry, Wildflower." With a gentle squeeze, he drops my hand and heads back downstairs.

I don't look back as I head into the backyard. I don't respond to the whistles or catcalling when I plop down next to Gwen. The chanting is replaced with cheering when Rome returns, and my cheeks blush when Gwen notices whose shirt I'm wearing.

"What the fuck just happened?" she asks in a hushed tone.

"I'm fucking cursed. That's what happened."

Chapter Eleven

Rome

Hoots and hollering erupt when I step outside without my shirt on. I glare at every single one of them, and they shut up immediately. Glancing over at Chrissy, I let my shoulders relax when I find her sitting next to Gwen.

From the pool, Zack lowers his sunglasses and examines his sister, then looks over at me with a thumbs-up. I'm assuming he's happy I got her to put a shirt on. If he knew how I managed it, I get the feeling he wouldn't be so thrilled.

I still feel her on my skin. I can still smell her faint strawberry perfume. She was so close, and I could've had her. The desire to tangle my hand in her curls and crash my lips against hers was blinding.

Thankfully, Chrissy came to her senses, and she stopped before we both made a terrible mistake. Usually, I can push down my wants, but it's getting harder. She's found a way to make me question my resolve. She's beautiful, but there's more to her than that. Her positive outlook and ideals are unlike anyone I've ever met. I'm drawn to her; I want Chrissy all to myself, and there's no avoiding that.

"That was quick, Carter." Malik punches me in the shoulder with a gross wink.

"Shut the fuck up," I growl at him.

My eyes land on Ash, and he tilts his head. He excuses himself from a group of people and walks over to me while wrapping a beach towel around himself.

"You look like you're about to explode. What's going on?"

"Nothing." I grab a hard seltzer and pop it open.

"Where did your shirt go?" he asks while eyeing me.

"Chrissy has it," I say before downing my drink in under five gulps.

Ash's eyes widen when he looks over at Gwen and Chrissy. Before he can question me further, I save him the breath. "I got tired of these perverts eyeing her like a piece of meat."

"She had her own shirt," he chuckles.

"I acted without thinking," I respond, trying to calm my emotions.

"There's something you're not telling me." And there he goes.

Ash isn't stupid. Life would be a whole lot easier if he were.

"I don't know what you're talking about." I try to throw him off the course he's on, but he's locked his sights in.

"You like her."

Hearing it out loud stings. Only because it means my feelings for Chrissy are stronger than the facade I try to maintain. I can no longer hide the way I feel for her. My demeanor has started to betray me.

"Even if I did, nothing can happen." My posture starts to relax, and my fury from earlier starts to diminish, but something worse takes its place.

"Why not?" Ash whispers.

Nodding toward Zack, Ash looks over and sighs.

"There's a reason Chrissy didn't tell Zack about Miles. I can't do that to him. He's my best friend."

"Zack is protective. There's no doubt about that. But you're a good guy, Rome. I know he's your best friend, but that doesn't mean you should ignore your feelings. What if you end up regretting this decision?" Ash's words strike a chord, but as much as I want to take his advice, I can't.

Walls begin to cement around my heart, and I feel myself become an emotionless shell. Pushing down my feelings for Chrissy, I focus on the past. I remember what happened the last time my heart broke. My mother left a lasting effect on me. She taught me not to love too deeply, and not to trust too easily. If she can leave her son without a second thought, who's to say Chrissy won't do the same thing?

Peering over at my Wildflower one last time, I work on memorizing her smile, her curls, and her rosy cheeks. I internalize her laugh and voice. Chrissy Willows is someone worthy of love, and I'm unsure if I can provide that to her. No matter how much I want to.

"Life is full of disappointments," I respond coldly.

Ash sighs and rakes his hand through his hair. "Only if you allow it."

Chapter Twelve

Chrissy

It's finally time. I've been waiting for this day for months. Walking across the Castle Brook campus, a sense of drive pushes me through the humidity. I'm at the top of my class in my major, and because of that, I got an exclusive invitation for a mentorship program this summer. Not only will it boost my résumé when I graduate, but it's also an amazing opportunity to start helping those who need assistance with their mental health.

I'm not sure which field of psychology I'll pursue after next May. I've been toying with becoming a child psychologist or helping teens and young adults, but nothing has called to me yet. I'm hoping this program will help me figure out where I'm meant to be.

Cool air rushes me when I open the humanities building door. I navigate the halls like a pro, not caring about the frizz that has taken over my hair. It's a good thing I pulled it back into a neat bun this morning. If I didn't, it would be three times its normal size.

Holding my notebook close to my chest, I stroll inside the

classroom and sit near the middle. A few other familiar faces are already in the room, but no one I'm acquainted with. This is perfect; I need to take this mentorship seriously, and I don't need any distractions.

"Oh, thank god, you're here," a familiar voice sighs.

A girl I recognize sits to my right. Raina has dark auburn hair and the kindest hazel eyes I've ever seen. She reminds me of Gwen, which makes me adore her even more.

Rubbing her stomach, Raina leans back in her chair and tries to breathe out her nerves.

"Have you tried ginger ale?" I ask.

Glancing over at me, she arches her right eyebrow in confusion.

"For the nerves. My best friend swears by it."

"That's one of the most genius things I've ever heard." Raina nods to herself, which is another gesture that reminds me of Gwen.

I met Raina last semester. We shared statistics and behavior science classes. We're both majoring in psychology but specializing in behavioral health. I'm surprised we didn't run into one another sooner.

"How has your summer break been so far?" I try to distract her.

"Good. I've been hiding inside where the air-conditioning is most days, watching way too much TV and playing way too many video games." Her response makes me smile.

Raina and Gwen would make great friends. I'll have to introduce them to each other one day.

"How about you?"

"I've been crashing at my friend's boyfriend's house. They have a pool, and it gives me an excuse to hang out with her. I plan on heading back once this is done for the day."

"That sounds wonderful."

"It would be even more wonderful if my brother and his friend would stop crashing as well . . ." I groan as I roll my eyes.

Rome has been a sore topic. Six days ago, I found myself in Rome's shirt. He tracked me down because not only did Gwen's plan work, it worked *too* well. I merely wanted to see if I could make Rome crave my attention. And boy, not only did I rile his desire, we almost kissed.

I can still feel his bare stomach on mine. The rush of chills that ravished my skin, the heat that pooled in my core. Sharing the same oxygen as him was intoxicating, and I wanted nothing more than to close the gap. I would have, too, if Rome hadn't brought my brother up.

He was right in the end. I was lying to myself when I said I didn't care what Zack thought. Zack has a record streak for freaking out about guys I date. He's the reason I keep my love life a secret. I know he worries because he cares, but I can't let his worry stop me from possibly finding love one day.

I want to explore things with Rome, but he was right when he said he couldn't do that to his best friend. I just wish he would stop showing up unexpectedly. These past few days, he and Zack have been glued at the hip. If Zack shows up out of the blue, so does Rome. If Rome shows up to raid the fridge, Zack isn't too far behind.

I tried not to let what happened between us cause a rift, but it naturally occurred. I peeked around every corner, scanning rooms before entering them. I don't want us to feel awkward around one another, but this is something that needs time to mend. I'm sure we can get back to where we were. Hopefully . . .

"That doesn't sound too bad," Raina admits. "Are they hot?"

I can't help but snort in response. Maybe she's not entirely like Gwen. I open my mouth to respond, but I'm cut off by a naturally soothing voice.

"Good morning, everyone," Professor Clastis announces.

Her heels clack against the tile as she strolls to the front of the room, and her black pinwheel curls bounce with her strides. Crossing her arms over her chest, she leans against the desk and examines the room. Her hot chocolate eyes land on me, and she flashes me her flawless smile.

"Who's ready to evaluate some football players?"

You've got to be kidding me.

Chapter Thirteen

Rome

The first week of practice is abnormally brutal. We spend the first day going over plays and drills. On the second day, we're on the field putting those plays into action. Today is our third day, and Coach Bradson is in a rare mood. And by that, I mean he's annoyed and cranky. So, instead of running plays inside since the weather is atrocious today, we're running laps up and down the field.

I pump my arms to push myself to finish this final lap, and my eyes burn as sweat and dirt fill my vision. My tank top clings to my body, and my shorts are drenched as I begin to sweat in places I didn't think were humanly possible.

"Move your ass, Carter!" Bradson shouts from the sideline.

I want to shout back and yell at him to pick on someone else, but there's a reason he's singling me out. He knows I'm one of his top players and wants me to be the best.

Pushing myself harder, I pass Malik and Levi. They curse as they try to overtake me, but I'm too fast.

I nearly stumble across the end zone. My knees buckle

when I come to a halt, and I gasp for air that doesn't satisfy my hunger for oxygen.

"That's how you do it!" Bradson claps as more guys collapse into the end zone.

Grabbing a bottle of scorching hot water, I down it without a care in the world.

"Keep that up, Carter, and you'll find yourself a first-round pick." Coach pats my back as I double over.

I give him a thumbs-up before wiping the sweat from my brow.

"All right, go shower and get changed. Meet me in the conference room in twenty minutes."

The field fills with groans and mumbles.

"What did we get ourselves into this time?" Levi whispers to me.

Standing upright, I scan the field to try and gauge the situation.

"Only one way to find out."

Washing off the grime was more than satisfying. I don't normally take cold showers, but today, I required one. I have to keep reminding the guys to hydrate. The last thing anyone needs is to succumb to heat stroke and dehydration.

Malik is the captain, but he doesn't take his responsibility as seriously as he should. I don't think he minds that I've stepped in to boost the team or assist the new players. I just wish he would show the team that he cares. A simple "Hey, did you drink water today?" goes a long way.

As I walk out of the locker room, I sigh when the frigid air envelopes me. I stroll across the hall and enter the conference room. Sitting near the back, I spin around in the office chair and savor my water.

"Whatcha do this time, Rome?" Malik asks as he plops down next to me.

"Shouldn't you be up front?" I ask with a bit of bite in my tone.

"Nah, Coach can handle this."

He knows what's about to happen, and he's relishing it. He wants me to ask so he can withhold the information. I won't fall into his trap, though. Coach Bradson will soon tell us what's going on.

"All right, let's get this over with." Bradson strolls into the room.

His gray hair is neatly trimmed, his eyes are dark, and while his features are stiff and stern, he is someone you can trust and go to about anything. Coach used to play for the Philadelphia Eagles, the same team I've had my eyes on since high school. After retiring from the field, he came to Castle Brook and has led this team to multiple playoffs and bowl games. I've been to a couple myself. We just haven't won one.

"I'm not going to go on about mental health and the rising depression statistics in men."

Multiple guys start to chuckle, which only makes Bradson more irritated.

"Silence! This is serious. Life is cruel, and I'm willing to bet that more than half of you in this room have felt some form of anxiety or depression at one point in your lives."

The room falls silent again. We're all itching to know what he'll tell us next.

"The head of the Psychology Department and I are joining forces this year. She has a mentorship program, and I volunteered the team to participate. There are seventy of you here, and she has seventy participating seniors who will treat you like guinea pigs. They will evaluate your psyche and help you discover ways to cope with anxiety, burnout, and depression. You will be respectful and take this opportunity seriously."

"What if we don't want our brains poked and prodded?" a senior-level player asks.

"If you don't want to help yourselves with this opportunity, I'll simply bench you and let one of the freshman players take your position. How does that sound, Everson?" The coach isn't putting up with anyone's bullshit.

Malik chuckles quietly beside me, and I glare over at him. "Isn't that blonde from the pool party a psych major?"

Fuck, he's right. Not only is she a psychology major, but she's also good at what she does. In one conversation, I almost spilled all my secrets to her. I wanted to share my past because she made me feel safe. I could tell she cared, and I knew she wouldn't have judged me if I told her. Even after the moment in the bathroom, I still find myself drawn to her. I've been going to Ash's almost every day, hoping to run into her. But every time she's there, we've avoided one another. And as much as it hurts, I know right now it's necessary.

"She is. Why does that matter?" I ask, noting the grit in my tone.

Stretching his arms out and sighing, he smirks at me. "If I see her, I'm making it my personal mission to partner up with her. You had fun. Now it's my turn."

"Now, get the fuck out of here and drink some water. I'll see everyone here tomorrow for the meet and greet," Coach states.

As everyone starts to stand, Malik firmly squeezes my shoulder. "See you tomorrow, Carter."

My fingernails dig into my palm. If Malik thinks he'll breathe the same air as Chrissy, he's wrong. I'll do everything possible to ensure she doesn't get paired with him. Even if it means I'm the one she ends up evaluating.

Chapter Fourteen

Chrissy

"What am I going to do?!" I ask while throwing Ash's bedroom door open. "Oh, it's you." The disappointment is blatant in my tone.

"Nice to see you too," Ash chuckles while closing his book.

"Where's Gwen? Oh, shit. Did I walk in on something nasty? I should've knocked." I backtrack out of the room.

"She has a shift at Tea and Kittens."

Popping my head back inside, I can practically see the wheels turning in Ash's head. "What the hell would we be up to? I'm reading a book."

"I don't know and don't want to know." I throw my hands in the air.

"What are you going to do about what?" Ash asks, returning to my first question.

"Uhh—"

Shit, do I tell him? Does he know? Can he keep a secret?

"Does this have anything to do with Rome?"

"Damn, you're smarter than you look," I say without thinking.

"Thanks?"

Walking over to his bed, I plop on the corner and sigh in defeat.

Ash swings his legs over the mattress and rests his elbows on his knees. "Want to talk to me about it, or do you want to wait for Gwen?"

Looking over at him, I come to a swift conclusion. "I'm going to bother both of you."

"It's not a bother." Ash's kind brown eyes meet mine, and he offers me a sweet smile.

"Promise not to tell Zack?" I offer him my pinkie, and he meets it without hesitation.

This boy has no idea what he's getting himself into. I start from the beginning, explaining how my feelings grew from a simple nickname. I inform him that I tried to avoid it, but no matter what I did, Rome would always manage his way back into my heart.

"You remember how I had his shirt at the party?" I ask, and he nods. "I was ignoring him to see if he would respond, and then we almost kissed in the bathroom."

Ash doesn't respond. His face is zoned in on mine, listening intently.

"We didn't because neither of us want to hurt Zack. He gave me his shirt because he was tired of the football team eye fucking me. Since then things have been weird, and it's about to get worse."

"How?"

"Remember my mentorship?" I ask, and he nods again. "We're going to be evaluating the football team."

"Oh, I see. And you're afraid you'll end up with Rome?"

"Bingo."

My palms meet my eyes, and I rake my fingers over my scalp. Ash sighs, and his silence makes my skin itch.

His leg starts to bounce, and he clears his throat. "You two are more alike than you realize . . . listen, Chrissy, Zack would understand—"

"I don't want to chance it. He's been through too much. He's finally getting over Rosalyn, and I can't ruin that. If he finds out I have feelings for Rome and that Rome might feel the same, he would have a heart attack."

"Chrissy . . ."

"No, Ash. Please, tell me what to do tomorrow. I can't end up as his partner," I plead.

My voice cracks, and my eyes water.

With another exhale, Ash presses his lips together. "So, don't. Do whatever you have to do to avoid being paired up with him. But let it be known that I disapprove of this idea. You two are adults, and so is Zack. This is a train wreck waiting to happen."

"What's a train wreck waiting to happen?" Gwen walks into the room with Pickles in tow.

"Chrissy and Rome," Ash answers for me.

"Oh, *that* train wreck." Gwen kicks off her shoes and picks up Pickles. "I don't know what's happening, but what's the plan?"

"Avoid him at all costs," I say, trying to summon as much confidence as possible.

"Brilliant, I see no flaws in this at all." Gwen's tone is coated in sarcasm.

I draw my eyebrows together and squint. "I find your lack of faith disturbing," I say in a deep voice.

Ash chuckles in response.

I knew that would get a rise out of one of them.

"My faith in you is fine. My faith in your plan? Now that's a different story." Gwen smirks at me as Pickles launches out of her arms.

"Five bucks that my plan works?" I extend my hand, and she meets it without a second thought.

"Five bucks that you two fail in this whole 'let's avoid one another' thing. And you end up together in the end." Ash coughs, and I give him a nasty side-eye.

Gwen accepts my bet with a knowing look. "Easiest five bucks I'll ever make."

Little does she know, I have an ace up my sleeve, and her name is Raina Bennett.

Walking into the sports center, I scan the hallway for my first target. The sooner I find her, the better. Professor Clastis told us to meet near the large conference room in the back. So, putting my ninja skills to the test, I sneak down the hall and peer around the corner.

"Gotcha," I whisper the moment I see her.

"Psst, Raina." Nothing. "Psst!" This woman, I swear. "Raina," I say a little too loudly.

Thankfully, only a few other students are lined up outside the room.

Raina grins when she sees me. I wave her over, and she follows suit.

"What are you doing?" she giggles when she reaches me.

"I need your help with something."

"Okay." Her smile grows in response.

"I need you to not let Rome Carter near me. He's tall, has gorgeous green eyes, blond hair, and huge muscles." I try not to sound swoony as I describe him, but it comes out nonetheless.

Raina's eyes focus behind me, and she tilts her head. "Is that him?"

I glance over my shoulder and mumble a curse. "Yes, that's him. He and I can't be partners. I really need your help with this. I can explain everything later."

"Oh, this is going to be fun. This is something I can totally handle, don't worry." Raina gives me a thumbs-up before linking her arm through mine and walking us back toward the conference room.

Professor Clastis informed us that this room hosts many press interviews and conferences, and I certainly believe her. The space is at least the size of two large lecture halls combined. In the front, an elevated stage with a long table, a podium, and the school's tapestry are. Multiple tables are spaced appropriately throughout the room. The dust makes my nose tickle, but other than that, this room is spotless.

Rome's voice filters into the room as Raina brings us to a table near the center. Thankfully, the space fills, and Rome hasn't caught sight of me. Sinking in my chair, Raina leans forward to cover me.

"Give me an update," I whisper while hiding my face with my hand.

"I lost track of him. Damn, I never noticed, but this team is *hot*." Raina swoons as more muscular guys fill the room.

"Focus, Raina," I hiss while peeking through my fingers.

The familiar clack of heels sounds from the hallway, and

Professor Clastis and an older gentleman with broad shoulders enter the room.

"Take a seat, everyone!" The professor instructs, and her students are quick to respond, leaving the players congregating in the center of the room.

"You heard the boss. Take a seat," the man, who I'm assuming is the coach, orders.

"Oh, hello," Raina utters.

Following her eyesight, I notice who has their eyes locked on me, and I groan. "Not him either."

"How many players are you trying to avoid?" Raina snickers as Malik strolls toward us.

"Just two, him and, oh crap—" My voice falters when Rome jogs past Malik.

I scramble out of my chair, and Raina quickly follows suit. She trails behind me as I hurry farther down the table.

Finding two empty chairs, I glance around the room. "Do you see them?" I ask.

"No, I think we're good." Raina sits in the chair, and just as I'm about to follow her lead, Rome pushes past Malik, and I stumble.

"Motherfucker," I curse to myself.

"I need to know what you did to those two because the hot blond just totally hip-checked the other one, and now he's running."

"God dammit, he's fast too. We have to hurry—"

"There you are." Rome greets us, pretending he's not out of breath. "I was looking for you." And there's that charming smile.

"Ms. Willows, please take a seat," Professor Clastis instructs me from the front of the room.

Obeying my instructor, I sit across from Rome. Avoiding his

gaze is difficult, so I zone in on my folded hands and focus on my breathing.

"What the fuck was that, Carter?" Malik grunts as he sits next to Rome, directly across from Raina.

"I guess this means we failed the mission?" She leans over to ask me, ensuring no one else hears her.

"We failed miserably," I groan.

Chapter Fifteen

Rome

Damn, my girl is fast. The moment I had my sights set on her, she would book it, and I would lose her in the crowd. I got lucky when I saw Malik. I wouldn't have reacted if I didn't know about his plan. Thankfully I knew, and because of that, I find myself sitting across from the girl he had his eyes on. I don't know how we'll be partnered up, but now I can keep a close eye on her.

Her expression leaves me curious. It reminds me of when I stepped off my first big roller coaster ride, plagued with a sudden case of nausea. The girl next to her leans in and nudges her gently. Chrissy nods at whatever she whispered in her ear.

"That wasn't cool, man," Malik hisses beside me.

"I don't know what you're talking about." I lower my tone and mask my smirk.

He scoffs in response and crosses his arms over his chest. "You owe me."

"I don't owe you shit," I bite back.

"Ladies and gentlemen, let's get started." The woman

wearing a navy power suit clasps her hands together and grins while looking out over the room.

Chrissy lifts her head and directs her gaze to the woman. Turning in my seat, I give my full attention to who I'm assuming is the leader of this mentorship and Coach Bradson.

"My name is Renee Clastis, and I'm beyond excited to have teamed up with Coach Bradson for this unique opportunity. Our goal here isn't to make anyone uncomfortable. We're here to educate you on the importance of mental health and possibly even teach you how to identify signs of depression or anxiety and teach you some coping techniques to help relieve those moments until you seek appropriate care. I could stand here and tell you about the rising statistics of untreated mental conditions in men. Or how men in professional sports tend to burn out faster than anyone else. But I won't bore you. I hope you like the person sitting across from you because they'll be your partner until the start of the fall semester."

I peer over at Chrissy, and our eyes lock. The professor's voice fades away, and the room becomes a bit brighter. Her lips quirk into a half smile, and I can't help but return the gesture. I don't often see her hair pulled back. It's always loose and wild. This is a different look, but she's just as gorgeous. She's wearing a white button-down blouse even though it's over ninety degrees outside. Sweat cascades down her neck, inching down toward her breasts. I follow the droplet like a kid watching rain race down a car window.

Chrissy clears her throat, and I dart my eyes back to hers. With a knowing look, she shakes her head and points back to the front of the room.

"You don't have to get to know one another here, but I expect you to spend at least an hour with your new partner today. Is that understood?" Coach Bradson asks, directing his instructions to his team. "Now, get out of here."

A few people stand when he dismisses us. Malik and I stay put, as do the women sitting across from us.

"I'll give you twenty dollars to partner up with this guy," Malik stares at the girl with hazel eyes and nods his head toward me.

"Don't I get a say in this?" Chrissy asks.

"I don't need your money, Mr. QB, but that makes me wonder, how often do you use that as a tactic to get what you want?" the girl asks, and my eyes widen.

"Malik, meet Raina. She's about to rock your psyche." Chrissy clicks her tongue, the sass rolling out of her mouth like it's her superpower.

"Forty bucks—"

"Nope."

"One hundred—"

"Not gonna happen. You're stuck with me." Raina giggles like an evil queen.

The two of them go back and forth.

Chrissy chuckles, and I immediately turn my attention to her. My lips turn upward, pulling on my cheeks, when Chrissy smiles widely. Reaching across the table, I take her hand, and sparks ignite along my skin.

"Want to get out of here?" I ask with a hopeful tone.

With an eager nod, Chrissy stands from her chair and grabs her stuff. "Let's go."

Chapter Sixteen

Chrissy

No one can say I didn't try, but Gwen might. The look she throws at me when Rome and I enter the cat café screams "I told you so." And now I owe that bitch five bucks.

The aroma of freshly brewed coffee and fresh, out-of-the-oven pastries wafts through the air. Rome sits in a booth, and I follow suit. I observe him as he looks over the menu, admiring how his sea-glass eyes dance along the words.

His hair is more relaxed today, not slicked back. It covers his forehead and ears, making my fingers itch with the desire to run them through his locks. His cologne tickles my nose, sandalwood and salty ocean air.

Closing my eyes, I can imagine the two of us on the beach, listening to the waves, and feeling the gritty sand on our skin. Him shirtless, and me wanting nothing more than to feel his power between my legs.

"Chrissy, are you okay?" Gwen interrupts my thoughts. "You look like you were having a *very* pleasant dream."

"I was thinking," I blurt out.

"Again?" Rome asks without looking at me.

Gwen chuckles. "Uh-huh, sure you were," she teases. "Anyway, since you're my two favorite people, I'll take your order here. Can I get you guys anything?"

"Iced vanilla coffee and a chocolate croissant, please." I bat my eyelashes at her as she jots it down.

"Rome?"

"Just water."

Both Gwen's and my eyebrows raise instantaneously. "That's it?" we ask at the same time, earning a baffled stare from Rome.

"What? I have to watch my figure." He rubs his stomach.

I know damn well that the last thing that boy is watching is his figure. He looks like he needs four thousand calories a day to maintain his weight.

"Can you bring him a blueberry muffin?" I ask, and Gwen winks at me.

"Chrissy, I have to be good." He sighs, and I roll my eyes.

"Shut up and eat the carbs, muscle man," I snap at him with a playful tone.

Rome drops the menu and raises his hands. "Damn, my girl's got a bite. Whatever you say, Wildflower."

My girl.

Wildflower.

These next couple of months are going to be rough.

Gwen is quick to bring us our drinks and pastries, and I chew on my straw as I bop my head to the song that comes on next, "Genie In A Bottle" by Christina Aguilera.

Clicking my pen, I flip my notebook to an empty page and write Rome's name on the top of the sheet with a few random doodles as he eats the muffin he *didn't* want.

"So, shall we start, Mr. Carter?"

"I guess so." He leans back in his seat and crosses his hands together to cradle the back of his head.

"Just a heads up, I hate scaling emotions. You'll probably hear a lot of your teammates talking about it. I don't agree with that technique. I'd rather you tell me your feelings. So, how do you feel about this program?" I keep my eyes on him, knowing the moment he starts talking, I'll be able to gauge whether he's lying or not.

"It doesn't bother me." He shrugs while picking at his muffin.

"Football practice started this week. How's that going?"

"It's good. Same old stuff."

He's keeping his answers straight to the point, but I need him to dig deeper.

"Do you have any responsibilities besides being an all-star

wide receiver?" I keep my tone even. The last thing I need is for him to curl up in his bubble of self-protection. He can't know I'm prying for more information.

"I memorize plays, help the coach develop strategies, and help the new players fit in and get used to the schedule. On top of that, I have to keep up with my own workout routine and meal regiment." Rome's eyes are on the empty muffin paper.

I notice then that his shoulders are tense. The fun-loving guy I started to fall for weeks ago seems to be disappearing, and I have a feeling I know why.

"Those sound like a captain's responsibilities. Were you promoted?" I ask even though I already know the answer.

"No."

"Did Malik hand some of these responsibilities off to you?"

"Not really. I noticed he was slacking, so I stepped in."

And now look at you, Rome. The once fun, bright-eyed, attention-seeking, beyond-extroverted guy I was reintroduced to months ago is slowly becoming a ball of stress and fatigue. My heart starts to break for him. I noticed a shift during the beach trip and even when I cooked him breakfast the next day. He won't survive if things continue as they're going.

"So you train and help the rookies, you review and memorize plays, and your days are planned to a T. Along with coursework and socializing with your friends. Hearing me say all that out loud, how does that make you feel?" I try to keep my voice level, but the emotion slips through.

Rome has taken on too much responsibility that isn't even his to bear. It doesn't surprise me that he wants to help the new guys or offered to help Malik initially. But he needs to start setting boundaries because, looking at him now, I see the deep bags under his eyes.

Rome looks up at me, and I offer him a faint smile. "You're tired already, aren't you?"

"I am," he mumbles.

"And classes haven't started yet. It's going to get worse." I want to reach out and take his hand, but I resist the temptation and focus on his expression instead. "Want to know what I'm thinking?"

He nods in response.

"You are a giver, Rome. You picked up Malik's slack. You wanted to help the new guys because you are kind and selfless. You work on the game plays with your coach because no one else is going to do it. *You* are the captain of your team, minus the official title. I don't know what your home life was like when you were a child, but I'm willing to guess you were a helper there as well. Rome, looking at you now, I can tell you're tired. But it's going to get worse when classes resume. My suggestion? Take a step back before it gets too hectic. Tell Malik he needs to resume some of his duties."

"I can't do that," he responds solemnly.

"Why not?" I ask, but silence is his only response. "If you don't stand up for yourself, Rome, you *will* burn out."

Chapter Seventeen

Rome

urnout. I've heard the term once before, but I don't fully understand what it means. Chrissy's expression stabs me in the chest. She's trying her best to keep a solid front, but I can see past her walls. Her lips offer me a kind, warm smile. She's worried about me, but there's no need. I know what I can handle. I've been through much worse than this.

"I'll think about it," I say, just to make her happy.

Chrissy nods, and her lips quirk up just a bit. "What do you do for fun? To unwind?"

I glance down at her notebook as she continues to ask me questions. Her handwriting is neat and curvy, just like her.

"I typically hang out at home when I'm not bothering you guys."

"You don't bother us." She looks at me like I have two heads.

"Then why were you dodging me all last week?" I know the answer, but I want to hear her say it. I want her to tell me to take it all back. We'll find a way to explore this strange connection and tell Zack.

"We both know why, but that doesn't mean I don't want you around. We're still friends."

That's far from the answer I was hoping for, but for now, it'll do.

"This cat is going to be the death of me!" A familiar redhead stalks from the back room, holding a white cat with blue eyes in his arms.

Ryan's face is scratched. Most are new, and some are healing.

"Is she being mean to you again?" Gwen walks over to Ryan and takes the cat from his arms.

"She hates people. If she doesn't stop attacking every customer who walks in here, we'll have to find her a different placement." Ryan sighs as Gwen cradles the cat in her arms.

"She sounds worse than Pickles," Chrissy whispers.

The cat locks her sights on me, and she leaps from Gwen's arms before Gwen can react.

"Korra, stop!" But Gwen's threat doesn't stop the ball of white fur from climbing up my leg.

I don't have much experience with pets. I didn't have any growing up. Pickles has been the only cat I've gotten to know, and he's a character. So, I don't know what to do when the cat curls up in my lap and starts kneading my thigh.

"Fuck, are you okay?" Gwen asks as she approaches us.

When she sees what the cat is doing, her facial expression shifts. "That's odd. She hates everyone. I'm only on her good side because I feed her."

"What is with our friend group and crazy cats?" Chrissy asks.

Reaching down, I offer the cat my finger so she can smell it. Korra rubs her nose across it and starts to purr.

"She's not crazy," I say while smiling down at her.

"Tell that to Ryan," Gwen jokes.

As I scratch the cat's chin, she melts into my palm and lies down.

"This doesn't surprise me one bit." Chrissy snickers as she starts to take more notes. "Crazy attracts crazy, and sweet attracts sweet. And you, my friend, just happen to be both."

"Rome, I will pay you to take that cat home," Ryan shouts from the other side of the room as he cleans his wounds.

"I don't know." I look up at Gwen, and she nods.

"Think about it. I don't think she'll be adopted anytime soon. Besides, I won't let it happen, not until you give me an answer." Gwen walks away to help Ryan, leaving me with Chrissy and a new cat friend on my lap.

"So, back to the previous question. What are you doing this weekend?"

I think it over, and nothing comes to mind. I planned on working out, just like I do every day. There is a new movie I wanted to see, but no one has wanted to go with me.

"I'm taking your silence as an answer. You and I are going to do something this weekend. We're going to get you back to where you were before all the stress bore down on you. How does that sound?" Chrissy beams across from me.

My brain is shouting and firing alarms, but my heart is speaking louder. "That sounds like fun."

I didn't want to leave Korra. I had to pry her off my lap when it was time to go so Gwen and Ryan could close up the café. The cat chased me to the door and started meowing as I walked away. I didn't let myself look back. I never thought of adopting a cat or dog. I'm home enough, but do I have enough time to provide them the care and love they require? It would be nice to come home and have someone there, even if it's a ball of white fur.

"This Saturday around noon work for you?" Chrissy asks as we walk back to campus.

"Yeah, that's great."

"Anything specific you want to do?"

"Well . . . never mind." I drop my gaze to the sidewalk.

"What is it?" she asks. "I'm up for anything. Well, maybe not *anything,* but you catch my drift."

"You wouldn't be into it." I shake my head, but Chrissy doesn't give up.

"Spill it, football boy."

"There's this movie I've been dying to see." I sigh. "No one has wanted to go with me though."

"What movie is it?" she asks with genuine interest.

"*Fearless,* the movie about the haunted manor," I answer while trying to hide my embarrassment.

"Seriously?" is all I need to hear to know it's a stupid idea. "I want to see that too!"

"What? Really?" She's left me speechless.

Everyone I've asked either didn't have the time or they simply weren't interested.

"Yes, really! Gwen and I want to see it, but she's been too busy. I'm sure she won't mind if I go without her. She can drag Ash the next time she's off work. Oh my gosh, I'm so excited." Chrissy bounces up and down, smiling wide.

"You really want to go?" I'm shocked. I was pretty sure she hated spooky things. She's the last person I was expecting to bring to such a movie.

"Yes! Gwen has me hooked on scary movies. Now, listen. I can't promise I won't be a big baby though. I might scream and cling onto you for dear life."

The idea of Chrissy throwing herself at me, needing me to protect her, makes me way too giddy.

"Oh, Wildflower. I'll protect you, don't worry." I can't help but shamelessly flirt with her.

Chrissy drops her gaze and blushes.

"I'd punch you in the arm, but all I'd do is hurt myself in the process."

Leaning in close, I say, "I'd never hurt you on purpose, and I hope you know that."

Chapter Eighteen

Chrissy

That son of a bitch was lying to me. Does he really think I can't tell? Not only did he lie, he did it terribly. His eyes darted around the room, his cheeks flushed, and his voice dropped an octave. Rome doesn't intend to put any boundaries in place, which means I need to keep working on him. I didn't expect a miracle in the first session. I hoped he would be more open to the opportunity, but I can work my magic on him.

Finishing combing the knots from my hair, I put on a purple V-neck and button my jeans. Rome should be here any minute, and even though I know this isn't a date, I can't push aside my nerves.

"Oh, Wildflower. I'll protect you, don't worry."

Following one of Gwen's techniques, I sip on some ginger ale to settle my stomach and try to breathe out the violent anxiety that has taken over.

"This isn't a date. Rome and I are two friends. I'm helping him get out more. That's all. Stop freaking out," I lecture myself.

My phone goes off beside me, and I nearly fall off my bed in response to the sudden interruption.

I'm right outside :)

Be right down.

I stand up and start to pace the room. I'm being ridiculous. For all I know, Rome isn't interested in me like that anymore.

Fuck, I can't even lie to myself.

Grabbing my phone, I head out of my dorm and take the stairs down to the foyer. I halt when I see him. Rome has his hands in his jeans pockets, staring up at the blue sky painted with white clouds. The sun seems to wrap around him instead of beating down on his body. It's almost as if the sun knows Rome is light himself, and he deserves the world to know just how glorious he is.

Strolling toward the door, Rome raises his hand and gently waves at me.

Gulping past the lump in my throat, I head outside and jog down the stairs.

"Hey, blondie."

My knees wobble when he flashes me his flawless smile.

"I'm starting to think I need more nicknames for you," I say with a grin. "Let's see. I have: football boy, Sir Eats A Lot, Carter, muscle man. Hmm, what else can I call you?"

"Dashing? Handsome? Irresistible?"

"How about captain?" I wink at him, and he purses his lips.

"Very funny."

"Too soon? How about—"

"Football legend?"

"Turtle licker." I smirk.

"I don't want to know how you landed on that one. Anyway, ready to go get spooked?"

"Absolutely."

But I really wanted to say, *"With you? I'm ready for anything."*

The car ride to the theater was silent, but it didn't feel awkward. It was nice. I caught myself smiling, just happy to be in his presence.

When we pull into the parking lot, I hop out of the car and psych myself up. The last time I was spooked, it involved a Horror Fest and a certain siren being punched in the face. I hope this outing doesn't end similarly.

"Do you have to use the bathroom or something?" Rome asks when he catches me jumping in place.

"What? No. Well, maybe. Wait, what is that for?" I point at the hoodie Rome grabs from the backseat. The same jacket he let me wear during the beach trip.

"It gets cold. Thought I'd bring it for you just in case."

And there goes my fucking heart. It melts into my bones and leaves me feeling wobbly.

"That's sweet of you." I smile, and we start to walk toward the entrance.

When we pass through the front doors, a gust of cold air washes over my body, and I inhale the aroma of freshly popped popcorn, artificial butter, and frozen drinks. The sound of arcade games bounces off the walls as Rome buys our tickets. Looking down at my feet, I grin at the classic nineties pattern. Random geometric shapes in all sorts of crazy colors. I follow Rome as he leads us to the concession stand.

"What, no diet today?" I tease while nudging into his arm.

"No diet today. We're going to eat as much as we can until we hurl. How does that sound?" Rome winks while clicking his tongue.

"Sounds like my kind of Saturday afternoon."

Rome orders a large popcorn, two large blue raspberry

frozen drinks, and way too many boxes of candy. We walk to our seats with our arms full. Sitting near the middle, we're both happy to discover only a few other people are seated.

I don't mind crowds, but something about movie theater crowds hits differently, and they can be irritating. Sipping on my frozen drink, I lean back and open a box of gummies. When the lights dim, Rome's relaxed expression turns eager, and I realize just how much he wanted to do this today.

A smile spreads across my face, and when he looks at me, he tosses his hoodie at my face. I peel it off and snort when I catch Rome holding back a violent laugh. I chuck a gummy at his face and press my lips together.

"I see how it is, turtle licker." I cross my arms over my chest and huff.

His chuckle is muted by the movie's volume.

"I'm sorry," he tries to whisper, but he's almost doubled over from laughing so hard.

Rome leans over and wraps his arms around me. I can't resist nuzzling into the crook of his neck and getting lost in his ocean-scented skin.

"I'm right here if you get scared." His words send a rush of hot chills over my body, and I nearly faint.

Pulling back, Rome offers me a kind smile before leaning back in his seat and tossing popcorn in his mouth like nothing just happened.

Chapter Nineteen

Rome

So far, the movie is everything I hoped it would be—the premise is what pulled me in. The main character's name is Shay, and she has a neurological condition that numbs her ability to feel fear. She enrolls in an experiment to visit a haunted manor, hoping the experts may be able to help her. Of course, there's a love interest, but I enjoy romance more than the average guy. We've already had a few jump scares, and each one has caused Chrissy and me to either scream or jolt in our seats.

Chrissy puts on the sweater and covers her face with the hood. I smirk when I catch her hiding behind the fabric. Just when I thought she couldn't get more adorable, she goes and proves me wrong.

I grab popcorn from the bucket mindlessly, and another hand reaches in, making me jump.

"It's just me," Chrissy reassures as our hands brush together.

Peeling my eyes off the screen, I look at her and become distracted from the movie. What would it be like to have someone like Chrissy in my life? Someone I could joke around with but who would still love me deeply. What would happen if I didn't let my fears get in the way?

The music hastens, and Chrissy's posture stiffens in response. Grabbing her slushie with her free hand, she slurps on it as her eyes widen.

With a lopsided smirk, I turn back to the screen just in time to see the main character enter a room that she discovered behind a portrait.

"That was amazing!" Chrissy cheers when we leave the theater. Her hair is slightly mussed from wearing the hood the entire time. "The ending?!" Chrissy makes a gesture like her head is exploding. "Did you enjoy it?"

"Yes, it was definitely worth the wait. Thank you for coming with me."

Chrissy nudges my arm as we walk side by side back to my car. Rushing ahead, I open the door for her, and her facial expression softens.

"Why, thank you, kind sir."

I close the door once she slides in.

Back in the driver's seat, I start the engine and fasten my

seat belt. After blasting the AC, I drum my hands on the steering wheel. The idea of going home makes my skin crawl. I don't want to be alone. I'm tired of being alone. I don't want to drag Chrissy around with me all day though. She's probably sick of me by this point.

"What's next?"

Her question catches me off guard.

"You don't want me to bring you home?"

"It's still early. Why don't we crash the Waylens' house, or maybe we can get some lunch?"

I'm baffled. That's the only word I can think of that accurately describes how I feel right now. My original plan was to drop her off and then do everything possible to avoid going home. I like this idea a lot better.

"Can I take you to one of my favorite places?"

Chrissy nods, so I shift the car into drive and start back toward the Castle Brook campus.

"Please tell me you're joking." Chrissy's unimpressed as I walk her toward the football stadium.

"Just trust me." I grab her hand and lead her down the walkway.

We step onto the field, and the space around us is open. The hash marks to designate the yard lines are freshly painted. The first time my cleats touched the dark green grass, I felt at home.

Chrissy takes a silent step forward, slowly spinning around to take in the brilliance of this place. The stadium can seat twenty thousand people. If the team is doing well, seats will fill, and the audience will roar. Their chanting and shouting used to be a distraction, but you learn to use it as motivation.

"I never noticed how huge this place is," Chrissy mutters in astonishment.

"You never come to any games," I remark.

"Well, you never invited me, now did you?" She purses her lips and places her hands on her hips.

"Would you come to opening day? You, Gwen, Ash, and Zack?"

I never have anyone in the crowd cheering me on. Sure, I have fans, but the idea of having someone who means something to me out there feels different. "I'd get you good seats, free food—"

"Can I get a jersey?" she cuts in.

"Absolutely. Which player do you want?"

"Yours, duh."

Chrissy goes back to admiring the field, completely clueless that she's left me breathless. She wants *my* number? She wants to wear *my* last name on her back? The image of her wearing one of my jerseys barrels into my mind, and my face burns.

"I'll give you whatever you want."

Chrissy beams in response, leaving me speechless. She skips over to the player's bench and sits down, patting the spot next to her.

"I have a question for you."

Following her gesture, I straddle the bench and face her.

"When did you start playing football?"

"Dad and I used to play catch and watch the games. I fell in love with it, so I begged my parents to sign me up. They didn't want to initially, but I always got what I wanted." Well, not *everything*.

I'm not your typical sports kid. My parents didn't force me into football. In fact, I begged them to let me play. They were concerned about the concussion rate, and they didn't want my body to bruise or my bones to break. I got my way in the end. Football is therapy in my own twisted way. Dad stopped caring after Mom left. He drowned himself in alcohol and TV. He got better over time, but he's always on the brink of a mental breakdown.

"They didn't push you into it?"

"No, not at all. They supported me even though they were terrified I might get hurt. It was only when—" Fuck, there she goes again. How does she manage to pull my secrets out of me? She must have a trick up her sleeve . . .

"Only when, what?"

Peering over her shoulder, I ponder whether I should tell her about my mother. Chrissy has good parents. Would she understand? Or would she throw me a pity party and offer me fake sympathy?

With a sigh, I meet her eyes again and decide to tell her. After all, this is what this mentorship is all about, right?

"My mom left when I was eight. My dad and I don't know why. All she said was that she needed time away. I don't think he was abusive. They seemed to love one another, but I don't know what happened behind closed doors. My dad withdrew after that. He went to work and provided for us, but emotionally, he was a ghost." I clear my throat to keep the emotions that bleed into my words at bay. I don't avert my gaze, and neither does Chrissy. I can't stop now, might as well get it all out.

"There's a reason I don't have a girlfriend or go out on dates. I'm afraid to open myself to the possibility of heartbreak because what if I do and the person ruins me just like my mom did to my dad?"

With a tiny smile, Chrissy reaches for my hand and holds it. "That's a lot to carry, Rome. And you've been carrying it for years, haven't you?"

I can only manage to nod. Tears threaten my eyes, and I know if I speak, they'll break free.

"Love is tricky, and it'll always be a risk. No one walks into a relationship knowing they'll be safe. Love is dangerous and exciting. But it's always scary. I understand why you feel that way, and know you're not alone."

I sigh, and the tears in my eyes slip free. Dropping Chrissy's hand, I wipe them away immediately. I was a fool to think she would judge me over my past. This is Chrissy. The sweet ray of sunshine who exudes love and warmth wherever she goes. She's good at this, and I hope she knows it.

"Want my advice?" she asks gently. "Don't force anything, but if there's someone you like, ask them on a date. It'll be terrifying, but no more than that movie we just saw."

I can't help but snicker, and she follows suit.

"One date might turn into two, and that might turn into three, and so on. You can't let your past determine your future." Chrissy runs her thumbs along my cheekbones to dry my tears.

I want to ask *her* on a date. I want to see if one date turns into two. I want to see if we become anything more than friends. But my past isn't the only thing holding me back from that. It's also my best friend and her brother.

"Don't worry. I still think you're cool, Captain." She messes with my hair and brings a smile to my face.

"Thank you, Chrissy. For everything."

Her shoulders relax, and her eyes brighten against the midday sun.

"That's what friends are for. Now, why don't we go raid the Waylens' and make Max order us dinner?" Jumping to her feet, she offers me her hand, and I take it.

Friends. Who knew such a simple word could hurt so much . . .

Chapter Twenty

Chrissy

"Hey, Lawyer Man!" I call as Rome and I stroll into the Waylens' house, knowing it's unlocked because I told Gwen to unlock the door for me.

We have an ongoing deal. She keeps the door unlocked whenever I want to crash their house, and I supply her with my company.

It's a win-win scenario.

"Max!" I continue shouting while peeking into the kitchen.

"Do you just stroll in and start shouting wherever you go?" Rome asks with a chuckle as he leans against the kitchen archway, crossing his arms over his chest.

"Pretty much," I answer while nodding, noticing the pattern the second Rome brings it up. "Max!"

"Chrissy!" Max hollers from somewhere upstairs.

When I grab his hand and pull him up the staircase, Rome arches his brows in response.

"Where are you, other Waylen?"

"Other Waylen?" Max snickers. "I was the first Waylen, thank you very much."

I knock on his door. "Housekeeping." I smirk before opening it.

My face contorts when I see Max lying in his bed with a book in his face and Pickles sprawled on his lap like he's the sidekick to an evil mastermind.

"Can we help you?" Max asks without looking up from his book.

"Your favorite football star is here." I grin, knowing that will get his attention.

Max drops his book and beams over at Rome. The two of them started off rocky. I mean, Rome practically raided the fridge and ate all his fancy yogurt the first day they met. Max has a soft spot for him though. I can't say for certain what it is yet, but I see it.

"What can I do for my two favorite people today?" he asks in a cheerful tone.

"Order us food? Pretty please." I offer him a wide smile in hopes of winning him over.

"I'm starting to think you only like me for my wallet," he grumbles.

"You know your life would be boring without me," I remark.

"Yeah, but his wallet would be happy," Rome chimes in, and my jaw drops.

"You're supposed to be on my side!" I punch him and flinch the second my fist touches his sculpted forearm.

"You never learn your lesson," he chuckles as I wince and shake my hand off.

"Where's Gwen and Ash? I need backup . . ."

"They went to see that movie you two saw today," Max responds as he stands.

Pickles stretches and sits at the foot of his bed, squinting his big green eyes at me like he knows something I don't.

"Alright, blondie, or should I say *blondies*." Max laughs at his lame joke.

As I roll my eyes, Rome chuckles and smiles wide.

Maybe that's why Max likes Rome; he laughs at his lame dad jokes.

"What do you guys want to order?"

I look over at Rome. "Whatcha think, Cap?"

His eyes widen and sparkle, and I can't help but broaden my smile. "Mexican?"

"Now we're talking! Why don't you two set up a movie while I order the food?"

"Can we watch something funny? I need something light after seeing that movie," I admit.

"Put on whatever you want." Max ruffles my hair before opening the app on his phone to start the food order.

"I like him," Rome tells me as we head back down the stairs.

"He has his moments."

I skip over to the couch, plop down, grab the TV remote, and hum. Rome sits down next to me, resting his knee against mine. The brief touch sets my body aflame, and I'd give anything to lean against him and snuggle close.

"What did you have in mind?" he asks, jarring me for a moment. "Geez, that movie left you jumpy."

My lips tilt upward as I try to clear the images of snuggling up to Rome out of my head. "Yeah, just a tad," I mumble while turning on *Rapunzel*.

"Oh, I love this movie!" Rome exclaims, and my brow raises.

"Really?" I was ready to hear bitching and complaining about putting a princess movie on. I was unprepared for a six-foot-five football player to get excited about my princess movie choice.

"Absolutely, just don't tell the other guys." He points at me in a teasing way.

"Yeah, yeah, whatever you say."

I don't start the film until the food arrives, and when it does, my eyes widen, and I fear they may fall out. Max ordered way too much food; he set it all up on the table in the living room, and there's still more food on the kitchen island.

Rome bounces in his seat in anticipation. My stomach growls even though I ate a ton of popcorn earlier today.

When Max sits on the floor across from us, I play the movie, and we dig in.

Three types of tacos, tostadas, elote, mole, refried beans, and rice, are laid out before us.

Rome doesn't waste a second piling his plate, and his glowing expression makes me sigh in relief. This is the Rome I know. He's kind, bright, and loves food and spending time with his friends. Malik put too much on his shoulders, and if it's up to me to help him realize that, then I will.

I would do anything for Rome, even if nothing romantically happens between us. Rome deserves to be happy. He deserves love, all the food he can get his hands on, and a girl who will love him to the ends of the earth. I'll do everything in my power to ensure he gets what he deserves.

Even if my heart breaks in the process.

Chapter Twenty-One

Rome

"How come whenever we return home, you guys always have food and are huddled around the TV?" Ash asks.

"Shh!" Max hushes his brother as the movie hits the final heart-wrenching scene.

I'm beginning to realize that smiling around this group is effortless. I don't think I've grinned this much in months, and I can thank Chrissy for that.

Gwen plops beside Chrissy and wraps her arms around her waist with a big smile. I glance over at Ash and grin when I find him looking at Gwen, almost in a daze.

My attention floats to Chrissy, and my heartbeat hammers in my eardrums. Today has been one of the best days I've had in a long time. When Coach told us about this mentorship, I was ready to get it over with. Little did I know it would bring Chrissy and me closer together. I know she didn't ask me to hang out today because she noticed I was in a rut. She asked because she cares about me and our friendship.

Friendship . . .

I'm beginning to despise that word. The thing is, though,

even if Zack wasn't in the picture, I'm not sure I would go after a girl like her. Not because she isn't everything I want, but simply because she is *more* than anything I could ever imagine.

It's plain and simple: I don't deserve a girl like her.

The credits roll, and my gaze is still fixed on the wildflower beside me.

"Can I talk now?" Ash asks with a hint of sass in his tone.

"Do you have something nice to say?" Max asks with an arched brow.

"To you? Never."

I snort out a laugh as Gwen snickers.

"Then no, dear brother, you may not speak." Max stands and starts to clean off the table.

"Oh, come on—"

"Can you guys hear that? It sounds like an annoying breeze." Max pretends to listen for something, and I laugh.

"You're supposed to be on my side." Ash side-eyes me, and I snicker harder.

"Rome, I have an opening for a brother. Are you interested?" Max offers, and Ash's jaw drops.

"You son of a bitch!"

He chases Max into the kitchen, and the two girls and I start cackling at the scene playing out before us.

"Rome! Help! There's some crazy ghost chasing me!" Max hollers as the two of them run around the kitchen island.

"This ghost is going to haunt your ass for all of eternity!"

"What about Gwen? You're supposed to be with her!" Max fires back, and Gwen doubles over.

"Who do you think is going to help me?" Ash shouts with a playful grin.

"She loves me too much!"

"Where are my blondies? Help your favorite lawyer!"

Chrissy falls against my shoulder and laughs harder when Gwen speaks up. "Pickles, no!"

Pickles charges in after Max and Ash and joins the fray. Max's screams get louder as Ash runs away from that ball of chaos.

"Pickles, help me get Max!"

The three of them burst into the living room as Ash gets Max into a headlock and digs his fist on top of his head. "Gotcha, sucker!"

"This is cruel and unusual punishment." Max struggles to get Ash off his back as Pickles starts to bat at his nose. "I'm suing for brother abuse."

"You know you love me," Ash says, planting a big kiss on Max's cheek before letting him go.

Max rubs it off his face with faux disgust. "Yeah, yeah, but you owe me."

Pickles crawls to Gwen's side as she catches her breath.

"Look what you did to my girlfriend. She can't breathe because of you." Ash gestures to Gwen, and she starts laughing again.

"Stop! I can't handle anymore."

Chrissy rights her posture as the three of them go back and forth. She turns to face me, her dazzling eyes meeting mine, and color rushes to my cheeks. "Welcome to our crazy family, Carter."

She ruffles my hair, and I allow my shoulders to relax.

"Did you have fun today?" she asks with hope tinging in her voice.

"Today has been a blast. Thank you again."

She wraps her arms around my neck and squeezes me. Without thinking, I hug her back and rest my chin on her shoulder.

"Anytime, but you know what this means now, right?" Her breath is warm against my ear.

I take in a deep breath, soaking in her scent before responding. "Tell me."

"You can never get rid of me. I'm going to bother you until the end of our days."

The idea sets my heart into overdrive, and my stomach flips.

"You could never bother me. It would be a pleasure to have you *bother me* until we part," I whisper in her ear.

Her back arches under my palms before she releases a puff of air.

"Don't say I didn't warn you, all-star."

"Don't say I never wanted it, Wildflower."

Chapter Twenty-Two

Rome

"Pick up the pace!" Coach orders from the sidelines.

Sweat drenches every inch of my body. The sun is relentless today, hammering down on us. Most of us are panting and on the verge of heat exhaustion.

"One last drill! Push it!"

I straighten and scan for the ball as it's thrown. Once I spot it, I arch toward it and grunt as I catch it and pull it in against my chest.

"That's it, Carter!" Coach Bradson shouts, his voice on the verge of giving out. "Do that if you want to get out of here! Carter and Faulkner, you're dismissed!"

I take a moment and fall on my back, my chest rising and falling while the other guys continue their drills. Pushing myself on my feet, I strip my shirt off and walk past the cheer-leaders pretending not to watch us.

When I walk into the tunnel to the locker room, I see someone jogging toward me out of the corner of my eye. Normally, I would turn around, smile, and engage in conversa-tion. But, right now, all I want is a cold shower and to change out of these damn clothes. So, I run into the locker room without looking back.

Not wasting another second, I kick off my shoes, remove my socks that are beyond saving, and peel off my white, grass-stained integrated pad pants.

I head into the showers and crank the temperature as cold as possible. Stepping under the showerhead, I moan as the water rushes down my back, rinsing away the sweat and grime. I hang my head low and let the water drench my hair before grabbing the soap bottle I keep here and washing my body.

"I can't wait for summer to be over," Levi sighs as he turns on the shower across the way. "I'm not sure how much more of this I can take."

"It'll be over soon. Just wait until we have our first game at the beginning of the semester. The stands will fill, and the cheering will make it all worth it. Plus, you might change your mind when we start practicing and playing in the snow."

"I can't wait for that."

With a gentle smile, I finish cooling off and cleaning my body. I turn the showerhead off and grab my towel.

"Hey, before you go."

I turn back around to face Levi, securing the towel around my waist.

"A cheerleader asked me for your number."

So that's who was following me . . . I should have known.

"Don't look so irritated about it," Levi chuckles. "You know how excited I got when she approached me? She's fucking hot—"

"You didn't."

Levi winces. "I did."

With an awkward smile, I groan and run my fingers through my hair. "It's fine," I sigh. "Please don't do that again."

"Yes, boss."

Back at my locker, I put on a pair of dark blue basketball shorts and a white tee, then tie my shoes before heading into the hall. As soon as I open the door, I see her, and my shoulders relax.

"You have no idea how happy I am to see you."

"Is everything okay?" Chrissy asks as her cheeks flush.

Before I can respond, my phone buzzes in my hand.

Hey Rome, this is Lindsay. You probably don't know me because I'm new, but I asked Levi for your number and was wondering if you'd like to hang out sometime.

Chapter Twenty-Three

Chrissy

Based on Rome's expression, either the heat got to him, or his phone threatened his life.

Stepping forward, I place my hand over his and soften my tone. "Let me see." He releases his grip, and I look at the text. "Why do you look as if you're about to faint? She asked you on a date not to marry her," I tease.

His eyes stay on me for a while, scanning my expression. "I don't want to go out with her."

"Why not?"

"She's not the woman I like."

My heart stills as time slows and blurs around us. If our circumstances were different, I would curl my hands in his hair and pull him against my lips. I would show him how much I want him, and I would die happily in his arms.

But that can't happen.

Rome and I wouldn't want to risk hurting Zack like that. The idea is too much to bear. I can imagine the look on his face if he found out and we didn't tell him, can hear his reaction if I talked to him about my feelings for his best friend. Neither scenario plays in my favor.

"Who do you like?" I mutter, and he only stares at me in response, answering my question without words.

I clear my throat and continue. "How do you know you don't like her when you don't know her?"

He shrugs.

"Go on one date. Have fun, and just forget your responsibilities for the night. What can go wrong?"

Rome groans. "I don't know."

"Oh, come on. One date. Think of it as an assignment from your mentor."

Rome observes me again, like he's waiting for me to catch him making the wrong decision.

I offer him a kind smile while holding up one finger. "Remember what I said? One date might turn into two, and that might turn into three, and so on. Take the chance."

His expression softens, and his lips turn into almost a sad smirk. "Fine. For you, I'll go on *one* date."

He returns his attention to his phone to text the girl.

We stroll outside, where a blast of hot air hits us, but his eyes remain on his screen. It's not until we leave campus grounds that he puts his phone back in his pocket and looks at me.

"So?" I ask with a teasing tone, even though my nerves are protesting with envy.

"We're going to get dinner Friday evening around seven."

"Where?"

"Rosamarie's Pizzeria—"

"The one with outdoor seating?" I fire back a tad too quickly.

"Yeah, you know the place?"

I smirk as an idea pops into my head. "I do know the place. You'll have a great time."

If I could laugh maniacally without raising concern, I totally would. Sometimes, my brain is on its best behavior, but most of the time, it's up to no good.

And right now, it's ready for trouble.

Chapter Twenty-Four

Chrissy

"**T**his is a bad idea," Gwen repeats like a broken record player.

"Code 'Spy on Carter' is not a bad idea. It's genius," I retort as we get ready in her and Ash's room.

"But why are we doing this?"

"I want to make sure everything goes well. It's part of the mentorship program," I lie.

In truth, I want to keep my eyes on him because I'm a jealous jerk. It was my idea for him to go on a date in the first place, and here I am, dressing up to spy on him with my best friend.

Selfishly, I want to ensure nothing romantic happens between them, but I don't know what I'll do if it does progress to that level. I'm a decent planner, so I'm sure I'll figure something out.

"And the disguises?" Gwen asks.

"What about them?"

She smirks at me while holding up a trench coat. "Are they necessary?"

"What's the fun in a stakeout if you can't dress incognito?"

Gwen nods before slipping on her sneakers. The two of us get dressed in what I must say, are killer outfits.

I wanted to wear a trench coat and a detective hat, but given that it's ninety degrees outside and humid, I decide to spare my body from additional sweat.

I tie the drawstring of the basketball shorts I stole from Zack, put on fake black-rimmed glasses, and tie my hair back. A Castle Brook baseball hat completes the ensemble.

Gwen is wearing matching black shorts, a baggy blue T-shirt, and a matching university cap.

I give her a thumbs-up before I leap past her. "I almost forgot!"

I pull a plastic bag out of my purse and offer her a fake mustache.

She looks at me like I've lost my mind. "Are you serious? No one is going to believe these are real."

"Oh, come on! They look so real, and no one will be up in our business. We just need to pull off the look from a distance."

"This is such a bad idea," she groans while accepting the handlebar mustache. "You two are going to end up together anyway. I feel it in my bones."

We stand in front of the mirror and secure our faux facial hair. When we finish, we look at one another in the mirror and laugh hysterically.

We look like absolute fools, but this is going to work. We look like two college kids with terrible mustaches going out to dinner. Rome won't spot us from a mile away.

The two of us head down the stairs and walk into the kitchen. Ash sputters out his water all over himself and the floor the second he sees us, and Max runs his hands down his face.

"What the fuck?" he asks as his lips turn upright.

"Whatever this is"—Max points at us while forming a circle —"I don't agree with it, and I don't want any part of it."

"I told you we look ridiculous," Gwen mutters as Ash starts to cackle.

"You guys look amazing!" he snorts while grabbing his phone.

"No pictures!" Gwen shouts, but Ash doesn't listen.

Pulling her into my arms, I flash a wide smile, and Ash takes a thousand pictures.

As he wipes his tears, Gwen smirks before looking at Max. "Max—"

"No way." He shakes his head before she can even ask her question.

"You don't even know what I'm going to ask." She pouts.

"You want to borrow my car, and the answer is no."

"Oh, come on. This is for Chrissy and Rome." She uses her most innocent tone and smiles at him. "Please, pretty please! We can't use Ash's car. Rome will spot us."

Max and Ash share a quick glance, communicating in their unspoken brother language. They know what we're up to, and neither likes the idea. That doesn't mean they don't find it entertaining, and they're both suckers for Gwen.

"Fine, just be careful." Max tosses her his keys, and she manages to catch them.

"Thank you!" she sings before running up and kissing him on his cheek.

"That was so scratchy." He shivers and scrubs his face.

She locks her eyes on Ash next, and before he can bolt, she crashes into his arms and plants her lips on his.

I let out a small laugh and smile. My heart flutters at the idea of Rome and me having moments like this, and I dare to wonder how he would react if I tried to kiss him while wearing a fake mustache.

Ash turns red, and when Gwen pulls away, she twirls the keys around her finger and loops her arm through mine.

"Ready, pretty lady?"

I walk in time with her, and we giggle when we overhear Ash say, "Why was I kinda into that?"

It's 6:35 p.m., and the sun has begun to set. The sky is pink and purple, interspersed with wisps of clouds. The engine's hum and the noise of the radio station Gwen turned on surround us. We blast the AC, and goose bumps quickly trail over my legs.

The pizzeria is twenty minutes from the Waylens', giving my anxiety enough time to go wild. I focus on the dashboard, the dark blue backlit gauges, dials, and displays. Gwen and I are silent during the drive.

"Thanks for doing this with me," I whisper while playing with my hands.

She grins without looking at me. "I may not approve of the idea, but that doesn't mean I won't support you."

My shoulders drop, and I close my eyes as my heart hammers against my ribcage. The thought of seeing Rome on a date with another girl conjures a potent mixture of emotions. If

I weren't such a coward, he and I would be on that date. All I have to do is talk to Zack. I mean, the worst he can say is no, right?

That's not the only thing holding me back though. I want Rome, and I know I can love him, but would that be enough? I'm no one special.

I'm not smart like Gwen, and I'm not gorgeous like the cheerleaders. Miles and I didn't work out because I knew he deserved more than I was giving him. But also, I didn't feel like what we had was progressing. I want what my parents and Gwen and Ash have, but it may never happen. So, why bother trying?

We pull in behind the restaurant and find parking near the end.

With a shaky breath, I look at Gwen and nod. "Ready for operation 'Spy on Carter'?"

With a smirk, Gwen fixes her cap and nods back. "Let's do this."

Chapter Twenty-Five

Rome

I don't remember the last time I went on a date. If I were to consider the movie outing with Chrissy a date, that would be my answer. And if I were to compare the two, the vibe is vastly different.

Here I am, sweating my ass off through my light running shirt and jeans. It must be a mixture of nerves and the heat. Either way, I'm uncomfortable. Something about Lindsay seems off, but I can't put my finger on it.

Don't get me wrong, she's pretty and seems nice, but I have a gut feeling she's not showing me her true self.

We get a table outside, and I sigh in relief when the sun begins to set.

The chairs and table are made from matching teakwood. The fence to my right is wrought iron and polished to perfection, with roses, vines, and fairy lights weaving across it. For a pizzeria, this place is very romantic and classy.

"So, Lindsay." I break the silence as she sips her water. "What are you majoring in?"

"Nursing."

I can't help but chuckle. It seems the majority of the girls at Castle Brook are majoring in nursing. There's nothing wrong with wanting to be a nurse, but I can't help but wonder why this generation is pulled toward the profession.

"What about you?"

I observe her frizz-free blonde hair and twinkling eyes. It's not long before a sting pierces my chest.

I miss Chrissy's wild curls and mischievous gleam. It should be her sitting across from me, not this stranger who managed to get my number from Levi.

If only I had a backbone.

"History," I respond with a small smile.

"History? Really? I would have thought business or some kind of physical therapy," she offers with a hint of chastising amusement.

"I'm a firm believer in doing what you love. I adore history. I always have. I mean, if you could go back to any significant historical event, wouldn't that be fantastic? Imagine being inside Independence Hall when the Founding Fathers signed the Declaration of Independence. Or on the field during the Battle of Yorktown."

"You've lost me." Lindsay shakes her head before dropping her gaze.

Looking down at my hands, a lingering sensation of someone watching me creeps along my left arm. Peering over, I squint when I catch a lanky guy with a terrible mustache staring at me. When he catches me looking, he and his friend scramble to pick up their menus and hide their faces.

Weird . . .

The pizza arrives, steaming from the brick oven, and my stomach rumbles. I've eaten today, but not nearly enough. If Chrissy were here, she would scold me, and the thought makes me grin.

The crust is rich golden-brown with some charred spots. The cheese is a gooey, molten blanket with bright slices of red garden tomatoes, green peppers, and sausages.

Not wasting another second, I cut the pizza into eight equal slices. Lindsay raises her plate, and I put two slices on it before I serve myself. When I pick the pizza up, I take a bite and stop myself from moaning. This is by far the best pizza I've ever had.

Silence engulfs us, and my skin starts to itch from the awkwardness. The glares coming from the two guys at the table across from us don't make things better.

"So—" I start but stop the second my phone vibrates on the table.

Lindsay looks over at me and smiles. "You can get that."

"Thanks," I say as I open the text, relieved to see it's from Chrissy.

> How's it going?

> It's okay . . . it's quiet.

> Is she quiet, or are you being quiet?

> Both?

> Get to know her!

> I don't know how!

> OMG, okay. Ask her if she likes being a cheerleader.

I start to type out my response but stop when I get another message.

> JUST DO IT.

"How do you like being a cheerleader?" I ask before Chrissy sends me another threatening message.

"I love it!" Her energy comes to life, and I can't help but smile because it reminds me of how Chrissy gets. "My favorite part is the energy. The crowd during game days, cheering on the players. It keeps me fit too."

"It is a vigorous sport—"

"Finally, someone gets it." She cuts me off and continues to beam at me.

"Do you enjoy football?"

"I do. My goal is to be drafted by the Philadelphia Eagles, but if that doesn't happen, I'll teach American history." As I grin, her expression drops and her forehead crinkles. "Everything okay?"

"You'll just give up if you don't get drafted?" she questions as her posture stiffens.

"Well, I enjoy football, but it's not something I'll run myself dry over. I figure wherever the universe wants me to be is where it'll put me. Either way, I'll be happy."

She squints, and the crease in her brow deepens. She did *not* like that answer.

"So you're giving up?" Her voice rises, and my eyes widen.

"No—"

"You'll quit after one rejection?"

"It's not quitting—"

"Yes, it is!" she shouts, and I'm taken aback.

"There's no reason to scream," I whisper before glancing over at the table where the two guys are and looking at them in wonder.

When the one in the blue shirt sees I'm watching them, he lowers his hat to hide his face and whispers something to his partner.

"I can't believe this," Lindsay scoffs, but I don't give her the time of day.

The guy in the red shirt peeks over at me, and I tilt my head as a strange sensation creeps over my body. The second he turns away, I smile.

You've got to be kidding me.

Looking back at my date, I stand up and place some bills on the table.

"I'd say it was a lovely time, but we both know it wasn't. Now, if you'll excuse me."

Before she can say anything, I walk across the way and tower over the two men hiding behind their hands.

Did these girls really think they could disguise themselves like this? Did Chrissy really think I wouldn't spot her curls from a mile away?

Placing my hand on the table, I lean forward and lift Chrissy's cap by the bill. I chuckle the second her glasses slide down her nose and laugh harder when her mustache comes into full view.

"What the fuck are you wearing?" I manage to ask.

Without a moment of hesitation, Chrissy points at Gwen and blurts out, "It was all her idea!"

"What?!" Gwen shrieks before the two of them go back and forth.

My smile grows as I watch these two point and throw each other under the bus.

"Okay, okay." I hold my hands in the air and snort. "Chrissy," I chide with a teasing tone.

"Rome," she mumbles as her leg jostles.

Holding out my hand, I meet her gaze and offer her a wide smile. "We need to talk."

"What if I don't want to talk?" She pouts while crossing her arms over her chest.

"Sorry, Wildflower, you don't have a choice." I grab her hand and pull her out of her chair with ease.

She doesn't fight back when I guide her to the side of the restaurant, toward the parking lot, and then stop at my car. She leans against the trunk and purses her lips.

"Okay, missy." I stop short and chuckle at her sweaty face. "Let's just take this off." I peel the mustache off her lips, and her jaw drops open.

"Son of a bitch!" She grunts before doubling over and pressing her hand against her mouth.

"Did you crazy glue that thing on?" I ask while crumbling it in my hand.

"Damn, and that's why I don't wax." She shakes it off before meeting my gaze again.

I stop myself from laughing at the red mark above her upper lip.

"Explain yourself, Willows. Why are you and Gwen here, dressed like—" I gesture toward her attire, bewildered. "This."

"I wanted to make sure the date was going well," she answers nonchalantly.

"Hence the text messages?" I ask with an arched brow.

"Yes."

"Were you eavesdropping?"

"Yes."

Her honesty makes me laugh while I rake my fingers through my hair.

"Why? Why all this?" I point toward her attire again, totally dumbfounded by everything that has happened this evening.

"I just wanted to make sure you were okay," she answers in a whisper.

Meeting her gaze, I sigh while I examine her. Her lips are pursed, and her nose is crinkled. She's hiding something.

"Honesty is the best policy. What aren't you telling me?"

She groans in response and tosses her cap on the ground. "Do you think she's pretty?"

My eyes widen, and it takes me a moment to process not only what she just said but an answer as well. "She's pretty, but only on the outside. I'm sure you overheard the conversation."

"Why did you go out with her?"

"Because you told me to."

She rolls her eyes. "You could have told me to fuck off . . . Whatever, I'll rephrase the question." She looks at me for a brief moment before continuing. "Is Zack the only barrier between us?"

Once again, her question is unexpected. Our chemistry is undeniable, but I thought she was moving on. Have I been misreading everything that has occurred between us? Does she still think about me in a romantic sense? This could explain why she dragged Gwen here tonight, not only to keep an eye on me but because she cares about me. *Was she jealous?*

I mean, she's also weird—in the best way possible—but that's not the point.

I open my mouth to respond, but she cuts me off. "Is it because you don't enjoy spending time with me?"

"The whole time I sat across from Lindsay, I could only think of you. All I wanted was to see *you*. To see your wild eyes, your mischievous grin, and your unruly curls. When I sat down, all I could think about was how much I thought you would like it here. I wanted to be with *you*, Chrissy. When I tell you that Zack is the only obstacle, I mean it wholeheartedly." Passion and desperation fill my words. I need her to believe me.

I never thought she wasn't pretty. Even in high school, I recognized her natural beauty. I want nothing more than to be with her. To pick her up, to feel her legs wrap around my waist as I guide her against my car, and to feel her lips crash against mine as I kiss her. Fuck, the urge makes my skin itch, and I know she's the only cure.

"You're not lying, are you?" she mumbles before sniffling back her tears.

"You tell me. Do you think I'm lying to you?"

She scans my expression, lingering over my lips, traveling to my eyes, then down to my hands. She's looking for signs, but she won't find any because I'm not lying. And I will do anything to ensure she believes me.

"You're not," she mutters before dropping her gaze to her feet.

Without giving it another thought, I step forward, tilt her head up with my fingers, and lock my gaze with hers.

"Never hide your eyes from me." I lower my tone as my stomach riots with nerves from being so close to her. "Don't ever look down, Wildflower. The world needs to see your beauty, but if it were up to me, I'd keep it all to myself."

She doesn't respond, so I pull her closer, and she stumbles into my chest. "Do you understand?" I trace small circles along her chin with my thumb.

"I do," she whispers.

"Good. Now, go find Gwen and get yourselves home. I'll see you at the cat café for a session on Monday, okay?"

"Okay." She glances down at my lips again, and I don't stop myself from looking at hers either.

"Go. Before I make a mistake we'll both regret."

With a solemn nod, she looks behind me, and I drop my hand. When she leaves, I focus on my breathing rather than the impulse brewing in my veins.

It's impossible to fight these feelings, and I can't deny it any longer.

It might be time to have a one-on-one with Zack . . .

Chapter Twenty-Six

Chrissy

"Why hat the hell happened?" Gwen asks while trying to keep up with me.

"I don't want to talk about it," I say without looking over my shoulder.

"I told you this was a bad idea." She uses her lecture voice and side-eyes me as she walks to the driver's side door.

"You were right, okay? Is that what you want to hear?" My voice raises, and she sighs.

"No, it's not what I want to hear. I just want to know that you're okay."

I'm far from okay. In fact, I'm the farthest from okay than I've ever been. Rome told me I was gorgeous and that he wanted to date me, sending a riot of frustrating feelings through me. Never, and I mean never, has anyone done anything like that to me, let alone in the span of ten minutes.

Miles was good with his words, but his actions infuriated me, or rather, his lack of actions. Sure, he would compliment me, but it never went beyond that. It never felt genuine because his words were never filled with passion. He never hugged me randomly, tilted my head upward when I glanced down at my shoes, offered me his coat, or pushed me against a wall to kiss me in a fit of desire.

Rome has done three out of those four things, and I feel like the fourth is inevitable, no matter how hard we try to fight it.

So, no, I'm not okay.

"Can you just take me home, please?" I murmur.

Gwen's expression softens, and she offers me a sincere smile. "Your place or mine?"

"Mine." There I know Rome won't randomly appear. I'll be safe and away from the temptation that plagues me when he's around.

"And that is how I know you're not okay."

We're silent the entire car ride back to Castle Brook. When she parks the car, I stare at my folded hands and squeeze my eyes shut, forcing the remaining tears to fall down my cheeks.

"Do you want me to stay?"

"No, thank you though." I offer her the best smile I can muster.

I put my hand on the door handle and push it open.

When I put one foot outside, Gwen wraps her hand around mine and stops me. "I'm going to need two favors from you."

I look back at her and nod.

"One, you'll text me first thing in the morning."

"I can do that," I mumble.

"Two, you will work on acknowledging your feelings for Rome."

I open my mouth, but she shushes me. "I don't want to hear it. You give everyone advice on their mental health, but you won't give yourself the time of day. Your feelings for him are growing, and there will be a point of no return if you continue to avoid them. I'm not saying jump his bones. All I want is for you to look at yourself in the mirror, say the words, and make a decision. Either follow those feelings or continue to avoid them and live to regret that choice."

I observe her for a moment, trying to figure out when she became so headstrong. Gwen has always cared about me, but she never pushed me outside my comfort zone. This is new, and while I want to tell her she's wrong, she's not. I walk through life examining people and encouraging them to work on themselves. I'll tell Gwen, Zack, and even Ash to practice self-care, even if it's something as simple as a face mask and a cup of tea. When was the last time I did something like that? I can't say because I don't think it's ever happened.

Gwen has grown up, and it wasn't all Ash's influence. She worked on herself because she knew that before she could love him, she had to learn to love herself. And while I'm proud of her progress, I can't help but feel like she left me behind. Here I am denying my feelings, crying over a boy, and not allowing myself to be happy because I'm worried about my brother and what he may think.

And there she is, growing to love her skin, standing up for herself and her loved ones, and showing me that I'm in the wrong. Gwen was always taking pages out of my playbook, so perhaps it's time I borrow some from hers.

"I think that's something I can do," I tell her with a weak smile.

"Promise?" She offers me her pinkie, just like she would back when we were kids.

And because I'm the adult I claim I am, I meet it because pinky promises are never to be broken. "I promise."

I don't wake up when the sun rises the next morning. If this were a regular day, I would be out of bed and jumping in the shower. When my eyes peel open, I immediately know today isn't a regular day. I stretch my legs and smile to myself at the sensation of the cool sheets against my skin. I shove my arms under my pillow and flop onto my stomach, closing my eyes once again.

I don't think I've ever slept in, not even in my angsty teen years. I was always up the second the sun rose, ready to start my day with a wide grin and a pep in my step.

So, when my eyes close again and my body sags from fatigue, I don't fight it. If my body is telling me that I need more rest, it's time I need to start listening to it. I don't have any plans today anyway, and no one will miss me if I sleep in.

I was right.

When I wake for the second time, I sigh in relief as I check my phone and don't see any messages or missed calls. A slight panic rises in my chest when I notice it's 11:00 a.m., but I remind myself I don't have anywhere to go and no one to see. Turning my head, I glance out the window and enjoy the silence. Birds are chirping, and the clouds are rolling in the endless baby-blue sky. I barely notice when my phone buzzes against my bed or when it starts to ring obnoxiously. I ignore it as best as I can, but when it doesn't stop, I groan.

"What do you want?!" I ask the device like it has a network of working nerves and cells.

Pain in the Ass appears on the screen, and I instinctively toss my phone across the room. It hits the floor with a *thud*, but between the tempered-glass screen protector and a solid phone case, it should be fine.

I'm not in the mood to talk to Zack. To be honest, I don't feel like talking to anyone, not even Gwen. As I stare at the ceiling, an idea pops into my head. It makes me sit straight up, hop out of bed, grab a change of clothes, and jump into the shower to prepare.

Gwen wants me to work on acknowledging my feelings for

Rome, right? I just happen to know the best way to do that, and it starts with going to my favorite store.

After showering, I put on a pair of jean shorts and a simple white T-shirt. Since my hair is curly, I work in some leave-in conditioner and run a fine-tooth comb through my crinkled locks. When I put the brush down, I look at my notes on the mirror and meet my reflection.

"I am willful. I am kind. My hair is unique, and my body is strong. I love me for me, and I'm special because no one else is like me." I have it memorized, but I rely on the notes for a reason.

Before I left for Castle Brook, my mom gave me a present. It was our mantra, handwritten on pink and purple sticky notes. When I miss her, I look at her handwriting, reminding myself that a little piece of her is always with me. Then I'll call her, and we'll talk for hours on end.

I was self-conscious growing up. In part because I was made fun of for my small boobs and my lack of ass. I've developed since then, but the words still haunt me.

Twig.

Flat-chested bitch.

No-ass Willows.

In the eyes of society, a woman's body is never perfect. You're either too skinny or too fat. Your breasts are either too small or too big. You're belittled no matter what you look like simply because you're a woman.

If I wasn't being tormented because of my body, I was being teased about my hair. Neither of my parents has tight curls, so I'm unsure where the gene came from. Most likely a long-lost ancestor.

Curly Q.

The Frizz.

The girl with the crazy hair.

Mom had to teach me to love my body and my hair. She would place me in front of a mirror and make me recite words of affirmation to boost my confidence. It didn't work right away, but I learned to love myself just as I am over time.

My hair is unique. Some people would kill to have the volume and curls I have, but that doesn't mean my self-consciousness doesn't rear its ugly head from time to time.

My phone rings again, and Zack's nickname pops up again. I'll never make my parents worry on purpose, but I don't mind letting Zack stew uncomfortably. It's his fault, anyway. He's the reason Rome and I can't explore our spark. I don't often feel anger or irritation toward anyone. Today is a day of self-care, and I'm letting myself be annoyed by my brother.

Gwen doesn't deserve my grumpiness, though, and I will never break a pinkie promise. I pick up my phone, ignore Zack's call, and text Gwen before looking for my sneakers.

> Hey, this is me texting you. I'm okay. Going to hang low and stay home.

> Alone?! Since when do you hang out by yourself?

A giggle slips past my lips as I put my shoes on.

> This is me trying something new. I'm going to be a self-care queen.

> Yes! I stand by this. I do have a question though. Does being a self-care queen include ignoring your brother?

For now. I'm working on my promises, and the first step is allowing myself to be annoyed with him. If Rome and I weren't worried about his feelings, who knows where we would be today.

I mean . . . I wouldn't put all the blame on him. You two are adults, you can talk to him.

Don't start, missy! I'm going to our favorite store to pick up a face mask, snacks, and a movie. Let me wallow in my feelings.

Okay, okay! I'll tell Zack you're on your period or something. Take all the time you need. Text me tomorrow :)

Thank you <3

After that, I silence my phone. With my purse over my shoulder, I step into the hall, lock my door, and start the trek toward my first stop for the day.

A blast of cool air envelopes me when I stroll through the automatic doors. There are many reasons why I chose to attend Castle Brook. One is that it has the best psychology department in the country. The second is that it's less than ten blocks from my favorite store.

The white floors glisten as if they were recently polished, and I breathe in the aroma of fresh coffee as I grab a cart, even though I don't need one. I grab the plastic bar and push the cart in the direction of facial care. When I reach the aisle I'm looking for "Sparks Fly" by Taylor Swift blares overhead, and I can't help but grin and hum along.

I ignore the lyrics when she mentions green eyes, my mind trying to summon a memory of Rome's beautiful irises. My body sways to the music, and I pick up a face mask before moving to the next aisle. I continue this motion and keep this headspace until I have everything I need, including some.

With my head in the clouds, I stand in line. My eyes wander nowhere in particular, but when I see a familiar figure, they stop and zone in. I want to curl in on myself. Today is definitely not the day I want to deal with him, but he sees me before I can turn around and book it farther into the store. At least he has a chaperone, and I know she'll rein him in if necessary.

"What's up, blondie?" Malik smiles at me.

From afar, it may seem like a kind gesture. However, this isn't a sweet expression or greeting. His grin makes me purse my lips in disgust.

"What did I say about having good intentions?" Raina lectures him like a toddler.

"All I did was say hi—"

"With that sly smile. Don't act like I didn't see it. Not every girl wants to fuck you, Malik. Get that out of your head." Raina massages her temples. "It's like I'm babysitting a child," she groans.

"I'm surprised to see you two here. You're not using the weekends as a break? The evaluations don't have to run seven days a week," I remark.

"This one needs extra lessons. Especially in the 'how to treat a woman' department."

"I didn't know that was a part of the program," I tease Raina before leaning toward her. "But you are doing God's work."

"Tell me about it," she sighs while rolling her eyes.

"You know I can hear you two, right? Women . . ." Malik grunts.

"What did I just say? Get it through your thick, jock skull. Women are equal, if not superior, to men."

Malik's lips turn upward, giving me a lopsided smirk. "I'm fine with that. If that means blondie here will take the charge. Tell me . . . are you a giver or a receiver?"

My face heats up, and rage simmers in my chest. Raina's complexion matches mine, but when she opens her mouth, I hold a finger up to stop her.

"You know, Malik. For an all-star quarterback, you really know how to pass off your responsibilities and claim the glory for work you didn't do." I smirk before looking toward the cashier. "Man, I'd give anything to sit in on your evaluations. Raina, you'll earn an award in excellence by the time we graduate." I glance at Malik and smile at him, trying my best to look as disgusting as he did five minutes prior. "Have a good day."

I walk away and start to put my stuff on the conveyor belt.

Raina looks over her shoulder and mouths *"Damn, girl!"*— amazed that Malik has shut his mouth.

I'm quick to defend my friends, and I try to do the same for myself, but I'm not perfect. It takes a lot to get under my skin. Malik is gross, and I don't trust his intentions. I'm glad Raina seems to have him under control. But if he does anything to upset her, I'll be sure he pays for it twofold.

I'm proud that I did that for myself. I don't aim to insult people on purpose, but Malik needed to be put in his place. Hopefully by the time Raina is done with him, he'll be more self-aware and not a menace.

I smile to myself when I get home. I don't care that I'm sweaty and sore from carrying four bags filled with things I don't need. These things will make me happy, and today is all about happiness. Spilling the items onto my bed, I grab my new pajamas and face mask. I haven't checked my phone in two hours, and honestly, it's freeing.

My feet lead me to the bathroom, where I remove my sweaty clothes, change into my new set of comfy clothes, and rinse my face. I apply the facemask and dance to the music in my head. Once I've coated on my face, I head back into my bedroom and plop on my bed. The jostle disturbs my phone, and it catches my attention. My heart skips a beat when I see his name, and when I read the message, any attempt at relaxation flies out the window.

> Hey, bubbles, can you meet me at the football field tomorrow around 4:00 p.m.? There's something I want to show you.

Chapter Twenty-Seven

Rome

Do I want to do this? No. Do I want to continue trying to avoid my feelings for Chrissy in an attempt to protect my best friend's feelings? Also no. It's a double-edged sword. But it's time I start considering my wants and what will make me happy. Fear can't keep holding me back. I won't allow it.

The way she looks at me sets my racing mind at ease. She wraps my heart in a warm blanket, melting the ice away. She laughs with me, not at me. She cares about me, and she enjoys being around me. She doesn't care that I'm a football player, a good one at that. She couldn't give two shits about it. I know she won't care if I ditch my dream of playing for the Philadelphia Eagles and become a history teacher. She would jump for joy and erase all my worries.

Ash was right, per usual. Zack is an adult, and it's time I start treating him as such. I pull out my phone and type out the message before second-guessing myself.

> Hey man, what are you up to today?

My phone vibrates within seconds after hitting the send button. It surprises me because sometimes this guy can be a pain to get a hold of. He must be holding it in his hand for some reason.

> About to head over to Ash's. Gwen promised to make me pizza if I stopped bothering Chrissy.

> What kind of pizza?

No, wait, shit. That's not the point. *Focus, Rome!*

> Scratch that. Can I stop by for a few minutes? I have something to talk to you about.

> Am I in trouble?

No, but I might be.

> No, lol. It's just not something I want to talk about over the phone. I'll be there in twenty minutes.

> Sounds good. I'll ask Gwen to make enough for you too!

His last message makes me smile. It's nice to have friends who think of you. Even small gestures, like having enough food, go a long way.

I don't turn on any music during the drive. I'm trying to figure out the best way to approach this conversation. Numerous scenarios play in my head, but only a handful end in a way I'm happy with.

The majority of the scenarios don't end well. I either lose Zack as my friend, or I lose the girl who is slowly capturing my heart. Neither instance is something I want. I hope Zack considers that I could have gone behind his back. I could have dated his sister without his knowledge, not caring about how he would feel about it. Chrissy and I didn't do that, though, because we care about him.

I'll keep it simple, not sugarcoat anything. I'll be upfront and honest. I'll explain that my feelings are genuine and that I won't do anything to hurt Chrissy. He knows the kind of person I am, so he should trust that my intentions are genuine.

Without thinking, I turn the car's engine off and play with my keys. I barely remember driving here . . . and that's scary for two different reasons. Not only did I drive here without a coherent thought of my surroundings, but I'm now one step closer to confronting the sole reason why I've been an anxious mess.

With a shaky release of air, I get out of the car and head toward the front door. I don't even get a second to prepare myself because the moment I approach, Zack opens the door and greets me with an innocent smile.

"What's up, man?" He steps to the side so I can walk in.

The aroma of fresh dough fills the air. Gwen must be trying really hard to maintain Zack's interest if she's making pizza from scratch. It reminds me of Mom, and I'm thrown back to my childhood against my will. We used to paint the kitchen with flour, not caring about the mess we would have to clean afterward. I miss those moments until the heartache sets in.

"Having fun?" I ask Zack before snickering at a splotch of flour on his chin.

"Loads. I haven't made pizza like this since I was a kid. Gwen is giving me special treatment since my sister doesn't want to talk to me."

"Why?" I ask with an arched brow.

Zack beckons me closer and lowers his voice. "She's on her period."

"Why are we whispering?" I smirk with a hint of amusement. "Periods aren't top secret, you know."

"Yeah, I know, but I don't want to summon her. She's always *super* cranky during her time of the month. It's best not to say her name, trust me."

Well, this is going to make today more difficult.

"Okay, sure, buddy." I pat his back before nodding toward the kitchen. "Can we talk out back? Just the two of us?"

"Absolutely, let's go."

I follow Zack as he leads us into the kitchen. Gwen stops me in my tracks, and I have to stop myself from doubling over in hysterics.

"You left me." She pouts, not caring about the flour scattered all over the countertop and her face. "Hi, Rome," she greets me in defeat.

"I barely recognized you without the mustache."

Gwen purses her lips at me while Zack spins around to look at us. "Mustache?"

"Ha, ha, very funny." She clicks her tongue at me.

"I don't get it. Gwen has never had a mustache." Zack observes the two of us.

"I'll tell you later, but don't think you can get out of helping me, Willows."

"Where's Ash?" I ask while Zack opens the patio door.

"He's watching *Star Wars: A New Hope* with Pickles. He wants to 'enlighten' him."

I squint. "Oh, okay." Yeah, I'm not touching that topic, not today.

Zack and I step across the threshold leading outside. The air is thick, and the sun is hot. One of the downsides of living in the Northeast is the humidity. Heat is never just heat. It's like you're trying to walk through the rain forest, but crank up the temperature and prepare for a sunburn.

The only solace we have is the pool. The water is clear, and the surface sparkles as the sun reflects off it. Zack sits on the edge and sinks his legs in. I don't waste any time and follow suit. My palms burn when I press down on them to get comfortable, but when I dip my toes in, the feeling fades away.

I sigh in relief when my legs become drenched, and I splash my hands in and use the water to cool off my neck.

"So, what did you want to talk about?" Zack starts.

The worry that this might ruin our friendship is real. Zack will protect his sister until his dying days. There's a reason she doesn't tell him about a lot of things. She doesn't want him to worry, and she doesn't want to deal with the backlash. Yet here I am, readying myself to face it head-on.

"You know I never dated much and why I don't open myself up to a lot of people," I start.

"Yeah, between you and Gwen, I'm ninety-nine percent sure our parents' generation is screwed in the head."

I chuckle awkwardly. "Yeah, that's one way to put it." I kick my feet back and forth, trying to summon the courage to do what I have to do. "I'm about to tell you something, but I need you to make me a promise first."

"Okay . . ." He sounds skeptical.

"No matter what I say or how you react, we'll remain friends. You can get angry, yell at me, or ignore me. I don't care. As long as we can get over it, we can go back to normal. Promise me nothing will change."

He watches me for a moment, not saying a word, probably trying to gauge where I'm going with this before I continue.

"I promise," he says without another thought.

I take in a deep breath and release it slowly. Because I'm a coward, I don't look at him. Instead, I look down at my hands and force the words to life. "I like Chrissy. I like her as more than a friend."

When I say it out loud, a physical weight is lifted from my shoulders. If I could, I would scream the words until everyone in this neighborhood knew how I felt. I wouldn't stop until I lost my voice.

I smile to myself when I think of her, and I speak without thinking. "I tried, Zack. I really did. I didn't want to like her because she's your sister, but I do. And I can't avoid these feelings anymore. We tried to create distance, but the universe keeps pushing us back together. She sees me for *me*. I want to see where it goes between her and me, but I can't do it without your support. You have to know, and you have to approve. But I have to be honest, if you don't, my feelings for her won't disappear. They'll continue to grow until they can't be contained. You know me, all I want is a chance to—"

"Dude, stop with the lecture," Zack speaks up, earning my attention.

When I look at him, his cheeks are red, and his eyes bore into mine. He tongues his cheek and lets out a small chuckle.

"You and Chrissy?" he asks, and my stomach knots.

He looks over my shoulder into the distance. My chest is heaving rapidly, waiting for him to explode.

"Rome and Chrissy . . . my best friend and my sister," he mumbles before looking back at me.

"You made a promise," I state calmly.

With a tiny laugh, he starts, "Are you out of your *fucking* mind?"

My heart sinks into my stomach, twisting into a knot that ties around my core.

"This is absolutely fantastic!" Zack cheers and claps his hands, shaking me from the void I was teetering into.

"Wait . . . What?"

"This is perfect! I don't have to worry anymore." He sounds like he's on the verge of tears. Throwing his hands to the sky, he looks up and beams. "Thank you! My torture is over! Oh, thank the fucking universe! You"—he redirects his attention my way—"are my savior. Come here. I could kiss you!" Zack wraps his arms around me and hugs me.

This was definitely not in any of the scenarios I considered. Zack is happy? The guy who would turn purple if anyone looked at his sister? I'm baffled. No, fuck that. I must have died. Zack must have killed me, and I'm in some sort of weird purgatory.

"Has the heat gotten to you?" I ask as he pulls back and plants his hands on my shoulders.

"Not at all. Do you really think I wouldn't approve of this? How did you think I was going to react?"

"I . . . Not like this." I wave my hands at him, gesturing to his wide smile. "You don't care if I ask Chrissy on a date? If we date or if we become something more than friends?"

"Not in the slightest," he says without hesitation.

"Huh." I click my tongue and look at the fence behind him. "So I went through all this emotional turmoil for weeks for nothing."

"That's what you get for lacking faith in your best friend." Zack jumps up and begins to head toward the door. "Come on, we can't leave Gwen alone for too long. She's a good cook, but she's a klutz."

"Zack," I call as I stand.

With his hand on the door handle, he turns to face me.

"Promise me this isn't a joke. You're really okay with this?" I keep my tone steady so he knows I'm not joking with him. I don't want him to think I'm messing around.

"I'm okay with this, Rome. You have my blessing." He nods toward the door as he opens it. "I'm not fucking around. Follow your heart. Just do me a favor, and don't let me see it." He shivers as if ideas are running through his head.

"I won't. Thank you," I say with a sincere smile.

"Text her, then head inside. We have pizzas to cook."

Zack heads inside, and I do exactly what he instructed. I pull my phone out of my pocket and send a long-overdue message.

> Hey, bubbles, can you meet me at the football field tomorrow around 4:00 p.m.? There's something I want to show you.

Chapter Twenty-Eight

Chrissy

A thousand and one thoughts run through my head as I walk toward the football stadium. What does Rome want to show me? Why is it at the football field? Why are we meeting on a Sunday? Could it not wait until our meeting tomorrow at the cat café? It looks like it's going to rain . . . should I have brought an umbrella?

Get back on track, Chrissy.

I haven't heard from Rome since I agreed to meet him via text. He told me to meet him by the main entrance around four o'clock. Checking the time, I walk a bit faster when I realize I'm running a little late.

Yesterday wasn't a total failure in the self-care department. Sure, his text left me reeling, but I still used the face mask, watched the animated version of *Anastasia*, and devoured all the snacks I bought. The emotional eater in me was awakened, and cheese curls are this woman's weakness.

I didn't tell Gwen that Rome reached out. Nor did I text my brother back. My mind is swimming, and I can only focus on one task at a time. See what Rome wants to show me, and then take the next moment one by one.

I work on clearing my head and slowing my breathing. The air is thick and sticky, and the clouds are dark and swollen. It's going to rain, but at least the football stadium is connected to the sports center. We can always seek shelter there until the storm calms down.

With fidgeting hands, I round the final bend. Rome appears in my line of sight, leaning against the railing on the stairs that lead into the center, and his appearance makes my heart falter. He is the definition of handsome with his mussed blond hair, sculpted jawline, broad shoulders, and lean core. He is what I expect a Greek god to look like, but that's not why I'm drawn to him. Rome is down-to-earth and easygoing. But if I had to pick one thing that pulled me in, it would be his smile. His smile is genuine and bright. He can make the sun appear on a gloomy day. When he looks at me, it seems different. Like he saves this certain gesture just for me. It's almost like everything he feels pours from him when he sees me. His green eyes glint, his features soften, and his smile . . . it's magic.

Rome looks up when I near him, almost as if he can sense my presence with his eyes closed. I stop in my tracks as we look at one another. He's wearing a navy tee and black basketball shorts. His hands are in his shorts' pockets, and his biceps are flexed.

With a nervous smile, I start toward him.

"Hey," I sound shyer than I intended.

"Willows," he greets me with a smile that turns my knees to jelly.

I take the stairs and stop at the step below him. "So, what did you want to show me?"

Rome offers me his hand and nods toward the stadium. "Follow me."

I glance down at his hand. My heart flutters, and my body tingles at the notion of touching him. I try to force Zack into the forefront of my mind, reminding myself not to let myself get too close.

But . . . I want more.

I want to hold Rome's hand and not have to worry about what others may think. I want to let myself fall into my feelings. I want him to hold me in his arms and never let go. I want to be happy. I don't want to fight this anymore.

The moment I touch Rome's hand, a rush of euphoria washes over me. A weight I didn't know was settled on my shoulders disappears, and a small smile makes itself at home on my lips.

He squeezes my hand and pulls me up the remaining stairs.

We remain silent as we pass through the doors and walk onto the field. Storm clouds roll across the sky, darkening the atmosphere and bringing the scent of impending rain. The field is empty, the only sound coming from us as we walk farther down the turf. When we near the players' benches, Rome drops my hand.

"You wanted to show me the football field? I've been here before."

I scan the area for any hint of what this surprise might be. Nothing is here. What could he possibly want to show me?

"You have, but I didn't tell you why I love it here so much."

Tilting my head, I step toward him as he grabs a ball.

"Since my mom left, nowhere felt like home. But when I'm here. . . I feel like I belong." He tosses the football in the air and catches it. "Dad used to play catch with me all the time. We would spend hours tossing the ball back and forth." With a few more steps back, he smiles wide. "Think fast!"

I manage to catch the football before it collides with my face. "Give a girl some proper warning!"

I shake off my hand from the force of the throw. With my dainty fingers, I'm surprised I didn't break anything from that throw.

"Sorry," he chuckles before walking farther down the field.

"Where are you going?!" I call after him.

"We're going to play catch," he shouts back, stopping at the 30 yard line.

"It's going to rain," I state while gesturing toward the sky.

"And?" He shrugs before pointing at the twenty yard line.

I scrunch my lips, and he laughs harder. "Get over there."

"Fine," I groan with a playful tone.

I plant myself on the line and place my fingers on the stitching.

"Don't judge me. I'm not a pro like a certain friend of mine," I tease.

I throw my arm back and launch the ball, far from surprised when he catches it with ease.

"Not bad." He nods in approval before tossing the ball back to me.

Scrambling to the right, I miss it by a hair. "You did that on purpose," I giggle as I reach to pick it up.

"Who me? Never," he chuckles.

Without giving him time to prepare, I hurl the ball as hard and long as I can down the field. With a simple leap, Rome catches it and lands gracefully.

"Oh, is that how you wanna play?" he asks with a hint of cockiness and amusement in his tone.

Rain starts trickling down, landing on my cheek and sliding toward my lips.

"It's funny that you think I stand a chance against you," I tell him with a snicker as more droplets come down.

"You can keep up with me. Want me to prove it to you?"

I eye him suspiciously as he smiles wider. "Go long."

Before I can comprehend what he means, he takes a few steps back and then, with a running start, hurls the ball down the field.

"Oh, shit," I mumble before running as fast as I can to chase after it.

My legs carry me down the field in a sprint. I'm not a fast runner and certainly far from fit, so when I pick up speed and my hair billows behind me, I'm shocked. The football starts to lose momentum, and I try to gauge where it will land. Putting myself under it, I jump and catch it against my chest. My feet meet the ground, and I smile wide when I look at Rome.

"I did it!" I cheer as giddiness courses through me.

"That's my girl!" He beams and claps as he runs toward me.

"Holy shit," I mutter in disbelief while looking down at the ball.

I now know why football players celebrate when they catch the ball in the end zone. Why they throw it down and dance like there's no tomorrow. I want to do just that, but Rome crashes into me.

I drop the ball when he wraps his arms around my waist, lifting me in the air and spinning me around. I embrace him, securing my arms around his neck and squealing.

The summer rain continues to drizzle down, dampening our hair and shirts.

Rome slows, our eyes lock, and our grins soften in an instant.

I become aware of his strong pecs against my breasts, his muscular arms hugging my lean waist.

Air hitches in my throat, and Rome licks his lips as he admires me.

"You surprise me every day, you know that, right?" he whispers.

"What did you want to show me?" I keep my voice low, hoping to mask the tremble from my nerves.

"If I show it to you, you have to promise me something," he starts.

I nod, trying not to seem as nervous as I really am.

"Whatever happens next won't change how we see one another."

I scan his eyes, unsure what he means. What could he possibly show me that would make me change how I see or feel about him? There's only one way to find out.

"I promise," I say as the rain starts to pour harder from the sky.

"Okay," Rome breathes while nodding.

With a deep inhale, he glances down at my lips, and my stomach tilts. Leaning in, he brushes his mouth against mine, and the faint contact leaves me feeling weightless. He doesn't make any further movement, like he's waiting for permission to seal the bond.

I close the distance a millimeter more, feathering our noses.

Our breathing is ragged, hot, and impatient.

I move my hand from his nape to his hair, curling my fingers in the short strands.

He presses his thumb into the small of my back, and as thunder booms in the sky, our lips crash together in a kiss.

His lips are soft, full, and powerful. He kisses me with slow, fierce passion, savoring our touch.

The knot in my stomach loosens, and my body tingles. I stop the whimper that wants to leave my chest. I've wanted this for too long, and now that I have it, I don't want to let it go. I press into him, kissing him back with equal desire. My hand travels around his shoulder blades as he holds me against him.

Sheets of rain come down on us, and I ready myself for him to pull away.

Chapter Twenty-Eight

Our lips part, and I begin to pull back.

"Where do you think you're going?" he asks, his voice husky.

"I—"

With a hand on the back of my head, Rome urges me back, taking my lips against his again and parting my mouth with his tongue.

I melt into his arms at the sensation. Never, and I mean never, have I ever been kissed like this. I've never felt so adored and wanted in my life. Rome Carter not only likes me, he wants me, and he's showing me rather than telling.

I welcome his tongue, letting him explore my mouth as I taste him. His body is hot against mine, and I moan as I breathe him in. Rome smirks as I release the sound into his mouth.

Thunder crashes in the sky, and I jolt. Rome tightens his grip around me in response. Breaking the kiss, we share the oxygen between us.

"I can't let you go," he rasps.

"I don't want you to," I admit.

The storm comes down harder, soaking us entirely. He opens his eyes and catches me watching him.

I don't want my focus to shift, but it does, and Zack appears unbidden in my mind. In Rome's arms, my joints lock, and my body stiffens. My eyes dance around his features, and my breathing becomes frantic.

Shit. Holy fuck! What did we just do?

He's going to be devastated. If he finds out Rome and I kissed, he'll never look at me the same way again. *Fuck!* I'm a selfish prick. After all he's gone through and done. This is the last thing he deserves: his best friend and sister betraying his trust. We're scum.

"I . . ." I try to separate from Rome while searching for the right words. "We can't do this." I drop my gaze and pull back from him.

"What? Why?"

My feet meet the ground, and I do everything to avoid his gaze. "You know why. I have to go."

I turn to leave, but Rome wraps his hand around my wrist. "No, wait," he begs.

"We can't do this, Rome, and you know that." I turn to face him, happy that the rain is hiding the tears that begin to fill my eyes. "Zack would—"

"I talked to Zack," he interrupts, leaving me desperate for answers.

"You . . . what?" I manage to stutter out.

"Yesterday, I talked to Zack. Right before I texted you," Rome says while reaching for me again. "I didn't believe it either. I was ready for him to lash out and lecture me to the day's end. But when he said 'This is perfect! I don't have to worry anymore!' I was speechless."

"Zack approves? Of us? Are you messing with me?"

The water starts to weigh down my hair, making it a sloppy mess. Rome doesn't pay attention to the wreck I'm becoming. Instead, he holds my gaze with unwavering attention.

"I wouldn't mess around about this," he whispers before brushing a curl behind my ear. "I wouldn't do anything to jeopardize what we could have together—"

"What we could have together?" I repeat, sounding out of breath.

Rome traces my jawline with his fingertips, not caring that we're both wet and red.

"Yes, what we could have together." He tilts my chin upward, and I look at him. "A spark has been brewing between us, trying to ignite and catch. We've been denying it for too long. I want to discover that fire with you. I can't avoid these feelings anymore, and I don't think you can either."

"I can't," I say without thinking first.

What does Rome have to gain by lying to me about Zack? If this was anyone else, I would worry he was aiming to get me into his bed. Men are like that. They'll lie to you just to get what they want, and once they get it, they'll toss you aside.

Rome Carter has never given me that vibe. His intentions are honest. He wouldn't lie about something like this because he cares about his friendship with Zack as much as I do. If he's lying to me, I would worry that someone brainwashed him. Besides, I've caught him in a lie before. His eyes darted around, avoiding contact. His breathing quickened, and his brow crinkled. Now, his voice is steady, his gaze is locked on mine, and while his breathing is quick, it's not erratic.

"You talked to Zack on your own," I say, mainly to convince myself.

"I did."

"And he's okay with this," I repeat.

"He is."

Raindrops cloud my vision, and a gust of wind makes me shiver. I lean into Rome's palm, and he inches his fingers into my curls.

"And you want us to be together?"

Rome nods and offers me a warm smile.

"Then what are we waiting for?"

Chapter Twenty-Nine

Rome

With Chrissy in my arms, we barrel inside my apartment. I barely manage to kick the door closed, and we're a mess of hands and heated kisses. The rain has soaked us. Her shirt is sticking to her skin, highlighting the curve of her breasts. We're keeping one another as warm as we can, but when we enter my room and the temperature drops from the air-conditioning, goose bumps cover our arms.

"I think we should get you out of this," I whisper while playing with the hem of her shirt.

"We should," she agrees while reaching under my shirt. "But only if I can get you out of yours."

"We can definitely do that," I say before taking her lips against mine again.

Balling her lilac shirt in my fists, I yank it over her head and toss it across the room. I'm trying to catch my breath while unclasping her bra. A lump forms in my throat, and her hands travel up my chest, taking my tee with her. She stands on the edge of her toes, and I help her get me out of my shirt. It drops to the floor, and her eyes linger down my body.

"Tell me this is real," she mumbles. Her fingertips barely touch my skin while she trails them down my body. "Tell me this isn't all in my head."

Lifting her chin with my fingers, I place a kiss on her lips. "This is real, Wildflower. You're finally mine."

A series of chills creeps over her skin, and she shivers. Her teeth begin to chatter while I wrap my arms around her. I scoop her in my arms and walk us toward the bathroom. "Let's get warm before we do anything," I say, kissing her cheek before placing her down to turn the shower on.

When I turn around, steam fills the room, fogging the mirror Chrissy is in front of. I approach her, like a beast stalking their prey. Except this pretty bird isn't scared of me. No, she's far from that. This girl looks me dead in the eyes and removes her shorts.

"Did I say you could take this off?" My voice drops as I stare down at her.

"I didn't know I had to ask permission," she sasses.

I reach behind her and pull her close by pressing the nape of her neck. She releases a tiny gasp when I yank her underwear down. "Take my shorts off, and then my boxers."

With a tiny nod, she looks down, but I twist my hands in her curls and tilt her head back up. "Did I say you could look away?" I smirk when she shakes her head.

She unties the drawstring of my shorts, and with a gentle tug, she slides them over my ass, and they pool around my ankles. Her fingertips dance around the waistband of my boxer briefs.

If she were to look down, she would see how hard I am. My cock is pressing against the fabric, begging for me to let it free so she can wrap her hand around it.

I'm going to savor this moment. I won't give in even though I *really* want to. I want to sink my cock inside her. I want to feel her walls pulsate and massage every inch of my length. I want to hear her scream my name as I fuck her.

But not yet.

My boxers cascade over my legs and fall on the floor.

Chrissy swallows before licking her lips.

I nod back toward the shower, and she peels herself away from me to obey. I turn around and let my eyes roam over her figure.

She's thin, but she has a subtle dip in her waistline that rolls over her hips. My hands are itching to cup her ass and massage it until she moans. My feet stick to the tile floor when I stroll toward her. She steps into the shower and leaves the glass door open so I can step in with her. Our gazes never leave one another, both hungry and desperate to get our hands on one another again.

I tower over her, and she sidesteps out of the water. Curling my hand in her hair, I guide her back under the showerhead, soaking her hair and her body.

"Better?" I ask.

"Much." She smiles, and the water trickles over her full lips. "Your turn."

I go to protest, but her hands land on my hips, and she maneuvers me around her with grace. The sweat and lingering chill wash away while I bend my head back and groan.

Chrissy's hands start to travel down my body, but I snatch her wrists and secure them against my chest.

"You're eager," I growl while brushing my nose against hers.

"You have no idea," she lets out in a single breath.

I toy with her lips, not making full contact. She tries to lean in to close the gap, but I pull away to tease her.

"Please, Rome," she begs.

"Please, what?"

Chapter Twenty-Nine

"Please let me kiss you."

"Hmm," I hum against her lips.

"Please," she murmurs.

I place my hand against her throat and crash my lips into hers. Our touch is wild, passionate, stomach tilting. I lick her lips, and she parts them for me. She tastes like strawberry ice cream. She moans into my mouth as our tongues whirl around one another. The sensation vibrates my core and makes my voice husky.

"Satisfied?" I ask when I pull away.

"Not in the slightest."

With a low hum, I reach behind me to turn off the shower. I move my hand from her neck back into her hair, and I lead her out of the shower and back into my bedroom. Her attention is glued to me, and when the backs of her legs hit the edge of my bed, we stop.

"At any point, if you want to stop, tell me. If I'm being too much, tell me." I loosen my hold and soften my expression.

In the past, my dominance wasn't always received well. I never pushed any boundaries, and I stop when I'm told to, but I don't want to scare her. I'll go as slow as this woman wants me to, but the need to relinquish all self-control is overpowering.

"Do you trust me?"

"I trust you, Rome. One hundred percent."

I nod before kissing her again. "Then get on the bed and open your legs."

Without questioning my motives, she settles near the pillows; her chest rises and falls in time with my heartbeat.

My knees sink into the mattress, and I part her legs with ease. I kiss her right leg, traveling down to her inner thigh.

She whimpers at my touch and stills when my breath closes in on her pussy.

I continue kissing around her core as I get comfortable on

my stomach. Looking up at her, I smirk when I catch her watching me.

"I'm going to savor you, Wildflower. I won't stop until you come all over my face. After that, I'm going to fill you with my cock and fuck you until you beg me to stop." I sweep my tongue over her, and the movement makes her arch closer against my mouth. "How does that sound?"

"Like heaven." Her tone is desperate. She's reeling, which is exactly what I want.

"Eyes on me, love."

I take a deep breath through my nose and secure my mouth against her. I hook my arms around her thighs and bring her as close as I can get her. A deep hum rumbles in my throat as I kiss her folds and run my tongue from her entrance to her clit.

"*Fuuuuck,*" she moans, and it's music to my ears.

I lap my tongue over her swollen clit, sucking it at random intervals so she never knows when to expect the electric pressure. I shake my head against her and increase my speed. My saliva, combined with her arousal, covers the lower half of my face. She tastes better than I imagined.

When I back up slightly, she whimpers and tries to inch back against my lips.

I chuckle and place my thumb exactly where my tongue is. "Patience, Wildflower."

"Rome, I can't—"

"Close already?"

She nods and throws her head back against the pillows.

"And what if I do this?" I sink my finger inside her, and her back arches off the bed.

"Fuck!" she cries, and I smirk.

I dive back in, running my tongue over her bud as I fuck her with my finger. Her walls contract around me, and a devilish thought comes to mind. I don't stop the motion. In fact, I increase the intensity. My lips close around her clit, sucking in time with my rhythm.

"Yes, yes, don't stop, fuck, please!" Her words are becoming incoherent.

As the wave of pleasure washes over her, I remove my finger and pull away from the girl, who has quickly become a puddle.

"No. Rome, come ba—Oh my god!"

I fill her with my cock, and with one thrust, she unravels around me. Her back lifts off the bed while I sink every inch inside her.

"That's my girl," I praise her as she rides out her orgasm.

I hold her against me until she's done rubbing her clit against my groin. My chest meets hers, and I nibble on her jawline before kissing up toward her earlobe.

"How was that?"

"I can't move. Fuck me," she rasps.

"If you insist."

I pull back and press back into her. Her legs drop to the side, but I scoot her down so they can rest around my waist. From this angle, she takes every centimeter I offer, and I mumble a curse as her pussy walls massage my cock.

"You're soaking, baby girl," I whisper against her lips.

"Please don't stop," she pleads while curling her hands around my neck.

I kiss her in a fit of desire as the muscles in my thighs start to tighten. "Not until you come again. I need you to come again," I order, and she releases a whimper.

I increase my pace, ramming into her until I know I hit her G-spot. "Fuck!"

I grunt in her ear and wrap my arms around her until her head is lifted off the bed. I take her lips against mine, and her cries fill my mouth while I kiss her. For extra measure, I pinch her nipple between my forefinger and thumb, earning myself a choked groan.

"Come for me," I command. "Right now."

"Rome!"

I thrust deep inside her and hold my position against her pleasure point. Her muscles spasm beneath me, and her arms splay against the mattress as she grinds against me.

"You're such a good girl for me," I growl against her throat.

My thrusts become sloppy, and with a grunt, I start to pull out so I can finish.

"Rome, wait." Chrissy shifts her body against me and holds me in place by squeezing my ass. "I need to feel you come inside me. I'm on the pill, I promise. *Please.*"

With her hands, she urges me to finish, guiding me back and forth, keeping me deep inside her. My eyes lock with hers. An overwhelming, carnal desire to fill her takes over. I know she wouldn't lie about this. She doesn't want to get pregnant; she's too focused on her major and the future. I trust her, and there's no doubt about that.

With a few more pumps, I grunt out a low curse, and my fingers dig into the base of her skull as I come inside her.

She gasps as my cock pulsates and fills her.

The muscles in my legs relax and sweat covers my brow even though the AC is cranked. I'm fighting for air when I offer her a small kiss.

"Fuck me . . ." I mumble while pulling out.

I see my cum inside her, and I don't stop myself from thumbing it and coating her entire pussy with it.

"You're so goddamn hot," I tell her before kissing her again.

"I can't formulate a coherent thought," she murmurs.

I collapse on my back next to her and stare at the ceiling while trying to catch my breath. She rolls on her side and cuddles against my arm. Her breasts cradle me while she trails her fingers along my jawline.

"You're something else, Carter," she whispers.

"Was I too much?" Worry fills me as I wait for her to answer, so I continue to blabber. "I think I tend to be overbearing in the bedroom because I don't have a lot of control over the rest of my life. Not that this happens often." I gesture toward our naked bodies. "I just. . . I feel safe with you, and I couldn't help it. Please, please tell me I didn't fuck up."

When she speaks, I turn my head so I can look into her gorgeous blue eyes.

She shakes her head. "Not at all. It was perfect."

My lips tilt upward, and I release a contented sigh. "And you are mine."

Chapter Thirty

Chrissy

I'm his.

I never belonged to anyone before. My heart was always mine. I kept control and wouldn't allow myself to fall headfirst because the love I sought was out of reach. Now I'm falling, and I know Rome won't let me collide with the ground. He'll catch me, hold me in his arms, and whisper reassuring words until I believe everything he says.

When he looks at me, it feels like he's committing me to memory.

I reach out and trace my knuckles over his sculpted jawline. His breathing is relaxed, and his nose crinkles occasionally while he sleeps.

Contentment seeps into my muscles. I have him. I am his, and he is mine. The man who has plagued my mind for seven months is finally with me, and I couldn't be happier. Everything is going in the direction I only dared wish it would. Zack was a massive bump in the road. At least, I thought he was going to be. Turns out he was a tiny obstacle, and our stubbornness was the biggest barrier. I don't allow the worry of my curse to resurface and ruin the moment. I push it to the back of my mind.

Rome and I should have been up front with our feelings, acknowledged them, and spoken to Zack like the adults we think we are. Rome took the step while I cowered. I claim to be an adult who can make big-girl decisions, yet I haven't made a single one yet. I have a lot of internal work I want to focus on, and I honestly think this is my first step.

The rain stopped pelting against the window about an hour ago. My body and mind are tired, but every time I close my eyes, I open them because I want to soak in this moment. I need to go to the bathroom though. I slip out of his bed, and chills coat my skin. Thankfully, Rome is a typical guy and he has clothes on his floor. I reach for a stray Castle Brook football jersey and do a quick sniff test. His natural musk and cologne fill my nostrils. I put it on and hurry toward his adjoining bathroom.

This was my first experience without a condom, and the first time anyone has ever come inside me. I'm not typically so reckless. Yes, I'm on the pill, but I follow precautions. The pill doesn't protect me against STIs or STDs, and I don't trust any of these college boys, except Rome. I don't know for certain that he's ever gone without protection, but I'm willing to bet the last thing he wants is to impregnate someone before he graduates. And I know he wouldn't knowingly pass something onto me. Hell, it was my idea for him to finish inside me.

Before I finish peeing, I rake my hands across my scalp. Without looking in the mirror, I wash my hands and then stand there, unsure if I want to look at my reflection.

Be a big girl.

Inching my gaze upward, I meet my parallel self, and I do the unexpected. I smile at myself. My lips are swollen from kissing Rome. My cheeks are stained pink from all the blushing

I did today. My hair is a mess, but when isn't it? I move my gaze down, and my fingers dance along the stitching across the jersey. The number 35 is red, and the rest of the fabric is black. I turn around and look over my shoulder. His last name is on my back, and I dare to imagine something out of character for me.

Chrissy Carter.

Has a nice ring to it . . .

I walk back into the bedroom. The carpet is warm under my feet, and a small smile spreads across my lips when I see Rome sleeping peacefully. My body is itching to curl up next to him, but my restless mind wants me to explore. I still don't know much about the blond man across from me. Other than how his mom left him and his dad when he was eight. What was he like when he was a kid? What is his dad like? What does Rome do other than play football and eat food?

If Rome has a roommate, he's either oblivious or not home. Rome and I barreled through the door without a care in the world, so I assume he doesn't have a roommate because he wouldn't do something like that.

I peer out of the bedroom before starting down the hall and running my hand along the wall. I note the lack of decor, but it doesn't raise any flags. I wouldn't expect him to have decorated. One, because he's a man, and two, because he barely has free time. Especially with Malik being a shit leader.

The kitchen is quaint, nothing special. There's no kitchen table or chairs, which makes sense if it's just him living here. Strolling into the living room, I chuckle when I notice the gaming system and forty-two-inch TV. He has the same taste in video games as Gwen. Loads of zombie shooters, and wait . . . is that a farming simulator? Huh, I wasn't expecting that.

I look at the bookshelf against the wall and zone in on the only picture in the apartment. An iron fist wraps around my heart when I focus on it. The woman has long golden hair and piercing green eyes. Her smile is wide, and she has a light trail of freckles over the bridge of her nose. The man has light brown hair, close to dirty blond. He has a neatly trimmed beard and looks at the woman with a loving expression. The boy is a perfect combination of his parents. His blond hair is messy, and he has his mother's eyes. He's smiling wide, showing a few missing baby teeth. It doesn't take a rocket scientist to put two and two together. If I were to guess, Rome is about seven in this picture. His mom would leave a year later, dismantling his family structure.

"There you are." His voice is deep and soothing, still husky from sleep, making him sound even sexier.

"You look just like her." I nod at the photo on the shelf before me without looking at him.

Silence fills the space; the only noise is his muffled footsteps as he approaches me. His shoulder brushes against mine, and a heavy sigh leaves his chest.

"What was she like?" I ask, being as careful as I can.

"She was . . . good. Until she left."

A hint of resentment fills his tone, and I don't blame him for it.

"I'm sorry you had to go through that. No one deserves to have their mother or father leave them without an explanation. I'm sure it still hurts. Not knowing why she left and dealing with that trauma."

He doesn't respond, but I can feel the tension radiating from his body.

I move my attention to his face. His jaw is clenched, and his cheeks are splotchy.

"You know it's not your fault, right?" I reach out and brush my hand against his. "You aren't to blame." I keep my tone low and tentative.

"I don't think I agree," he murmurs.

"And why is that?"

He furrows his brow, and his eyes don't leave the framed photograph. "They loved one another. I mean, look at them."

I glance back at the picture before returning my focus to him.

"If she loved him, and if he loved her, she wouldn't have left. I'm the only factor I can think of. I wasn't an easy child. I begged them to let me play football. I threw tantrums, screamed, and cried if I didn't get what I wanted. They never fought, so there's only one explanation. She left because of me."

Keeping my emotions in check, I take a moment to curb my defensiveness. I graze his jawline with my knuckles before tilting his head so he's looking at me.

"Listen to me," I start, trying to keep my voice steady. "You are not the reason she left. I will not speak ill of her even though I *really* want to. Do you know what children do, Rome? They cry, they scream, and they drive their parents up the wall. You are *not* at fault. You don't know what happened between your mom and dad. For all you know, they weren't as in love as they seemed. Even if they were in love, even if they never argued, she made the conscious decision to leave you and your dad. She's an adult, and she is the *only* one to blame. You may never find the answer you're looking for, but you must start accepting that it's not your fault."

He tries to look away from me, but I guide his focus back. "And no, this isn't me evaluating you. This is me protecting the man who deserves nothing but the best in the world."

"No one has ever said that to me before, not even my dad," he mumbles, tears coating his eyes.

"I will tell you every day until you believe me. I will remind you that you are worth everything the universe has to offer. And you are not the reason she left. You never were."

"I don't know if I can believe you." Tears slip down his cheek, and I catch them with my thumb.

"You won't right away. You can't undo a lifetime of beliefs in a day. It's going to take time, but I can promise you that with work, you will begin to believe me." I offer him a kind smile before he rests his chin on my head.

"You know, I wasn't prepared for this. When I saw you in my jersey with bare legs, I planned on taking you in my arms and throwing your fine ass back into bed."

I snicker and start to soften when his lips tilt upward, showing me his flawless grin. "Sorry, handsome. I can't help it. Helping people is in my DNA." I stand on my tiptoes and kiss his cheek. "Want to go back to bed?"

With a sniffle, he nods and places a kiss on my forehead. "I would love that, but you owe me for both turning me on and making me cry."

I wrap my arms around his bare waist and follow him back into the bedroom. "Yes, Captain," I giggle.

We climb back into bed, and I rest my head on his chest, listening to his heartbeat. He runs his fingers up and down my arm, and my eyes start to flutter closed as sleep overtakes my body.

"If I knew the trouble you would cause me, I would have better prepared myself. I'm going to trust you because I know you'll change my life," Rome says as he wraps his arms around me, securing me against his body.

Fatigue settles in my bones, and my mind starts to sway.

"And because I'm falling for you, Wildflower. Harder than I want to admit."

That's the last thing that registers in my mind before I succumb to exhaustion.

The bed shifts, and I begin to stir. I flop onto my stomach and shove my arms under the cool pillow with a long release of air. I'm about to fall back asleep when Rome squeezes his hand against my belly and inches it downward. He brushes my hair away from my neck and trails his lips along my skin.

"Wake up," he hums in my ear, and chills run up my spine.

"No," I whine and shake my head.

"You have a debt to settle," he says before nibbling on my earlobe. "And you made the grave mistake of falling asleep in my jersey. I need to fuck you, princess."

Pulling on my hips, he lifts my bare ass and presses his cock against me. I shiver when his finger glides through my folds to my clit, tracing small agonizing circles.

"Do you have any objections?" he growls in my ear.

"No," I breathe.

"Did I leave *the* Chrissy Willows speechless? Huh, who knew it was that easy."

I go to sass the shit out of him but end up gasping when he drives his cock inside me. "Fuck!" I ball the sheets in my fists.

"So fucking tight," he grunts as he drives in and out of me.

My walls massage his erection, trying to accommodate the girth and impressive length. I've never been with anyone as big as him, and there's no going back. Rome has ruined me in the best way possible.

My back arches, and I moan as he hits that sensitive spot. "Right there, please," I plead while bouncing off him in time with his rhythm.

"Shh."

I purse my lips in response and turn around, only for him to wrap my curls in his fist and hold my head still, forcing me to watch him fuck me.

"Whose pussy is this?"

I fight back the moans of pleasure that threaten to leave my lips. When I don't respond, his movements quicken.

"Answer me, Willows."

"I'm sorry." I smirk at him. "I thought you wanted me to be quiet."

He grips my hips and presses deeper into me. When he stills, I shudder as he hits my pleasure point. "Rome!"

He wraps his hand around my throat and pulls my back against his chest. "I'll ask you again. Whose pussy is this?"

With a staggering breath, I whimper, "Yours."

"That's my girl."

He guides me back in place, and his abs press into the small of my back as he folds his body over mine and kisses my shoulder.

I expect him to continue ravaging me, but he pulls out. I start to beg him to come back but stop when he flips me on my back and kisses me with every ounce of passion he can.

"You are gorgeous. I hope you know that."

I look into his eyes and offer him a warm smile. "You make me believe that I am."

He trails his lips down my neck and hums against my pulse. "Tell me if I get too rough."

"I will," I reassure him.

The tip of his length settles into my entrance, and I dig my fingernails into his back when he presses inside me once again.

Rome grunts, and his eyes darken to a sinister shade of green. He enjoys seeing me writhe under him, hearing me moan and whimper, screaming his name.

I'm normally someone who takes control, always have been. I've never been with someone who is so . . . dominant. I wasn't prepared for this, but it's a more than pleasant surprise. Rome can take the power he wants, but he's a fool to think it will always be like this.

His shoulder blades flex under my palms as he rams his cock into me repeatedly. Rome moans, and it sends a coil of desire to my core, another explosion building within me.

"Rome," I manage to say before releasing a muffled curse.

He looks at me, and I cup his cheeks and kiss him with all the desire I feel. Wrapping my arms around him, I shove my face in the crook of his neck and groan against his skin. Rome presses the side of his face against my temple and groans in my ear.

"Harder, I need you harder." My words are desperate as I near the peak.

Unlike most guys, Rome obeys. He listens to my needs and obliges without a second thought.

He increases his pace, his pelvis meeting mine, his balls hitting my ass while my grasp around him tightens. He hooks his arm under my left leg, allowing him to hit the spot I need him to reach.

"Yes, yes, right there!" My jaw hangs open as the muscles in my thighs tighten, and my toes curl. I gasp before the tension releases, and I'm left with stars in my eyes.

"Fuck," I squeal while I hold onto him, unwilling to let go.

"Can I come inside you again?" he manages to ask, and I nod.

Not a second later, Rome groans in finality, and his cock pulses inside me as he comes. Warmth fills my core, leaving me wetter than I was moments before. He doesn't pull out right away. Instead, he rests his forehead against mine and gives me a sloppy smile.

"You've ruined me." He laughs darkly. "I can never go back now. I'm officially addicted to fucking you bare and coming inside you."

I weave my fingers in his short hair and gently kiss his swollen lips. "Good thing I don't plan on going anywhere."

With a small smirk, he pulls out and collapses on his back next to me. We look at one another at the same time, neither of us moving.

"We have a date today. Remember?" I start.

He raises his eyebrows in confusion.

"The cat café. You, me, and my notebook." I bop his nose before hopping out of bed.

"Does this mean I'm sleeping with my therapist?" he quips.

Spinning around, I walk over to him and kiss him. "No, it means you're dating your therapist."

Chapter Thirty-One

Rome

I don't want to go to practice today. Leaving Chrissy was harder than I was ready for it to be. Especially since she was in the shower when I had to book it out the door. The only motivation I have to get today over with is knowing I'll see her later in the afternoon. I don't mind that she'll try to dig through my messy childhood and painful memories. I trust that she's going to do it with grace and consideration.

It's the last week of June, and July fourth is next Friday. I usually hate the holidays, solely because I spend them alone, but I'm not alone this year, and that reminder brings a smile to my face. We don't have any plans. Hell, we just lit the spark between us. Knowing Chrissy and the crew, though, they'll want to do something, and I know they'll drag me along.

I dig my feet into the turf when I jog toward the other players across the field. Just before I reach them, Malik rushes toward me and stops me in my tracks.

"Did you review those new game plays?" he asks, out of breath.

"What?" My brow creases.

"The plays. Remember? The ones I asked you to review for me? Coach wants my notes first thing after practice."

Fuck . . . I completely forgot about those. I lost track of time between the abrupt decision to talk to Zack, the conversation with him, and then Chrissy.

"Dude, I'm so sorry. I—"

"Shit!" He walks away just to come back. "Did you look at them at all?"

I shake my head, and his cheeks flush.

"Coach is going to tear me a new one," he growls.

"I'm sorry. It slipped my mind."

Malik shoots daggers at me before storming off, grumbling.

This is what he gets for passing his shit onto someone else. It's not my responsibility to review the plays. He's the QB and the captain. All I do is catch the ball and run it as far down the field as I can before getting tackled. I stepped up to assist him because I noticed he was drowning. He took my kindness for granted, and now he has to pay for slacking off.

"Warm up, boys! After that, get into formation. We're running some plays from last year, and I want to see perfection!"

Malik hurls the ball across the opposite side of the field, directly at a rookie who is surrounded by the defense. He catches the ball but is tackled instantly.

"What are you doing, Chen?! Carter is wide open!" Coach shouts from the sidelines. The vein in his forehead pops out as his face turns beet red.

Coach blows the whistle, and I wince as it pierces my ears.

"Chen! I will bench your ass if you don't get your head screwed on. Do you hear me?!"

Malik doesn't acknowledge Bradson. He glares over at me and wipes the sweat from his forehead. "Sorry, Coach. Carter told me he wasn't feeling too well. I was trying to give him a break."

What the fuck are you doing?

I fumble my helmet off and clutch it in my hand.

"Carter! If you're not feeling well, you have to sit out. The weather is too brutal for you to be pushing anything."

"I'm fine! I don't know what the fuck he's talking about!" I hiss while pointing at a smirking Malik.

"You told me before we started that you were up all night with a stomach virus, and you were afraid you were dehydrated. You asked me to go easy on you. Did you forget?"

I throw my helmet to the ground, and with a crack, it bounces back up only to land farther down the grass.

"You entitled son of a bitch!" I close the distance between us before anyone can stop me. I grab him by his jersey and force him to look me in the eyes. "You're just pissed because I didn't do your work. You fucking snake!" I holler, my throat scratching from the volume and intensity.

Malik pushes me off him, but I don't stumble. I ram my hands against his chest, pushing him harder. Tripping over his feet, he collides with another player.

"Fucking do that again!" He comes back at me, flexing his hand until he forms a fist.

I chuckle harshly. "Oh, I will." I go to throw the first punch, but Blake forces my arm back and holds it behind me.

The player Malik tripped into holds him back.

"Let me go! He's lying!"

"Fucking, prove it! Tell me he's not acting like himself! He's a danger to this team and himself!"

"Shut the fuck up!" Coach shouts, and the two of us close our mouths. "I don't know what's going on between you two, but you better get your shit straight. If you don't, I will bench you both and have the freshmen take your spots. Is that understood?"

My nostrils flare as my lungs suck in and release as much oxygen as possible. "Yes, sir," I answer before Malik.

"Carter, hit the showers. I don't care if he's lying. You need to cool off. Chen, go to the other locker room and get your shit together. I want my review of the plays by early evening. Now, go. Before I lose my fucking shit."

Blake escorts me into the locker room while Malik storms toward the opposite end of the field. I rip my jersey over my shoulders and remove my shoulder guards. Without looking back, I finish undressing and stand under the cold water until the muscles in my jaw relax.

"Care to tell me what happened out there?" Blake asks as I hang my head low, letting the water wash over my neck.

"Not really," I grumble.

"That wasn't like you. You and I both know that."

"I know," I respond. "But he lied."

"It's Malik, of course he lied. When has that ever bothered you?"

"He was going to get me benched for the day. I wasn't going to stand for that."

"Well, look where that got you."

"Fuck you, Blake," I snap.

"How about you talk to me when you regain your wits? This isn't you; we both know it."

After that, I'm met with silence. I cool off for a few more moments before turning the shower off. I'm drying off with a scratchy white towel and changing into casual clothes when my phone lights up. My heart flutters, and I look at the notification without a second thought.

> If you want to keep your position, if you want me to keep throwing the ball your way, you'll get me those review notes. Tonight.

Is he threatening me? Really? He's stooping this low? I wouldn't take his threat seriously, but he proved earlier that he intends on fucking me over. He didn't throw the ball my way once during practice. He called me out, and Coach seemingly believed him. One wrong word or action will get me benched or out of the game, and my future will be jeopardized.

I have to succeed. Not only for myself, but for my dad. He was shit, but he raised me after Mom left. He deserves a break and any relief I can provide him. It all starts with me getting drafted, and Malik is threatening to take that away from me.

Gripping my phone, the snap of plastic fills the quiet while I text this prick back.

> Fine. Give me until five. I'll get you your play notes.

Fucking son of a bitch.

Chapter Thirty-Two

Chrissy

It's 3:30 p.m. when I stroll into Tea and Kittens, and I'm walking on air. These feelings coursing through me are new. I've never felt on top of the world. It's like the little butterflies in my stomach are spreading serotonin through my body.

When Gwen strolls out from the back room, she smirks at me. "You just got plowed, didn't you?" She clicks her tongue and shimmies her shoulders.

"Shut up, woman." I try adding some bite to my tone, but I can't wipe the wide smile off my face.

I settle in a booth across the room and sort through my notebook. Gwen slides into the seat across from me and leans across the table, resting on her elbows.

"If I recall, the last time we talked, you were taking a day for self-care. Did that include sleeping with a certain blond football player?"

"Initially, no . . ."

"Spill the tea, missy."

Talking to Gwen is easy; there's a reason we're best friends. I start by telling her about my trip to the store and then the run-in with Raina and Malik. It didn't surprise her that I put him in his place, not as much as it surprised me.

What did leave her baffled was when I told her what Rome did.

"He talked to Zack?"

I nod.

"Alone?"

I nod again.

"Holy shit, he's really into you."

I blush and look at my hands folded over my notebook. "Yeah, he is."

"And you feel the same? You're not feeling any regret?"

I look up at my best friend and shake my head. "No, I'm not. It feels different, Gwen. He's making me feel things that I've never felt before. It's. . . It feels like my heart has flown out of my chest. He's stolen it, and I don't want it back. Is that crazy?"

"Not even a little." Gwen reaches for my hand and offers me a warm grin. "I'm here for you, even if you get scared. Don't push him away, you hear me? You deserve every second of this."

"I believe you, and I'll come to you if I catch myself falling into old habits."

"Good." The corners of her eyes crinkle, and she squeals. "Fucking finally! The tension between the two of you was becoming insufferable! Whenever you were in the same room, I was waiting for one of you to jump the other's bones. And the *master* plans? Thank god those are done! Is he meeting you here?"

"Yes, should be here any minute now."

Her eyes dart toward the door.

"Coffee, tea, muffins, whatever you two want, it's on me. Can I text Ash?" She asks as she fumbles for her phone.

"Go ahead, but let me talk to Zack before you do."

"Easy. Oh my god, he's going to flip!" Gwen leaps out of the booth and starts to text the love of her life.

I reach for my own phone and send a quick message, thanking the man who is not only the reason I'm smiling so much but also the reason I'm pleasantly sore.

I've ended up on the floor, letting a group of kittens tangle themselves in my hair and stomp all over my stomach. I bring my phone to my face and check the time: 5:00 p.m. on the dot. This isn't like him. He knew we were supposed to meet almost an hour and a half ago. Where the hell is he? I open my messages and the last three I sent are still unanswered.

> This is a friendly reminder that you are ten minutes late to your appointment. Where are you, Captain?

> This is a not-so-friendly reminder that you are forty-five minutes late. Where are you? Are you okay?

> Rome Carter, where the fuck are you?! I've been waiting for an hour now.

So, I send one final message.

> I'm really worried. Please tell me you're okay.
> I promise I won't get mad.

Dropping my arms, I cradle my device while a cat licks my cheek. It is hot today; did he faint from dehydration? Did he succumb to heat stroke? Fuck, did someone tackle him the wrong way, and he's currently lying in a hospital bed with a multitude of broken bones . . . or worse, in a coma?

I sit straight up. Worst-case scenarios are running rampant through my mind, and they won't stop.

As I scramble to my feet, I gather my notebook and bag. "Gwen, I'm going to the sports center. If Rome shows up, tell him to call me."

I storm out the door before she can respond.

The sun has set, cooling the air to a still-warm seventy-nine degrees. The humidity is still thick, but I'm not soaked with perspiration when I push open the doors and strut down the hall. I aim for the locker room, and without a care, I open the door and make my presence known.

"Y'all better be dressed in here because I'm coming in!" When I round the bend, I don't see Rome or anyone who can help me find him.

"Where the fuck are you?" I whisper.

A door near the back opens, and voices spill into the locker room. I walk toward them without a second thought.

"Here you go, Coach. I went over the plays and made some suggestions I think will be useful."

My upper lip twitches at the sound of his voice. He's the last person I want to see.

"You're an hour late in getting these me to," Coach Bradson lectures.

"Sorry, I was showing a rookie how I go over the plays. He wanted to learn."

I peek around the corner and see Coach nod in approval at Malik. "Very good. I'll review your notes and see if I can recommend you for that position you want to get into."

"Thanks, Coach." Malik turns and locks his dark brown eyes on mine. Without saying anything, he winks at me, and I flip him off.

Before the coach can return to his office, I call out for him. "Coach Bradson, please wait a moment."

His brow wrinkles when he looks at me. His messy hair is sticking up from the heat and being outside. He has kind eyes, but I know he's stern. He seems like the kind of guy who offers tough love, but I don't get the feeling that he's cruel. His aura feels too warm.

"I'm sorry. I know I shouldn't be in here," I start.

"Are you lost? The women's locker room is on the other end of the hall."

"What? No. I'm looking for Rome. Rome Carter. Do you know where he is?"

Realization hits him, and his stance softens. "You're his psych mentor. I remember you. Good, this is good." He looks around the room before continuing. "Something is going on between him and Malik Chen. I'm not as big of a fool as they think I am. Malik claimed Rome was sick; I can't take those claims lightly. Not in this weather. Before I could bench him, Rome started yelling about Malik lying. The two of them clashed. I haven't seen Rome since. I talked to Chen before he gave me this—" He gestures at the packet.

Glancing down, I sigh when I recognize his handwriting. I haven't seen it often, but I would recognize those fancy curves anywhere.

Oh, Rome, we talked about this.

"Rome is being very cooperative with the mentorship. I'll talk to him once I find him."

I want to tell him Rome provided the notes on the plays. He's been helping the rookies get acclimated and ensuring everyone is okay during and after practice. But then I would be stepping on Rome's toes. He's finally opening up to me. I don't want to push him away by crossing a boundary.

"Thank you."

I offer him a small smile before turning around and heading back into the hallway.

I'm at a loss. I have no idea where even to start looking for him. I'm pulling out my phone when the urge to look up overwhelms me.

"You have no idea how happy I am to see you." Rome crashes into me and wraps his arms around my waist, lifting me off my feet. "I'm so sorry. I didn't mean to stand you up. I had to help one of the freshmen with his workout regimen. My phone was in my bag. I got distracted." He puts me on the ground and places his hands on my cheeks. "Please forgive me." His voice falters, making my heart ache.

With a sigh, I nod and force myself to smile through the pain. "I'm not mad. You just scared me." I run my fingers through his hair. "You look like you need to go to bed."

His jaw is lax, and his eyes are tired. He looks defeated, and I bet he has no intentions of telling me what happened between him and Malik.

"You have no idea." He rests his forehead against mine and closes his eyes.

"Want me to drive you home? I can walk back to my dorm. It's not far."

Without opening his eyes, he nods. "Can you stay with me? I need to hold you."

Chapter Thirty-Two

"I would love that." I kiss his cheek, and he hands me his keys.

We walk to his car, his arm wrapped around my waist the entire time. When we approach his old-school Jeep, he rushes forward and opens the door for me, even though it looks like he's about to collapse.

My heart swells, and I smile at him. "Thank you. Now, sit before you pass out."

"Yes, boss."

The drive home is silent. Rome fell asleep within five minutes of getting in the car.

When I stop at a red light, I glance at him and drop my shoulders. Why did he not tell me what happened? Why hasn't he told me what Malik did? Why lie?

Reaching out, I trace his jawline with my knuckles. "I'll take care of you," I whisper. "Even if you don't want me to, I'll take care of you. Always."

Chapter Thirty-Three

Rome

She knew.

My girl knows me better than I know myself.

I had to review those plans and give Malik the notes. I couldn't chance him screwing me over when the season starts. People like him can ruin people like me. My future is mine, and I won't let him touch it. Even if that means I go against my moral code. If he wants me to do his task, then fine, I'll do it.

My eyes were strained when I walked out of the conference room. Malik took the packet without a thank-you, but I didn't care. I just wanted to get away from him and be with my sunshine.

The car slows, and the engine turns off. I stir in my seat when she places her hand on my shoulder and gives me a gentle shake.

"Hey." Her tone is comforting, and it soothes my pounding headache. "Let's get you to bed, come on."

I open my eyes and unfasten my seat belt. The left side of my head pulses and pain trickles down to my eye.

"I think I have a migraine," I mumble and wince as she closes the driver-side door.

"Do you get them often?" she asks while opening my door.

"Sometimes, if I focus too hard."

She doesn't respond.

I barely remember entering my apartment or sitting in bed. My back hits my bed, and Chrissy pulls my shoes and socks off.

"I'm going to get you some medicine. When I get back, I want to see you under those blankets and super cozy."

"Okay," I mumble.

Pushing myself up, I crawl under my comforter. The fabric is cool against my bare skin. I didn't realize how tense my shoulders felt until the mattress cushioned my frame. With my eyes closed, I work on pushing away my negative thoughts.

The sound of footsteps inches toward me. I start to open my eyes, but she stops me.

"Keep those things closed, mister," she instructs me. "Give me your hand."

When I hold my hand out, she puts some medicine in my palm. I pop the pills in my mouth and accept the glass of water.

"That should help, along with a nap and a dark room."

"Thank you," I mutter before lying back down.

"Oh, Rome," she sighs before sitting next to me. "I told you this might happen. You're pushing yourself too hard."

She brushes the hair away from my forehead and rests the back of her hand on my forehead. She's cold to the touch, and it cools my forehead instantly.

"Mmm, that's nice."

"I'll have dinner for you when you wake up. Just rest, don't worry about anything right now."

She goes to leave, but I reach out and grab her hand. "Please stay." My eyes throb when I look at her, but I need her to know I want her with me. "Just until I fall asleep."

"Of course," she says with a soft smile.

I scoot over and lift the blanket for her. She lies down and presses her body against mine.

Draping my arm over her waist, I rest my forehead against her shoulder. "Chrissy?"

She squeezes my hand and tilts her head back. "Rome."

"I'm about to ask you something, and it's going to sound childish."

Shifting against me, she flips onto her other side and takes my hand. "Let me see your handsome eyes, just for a moment."

I squint my eyes open and look into her blue irises. She places my hand against her lips and kisses it.

"Nothing you say could ever sound childish. Don't ever feel that way, not with me. You can tell me anything."

Staring into her eyes, I smile softly and smother my nerves to the best of my ability. "Will you be mine?"

When the question leaves my lips, my stomach twists. I haven't asked something as important as this since high school, and I haven't had any love interests since then, either. Nothing has ever gone this far. For all I know, she'll say no, and I'll be left alone and broken like I was when I was younger.

Chrissy inches forward and feathers her nose against mine. "Oh, Rome. I'm already yours."

A comforting warmth spreads through my chest, easing my worry, and I smile widely. "Really?"

"Yes, really," she chuckles and kisses the tip of my nose. "I'm yours, and you're mine. Plain and simple, darling."

I tangle my hand in her hair and pull her against my lips, kissing her with blind devotion.

She grins against my mouth and traces tiny circles on my arm. "Now sleep. We can kiss more once that headache of yours goes away, deal?"

"Deal."

Chapter Thirty-Three

"It's all your fault!" Father shouts at me, wagging his finger in my face.

"I'm sorry!" I cry before falling to my knees.

"She left because of you. Everything was fine until you were born."

My palms meet my tear-drenched eyes, trying to scrub the tears away. "I'm sorry."

"You should have been the one to leave, not her. Anyone but her."

"I know."

"You're the one to blame."

"I know."

"You're the reason this family is broken."

"I know."

"She left because of you."

"I know."

"It's all your fault."

"I know . . ."

My eyes are wet when I open them. The room is dark, and my heart feels like someone is squeezing it. That's not the first time I've had that dream. It returns when I'm stressed or tired. Dad never said those things to me, but I know that's what he thinks when he looks at me. That's the reason he only calls or texts me once a month. In his eyes, I'm the reason the love of his life left. I'm the reason we're not happy.

I sit up and rub my eyes, clearing away the tears in the process.

The aroma of fresh bakery rolls and meat filters into my room, piquing my interest.

"Wildflower?" I call out, and she appears in the doorway not a moment later.

"You're up! How do you feel?" she asks while rushing toward me.

"My eyes are sore, but my headache is almost gone."

"Good, are you hungry?"

I look at her with a knowing smile. "Do you really need to ask me that?"

"Jeez, the sass master has returned. Stay right there, and I'll be right back."

She hurries out of my room, and the clatter of plates and the rustling of paper comes a minute later.

When she returns, she puts two plates down on the bed, along with a brown paper bag.

"One more second." She walks back out and returns with some ginger ale. "Dinner is served." She rests her hands on her hips and smiles triumphantly. "Cheesesteaks and french fries. Hope that's okay. I haven't had a decent one since my last trip to Pennsylvania."

"This is perfect, thank you."

Chrissy turns the TV on while I set our plates up, being super careful not to hit the plates together. When she puts on a true crime doc, I laugh to myself. Now I understand what Ash means when he talks about Gwen putting these shows on when they're eating or unwinding from a long day.

Her eyes are glued to the screen while we eat. She's holding her cheesesteak in both hands, blindly taking bites as she watches the TV.

I smile to myself while eating my own food. This is new, but it feels familiar. I'm not uncomfortable or itching to get out. My heart feels at peace, and the dream from earlier isn't at the forefront of my mind.

"Can I ask you something?"

"Sure," she answers without looking at me.

"Eyes on me, baby girl," I chuckle.

"Oh, sorry." She pauses the show and fixes her gaze on me.

"Do you have plans for the Fourth of July?"

"Hmm, I don't think so," she responds while tilting her head back and forth.

"Could I offer an idea?"

"Absolutely! What did you have in mind?" Her excitement spurs on my own.

"Well, I saw a poster for a carnival. It's a few minutes away from Ash's. There will be rides, fireworks—"

"I'm in," she bursts in with a wide smile.

"Want to invite the rest of the family? Gwen, Ash, Zack, maybe Max?"

"Yes! Oh my gosh, we haven't done something like this in years! Let alone with all of us! Can I text them now?" she asks while reaching for her phone.

"Yes, go ahead," I respond, feeling like I've done something worthwhile.

Not a minute later, I get a notification. The chat's title, *My Crazy Family,* makes me beyond happy.

Chrissy: We're all going to the carnival by the Waylens' for the Fourth of July! No ifs, ands, or buts!

Max: I have to work!

Chrissy: On a federal holiday?!

Max: Crime never sleeps!

Chrissy: This is Rome's idea.

Max: I'll think about it. . .

Gwen: Yes! I'm so excited! This is a great idea, Rome :D

Ash: I'll bring the barf bags.

Zack: Does this mean I'm the fifth wheel?

Ash: Not if Max comes.

Zack: Max, you better be free. I need a date!

Max: I said I'll think about it!

The messages don't stop after that. Chrissy smiles and giggles as she types away on her phone screen.

I don't jump in only because my head aches again. Leaning back, I close my eyes and fall asleep, feeling content and at peace.

Chapter Thirty-Four

Chrissy

"What do you mean you're not coming?!" I burst through Max's bedroom door.

Thankfully, he's decent.

"Chrissy! Jeez, woman." He grasps at his chest with wide eyes. "What if I was naked?"

"That's not the point! Ash said you're not coming tonight?"

"I have to work. I have a high-profile case that needs my immediate attention."

"It's a federal holiday," I pout and stomp my foot like a toddler.

"And I'm a federal lawyer. This case requires my attention, even on days off."

"I call bullshit. Where's Gwen?"

Before he can answer, I walk into Ash's room and find Gwen tying her sneakers.

"Did you know?" I ask, more upset than angry.

"Know what?" she responds.

"That Max isn't coming tonight."

"What?! Maxim Waylen!" She storms past me and into his room.

"When did my mother get here?"

"I knew you two were up to something." She pokes at his chest. "When was someone going to tell us?"

"Fuck me. Ash!" Max calls for support, but it's fruitless.

"Get your ass into some casual attire and bring your ass downstairs before I—"

"Gwen, Chrissy, I have work."

"One night, please," Gwen begs, and I join her.

"Come on, celebrate America with us." I quiver my lower lip.

"Jesus, where's Ash? Ash!"

"Please, Max," Gwen whines. "*Pleeeeeease.*"

"Gwen, you're breaking my heart. I really can't—"

"Come on, spend the night with your favorite people. What happened to family sticks together?" I feign some tears.

"Oh my god," Max sighs and drags his hand over his face.

"*Maaaaax*, please!" we both plead, hoping to break down his stubborn resolve.

"What the hell is going on?" Ash asks from the bottom of the stairs, holding back a chuckle when he sees Gwen and me pleading with his older brother.

"Someone forgot to tell the girls I wasn't coming tonight," Max chastises Ash.

"I didn't forget. I was hoping they would sucker you into going."

"Fuck me . . ." Max grumbles.

"Oh, I wasn't expecting this," Rome blurts out when he appears in front of the doorway.

"Rome! My favorite blondie, please tell the girls I can't go. You'll have fun without me."

Rome's expression falls. "You're not coming with us?"

"Oh. . . fucking, fine! Fine, you win. I'll get changed."

"Really?!" Gwen and I squeal at the same time.

"Yes, I accept defeat. Give me ten minutes."

"Thank you!" I kiss his cheek obnoxiously, and he cringes.

"Family outing!" Ash cheers while Zack appears next to Rome.

"Looks like you won't be fifth wheeling it tonight." Rome nudges Zack's arm and smirks.

"Thank god. Before we go, though, you." My brother points at me. "We need to talk."

I follow Zack into the kitchen while the others finish getting ready.

I had to fight the desire to hug Rome and kiss him until my lips went numb. His ocean-scented skin is intoxicating, proving tonight is going to be a challenge.

Zack pulls a stool out and gestures for me to sit. As I get comfortable, he settles beside me and rests his elbow on the counter. He looks at me for a moment.

When I look at him, I still see the boy I grew up with.

Zack and I aren't identical twins. He has black hair, while mine is gold. I don't have my freckles anymore, but my eyes are the same as his.

We've been through it all together. Looking back, our relationship was never strained. Sure, we had our ups and downs, and his protective streak kicked into high gear when I started dating in middle school. But it never drove a wedge between us. He never took his frustration out on me. He would voice his concerns about the guys I was interested in and then tell me he was there if I needed him. The snide remarks didn't come until later, and it was only because I started taunting and teasing him about his protectiveness. I knew and still know that I can go to him about anything. He only has my best interest at heart.

"I'm sorry we haven't gotten the chance to talk yet. We've

both been understandably busy," he starts. "I wish you had told me about your feelings toward Rome."

"I didn't want to hurt you. I didn't want you to think I was betraying you."

"When have I ever put something like that into your head?" He turns to face me, his expression soft yet full of disappointment.

"Never. You never made me feel like I couldn't tell you anything."

"So why? Why didn't you tell me? Why did I have to learn about this from Rome?"

"I was scared." I stumble over my words. "I didn't want you to feel like I wasn't taking your feelings into consideration. I passed the feelings off as nothing more than a crush. For seven months—"

"Seven months?" His voice raises slightly in shock. "Chrissy..."

"I—I don't have a valid reason other than I was scared of pushing you away."

"I know how I am. It started becoming abundantly clear when Gwen started seeing Ash. I'm too protective, and it comes across as toxic. I'm trying to be better. I don't want either of you to be scared to tell me anything because you're afraid of how I'll react."

I nod solemnly. "I'm sorry. You're right. I should have talked to you sooner."

Zack reaches out and squeezes my shoulder. "I'm happy for you. Rome is a good guy. I know he'll take care of you and that you'll take care of him. But please, for the love of the universe, don't let me catch you two making out or fucking on the other side of the door. I don't want another Gwen and Ash flashback."

"I promise," I giggle as I recall last Halloween. "While

we're on this topic. There is something I have to tell you." I hold his stare while sucking in as much courage as I can. "Miles and I had a thing last summer, and we semi-dated in the fall."

He's still for a moment like he's processing. "Semi?"

"We went on a few dates. I ended things with him in early December."

"He was there at Horror Fest. Why didn't I put two and two together?" he asks himself while looking off into space.

"You were under a spell. I'm surprised you remember any of that night."

"Yeah, well, I'm sorry you felt like you couldn't tell me about Miles. It makes sense now why he was so upset at the end of the semester."

"It was my fault," I mutter.

"No, no, it wasn't," Zack states without hesitation. "You did the right thing. You shouldn't have forced yourself to stay if you weren't feeling the way he was. You did the right thing for yourself. Which, in itself, is commendable."

Tears sting my eyes. I lean across the gap between us and wrap my arms around him. "What did I do to deserve a brother like you?" I ask before sniffling.

He hugs me and pats my head. "You're you, and while I may want to shake you sometimes, I love you and that's enough."

Pulling back, he messes with my hair while I wipe my tears away. "Thank you. It means a lot."

"I've only ever wanted you to be happy. If Rome makes you happy, if he's the one you want, all you had to do was tell me."

"He makes me happy, trust me." I smile at Zack before smirking mischievously. "*Very* happy, if you know what I mean." And I give him a sloppy wink.

"Oh, come on, gross!" He gags and pushes me away from him. "Ash, I need that barf bag!"

I cackle and almost fall off my stool as Zack continues to pretend to throw up. He gets up and starts to walk away from me.

"Wait, come back! I have more to share."

"No! Stay away from me, you freak!"

"Let me love you!" I chase him into the living room and giggle manically.

"Where do you think you're going?" Rome catches me in his arms and weaves his fingers into the hair at the base of my neck before tugging.

"Hey, you." I greet him as he lifts me off my feet.

His pecs press into my chest while his arms secure me close. He's wearing a red Castle Brook football shirt and black shorts, and his hair is damp from the shower, messy yet sexy.

"Have I told you how stunning you are?"

My cheeks flush. "Multiple times."

"Well, you are beautiful." Rome kisses me, and the butter-flies in my stomach flutter rapidly into my chest.

"I think I'm gonna cry," Gwen whimpers.

Our lips part, and I turn to face the audience gathered by the front door. Gwen pretends to dab the tears from her eyes, and Ash is slipping on a pair of sandals while Max scrolls through his phone.

When Zack peeks into the room, he purses his lips. "I lied. *Now*, I need the barf bag."

Chapter Thirty-Five

Rome

I'm not sure how this happened. It was like I blinked, and Zack shouted "Shotgun!" and then he was in the front seat, leaving Chrissy in the back. Ash, Max, and Gwen are following in Max's car. Zack is drumming his hands on his legs while I focus on the road. It feels weird not having Chrissy next to me while I drive. She's only been in the passenger seat a handful of times, but to me, it's her seat, and now, a hyperactive golden retriever is sitting next to me.

Going to a carnival on the Fourth of July probably wasn't the greatest idea. Everyone and their grandmothers are going to be here today. The traffic to find parking is a headache, but we find a spot in the back so we can park next to one another. Everyone gets out of the car, and Chrissy leaps on my back and kisses my cheek.

"This is going to be so much fun!" she squeals and holds onto me while we start our trek to the front gate.

"Comfy up there?" I ask while peering over my shoulder, happy to see her smiling ear to ear.

"Extremely," she says in my ear with a seductive edge to her voice.

I run my calloused palms along her smooth legs, which she's wrapped around my waist.

I tried not to admire her in front of Zack, but my eyes wandered, and when she ran into the foyer at the Waylens' house, I had to swoop in and hold her in my arms.

She's wearing light-washed jean shorts and a cropped cream-colored knitted tank top. She left her hair down, and a few loose strands tickle my cheek when she leans over to squish her face against mine. Her skin smells like fresh strawberries, and I'd give anything to have her to myself. To taste her and make her lips swell from kissing me. To have her mouth around my co—

"Gwen, get off me!" Zack struggles to get Gwen off his back.

"Carry me! Ash hurt his back, and my feet hurt from the café today," she whines as she clings onto him.

With a fake groan, Zack's expression melts, and he gives in. "You're lucky I love you."

"Yay!" She kisses his cheek repeatedly and messes with his hair.

"Max?" Ash asks with a lifted eyebrow.

"Do not even think about it!" Max raises his voice, making Ash chuckle.

After waiting in line, we have our tickets and gather in a deserted spot near the entrance. As everyone formulates a game plan, I take in the sights and smells.

The sun is starting to drop below the horizon, casting a warm, golden glow across the grounds. The air is sticky and filled with the sweet scent of cotton candy and fried foods. The distant sound of cheerful music from the merry-go-round drifts through the air, along with gleeful screams. The carnival is a kaleidoscope of colors and energy. The Ferris wheel towers over everything, adorned with multicolored lights. Strings of fairy lights illuminate the pathways, and the neon glowing from rides paints the scene in a vibrant palette.

I can't recall the last time I went to a fair like this. It must have been before Mom left and Dad succumbed to his darkness. Now, I'm with a different kind of family, and my heart swells as I watch them go back and forth with one another.

"We can always separate." Max butts in between Zack and Chrissy.

"No way!" Chrissy and Gwen say at the same time.

"Family sticks together. Instill that in your brain, older Waylen." Gwen nudges his arm before hugging him.

"Let's just start walking. We have a few hours before the fireworks. We can do as much as possible before then," Ash offers like the leader he is.

"As long as we start moving, I don't care. I'm beginning to sweat in places I'd rather not admit to." Zack cringes.

Gwen and Chrissy make a face at Zack, who shrugs.

I snicker before pointing at him. "Let's go before Zack starts stripping and people start throwing singles at him," I tease and dodge his attempt at punching me in the arm.

What's with the Willowses wanting to punch me all the time?

We start down the path, passing a few food and game stands. Chrissy secures herself by my side, squeezing my hand and resting her head on my shoulder while we walk. The air is buzzing with thrills and too much sugar.

Gwen stops the group abruptly when she sees a stuffed raccoon hanging from a tent. She looks at Ash, and with a simple look, he whips out his wallet and offers her money to play the water gun game.

"Max, come play with me!" she calls while patting the stool next to her. "Blondie, you too!"

Chrissy peels herself from my arm, but before she walks away, I wrap my hand around her wrist to stop her. "Here, this one's on me." I offer her a five, and she responds by hugging me a little too tightly.

"Thank you!" She kisses my cheek before running toward Gwen.

Ash, Zack, and I watch they go head-to-head against another family on the other side. Max nudges into Gwen to try and ruin her impressive aim. Chrissy is on her knees on the seat, squinting her eyes and squealing as the three of them near the top. When the winner's bell rings, no one is surprised that Gwen popped her balloon first. She is, after all, a self-proclaimed video game professional.

With a huge grin, Gwen hugs her raccoon plushie and crashes into Ash's arms. "Isn't it cute?" she asks.

"It's something . . ." He plasters on a fake smile and nods. "Since when did you start liking raccoons?"

"Since I discovered they're basically outdoor cats who live in trash cans."

"Oh, boy," Zack grumbles with a hint of amusement.

"Gwen, darling." Max places his hands on her shoulders and stares into her eyes. "I love you, you know that, right?"

She nods excitedly.

"Good, and you love me?"

Another nod.

"Good, very good. I don't want to come home one day and see a raccoon raiding my refrigerator. Deal?"

"Oh, please." She dismisses him. "You have nothing to worry about. Besides, I don't know how to catch one . . . yet."

"I'd pay to watch you try." Ash snickers louder and louder as the scene plays out in his head.

"There's my girl." I hold my arms out for Chrissy, and she crashes against my chest. I rest my chin on top of her head and let a wave of butterflies swirl from my stomach into my heart.

She was not even five feet away from my side, and she missed me like we'd been apart for days. I've never felt this way before, and I avoided it for so long because I was afraid of inevitable heartbreak. Now? I don't foresee that happening between us.

"Whatcha thinking about?" she asks me, pulling me from my thoughts.

Her cheeks are pink from the heat, laughter, and maybe something else. She has a twinkle in her eyes, and her tone suggests she's up to something.

"Want the honest answer or a lie I can throw together?"

The crew starts to walk away, assuming we're right behind them.

"You know what I want." She stands on her tiptoes, and our noses touch. "The truth, Carter. Nothing but the truth."

"You," I whisper against her lips.

"What about me?"

The hum of carnival buzzers, mechanical rides, and chatter ceases. It's just me and my wildflower. No one else is here. Nothing else matters.

"How your mouth would look wrapped around my cock."

"Hmm." She smirks before she starts scanning our surroundings. "Want to make that thought a reality?"

Without giving me a chance to reply, she takes my hand and urges me to follow her, and I happily oblige.

Chapter Thirty-Six

Chrissy

Rome motherfucking Carter.

He's making me reckless. Don't get me wrong; I know the kind of girl I am. I crave adventure and mischief, but this is new, even for me.

His hands are trailing over my bare stomach, inching downward as he kisses and licks my neck. Behind a vacant tent, I'm trembling beneath his touch as he curls his hands in my hair, urging me closer.

"Wait," I say between our hungry kisses.

"What's wrong?" He's in a daze of desire. I'm the only one capable of rational thinking—barely.

"We need structure."

"What?" He laughs.

"Just trust me." I tug on his hand before he can pull me under his spell.

He brushes his fingers against my skin as he pushes my hair to the side, exposing my neck.

"Rome," I threaten before my mouth drops open.

"Hurry, woman. I *need* you."

I increase my pace and aim toward a shed that's closed off. We ignore the Employees Only sign and stumble inside. Rome pushes me against the door, not giving two shits that we may or may not be alone right now.

"Slow down." I place my hand on his chest and fumble for my phone.

As soon as I turn on the flashlight, I jolt and drop my phone. "Fuck!"

"What? What's wrong?" Rome asks while picking up my phone and spinning around.

A bunch of beady-eyed stuffed animals stare back at us. Some are missing heads; others have stuffing falling out of their stomachs. They're piled high, toppling over one another.

"Well, this is interesting," he states.

"And terrifying. Turn the light back off." I take the phone away from Rome and turn the light off. "That's better." I crash my lips against his, pressing my body against him.

Rome takes a deep breath through his nose as he parts my lips with his tongue. I moan into his mouth at the sensation of his tongue dancing around mine.

My hands dip down his body until I reach the waistband of his shorts. "You want to see me on my knees, right?"

"I do, but I can't see you too well."

I continue to travel my hand down, and when I reach my goal, Rome grunts.

Leaning into his ear, I nibble on his earlobe and whisper, "Light on me and only me. I want you to watch me suck your cock."

I can't make out his expression in the dark, so I drop to my knees and start to untie his shorts. My fingers work the knot loose, but before I tug his shorts down, I take a moment to gather myself.

I'm not sure I can please him like he's hoping I can. I've

given blow jobs before, but I worry he won't enjoy it. What if I'm terrible at it and no one ever told me before? Rome is special, and I want him to know that, to feel that.

With a sharp intake of air, I pull his shorts down. Already, his length is bulging against his black boxer briefs.

"Completely off or—"

"All the way," he interrupts.

"Okay," I mumble under my breath.

I work his boxers over his form. When I get them over his thighs, they gather in his shorts, and I hold back a huff through my pursed lips. The flashlight turns on and dims. With as much confidence as I can summon, I look up at him as I start at the base of his shaft, kissing his cock to the tip.

"So fucking pretty." His voice drops. "Keep going."

I wrap my lips around the tip, kissing and teasing it with my tongue. With a satisfied hum, I repeat this motion until my body relaxes. Looking up at Rome, seeing his head resting against the wall and his flushed cheeks, I begin to doubt that anything I do could dissatisfy him, but let's test the water—for my own curiosity.

I take his cock in my right hand and slowly take him in my mouth. With each inch, I pull back and suck, and I'm pleased as his expression tenses. With a few more motions like this, I find my stopping point, which is less than his entire length. If I push myself, I can take more, but I know I'll gag.

I time my strokes with my mouth, and because I know he enjoys my tongue, I use it to my advantage. A moan leaves my mouth and vibrates against him.

Looking down at me, he uses his free hand and balls my curls in his fist.

"That's it, baby. Such a good girl."

He tightens his grip and arches his hips, forcing more of his length down my throat. When I choke, I drench his cock, and he chuckles deeply.

I keep stroking him while I pull back, making sure not to leave an inch of him untouched by my hand.

"Are you okay?" he asks.

I smile and nod while maintaining eye contact. "I'm fine; I just need a moment."

"Okay . . . *fuck*, that's good."

I move back to kiss the side of his length. "Let me know if you don't like this, okay?"

Before he can respond, I lick his balls before placing one in my mouth and sucking gently.

"Oh, shit!" He quivers, and I increase the pace of my strokes. "Just like that." His voice grows louder, and my core tightens at his praise. "Let me see your eyes."

Looking up, I change sides and take his other ball in my mouth, sucking with the same pressure.

With a series of grunts and incoherent curses from Rome, I shift my position and take his cock in my mouth again, taking as much of his length as possible.

"You're going to make me come, Wildflower. Is that what you want?"

I hum against his erection, and the rumble makes him smirk.

"That's my girl." Using the fist tangled in my hair, he encourages me to take more.

I take another half inch before I gag, but that doesn't stop me.

"Love, you can stop."

But I don't. I work my head farther and hasten my movement. My eyes water, and my knees begin to ache from the rough hardwood floor.

Rome's muscles tense under me, and his face contorts as his mouth drops open. "Fuck, that's it, baby. Yes, yes, fuck!"

With a deep and dark murmur, he comes in my mouth. His cock pulses against my tongue. He tastes salty with a hint of sweat; it doesn't stop me from swallowing and licking his tip before collapsing onto my butt.

"Shit," I mutter while working on catching my breath.

Sweat covers every inch of my body. The air is thick in the shed, and the heat from the flashlight is no help.

"Can you turn that off now? I don't want to be reminded of our audience."

"Oh, yeah." Rome snickers and turns off the light.

He fixes himself as I stand back up. Our eyes meet at the same time, and even in the dark, I can see his loving gaze and smile.

"You, my love," he says while reaching for me, "are too good."

I giggle and rest my head over his chest, listening to his rapid heartbeat. "A plus?" I ask with a hint of playfulness.

"Off the charts. My life has been changed for the better. Everything before you was in black and white. With you, I can see color. Vibrant, beautiful, stunning, absolutely breathtaking."

"Wow, if I knew one blow job would change your life, I might have offered one sooner," I giggle, but his expression stays soft and loving.

"You are what's changing my life. *You*. Nothing else."

My features soften, and I release a small breath. "I adore you. Every inch, every hair, every glance. You're everything I hoped you would be and more."

He runs his thumbs over my cheekbones. "Let's get out of here and get you some water and food."

"Shall I text the others?" I ask as Rome opens the door.

"Hmm, probably for the best. We don't want Max to file a missing children report."

The sun has set when we step back outside. I link my arm through Rome's, letting him guide the way to the nearest food stand.

> Y'all shouldn't have left the two blondes behind. Rome and I got lost. Meet us at the Ferris wheel.

> Zack: They're alive! Max, you don't have to go to security!

> Max: And this is why I don't have kids!

I lean against Rome as we get in line, and I get a separate message from Gwen.

> I got you a snow cone. Something tells me you need it ;)

Chapter Thirty-Seven

Rome

Chrissy is eating her snow cone while I devour a bag full of cheesy french fries, more than happy to offer some to Gwen.

"Now that we have the blondies back and food, what's next?" Zack claps his hands together while looking at each of us individually.

"Well, we were on our way to the roller coaster before a certain pair got 'lost.'" Ash eyes Chrissy and me with a hint of knowing amusement.

Chrissy side-eyes Gwen, who is in her happy place while eating two fries at once. "You, on a roller coaster?"

"Who? Me?" Gwen asks while pointing at herself. "Ash said he would give me five bucks if I went."

"Wait, *I* offered you five bucks," Max chimes in.

Gwen smirks at Ash and Max. "Easiest ten dollars I ever made."

"This woman . . ." Ash sighs before sweeping her into his arms.

"No!" she giggles as he starts toward the ride that towers

over the Ferris wheel. "Wait! I changed my mind; you guys can keep your money!" She kicks her feet, but Ash keeps a hold on her.

"Not happening, sneaky girl. You're going to sit right in the middle between Max and me and suffer with us."

"Wait, don't leave me with the love birds!" Zack chases after them, leaving Chrissy and me behind again.

"Just so you know," Chrissy starts while looping her arm through mine. "I'm going to scream, and I apologize in advance for your eardrums."

After tossing out the brown paper bag my fries were in, I lick my fingers and tilt my head from side to side. "That's fine. If my eardrum pops, you'll have to nurse me back to health. It's a lose-win scenario."

"I'm not wearing a nurse outfit," Chrissy threatens playfully.

I open my mouth, and she feeds me some of her shaved ice. "What if both of my eardrums burst?"

"Not going to happen."

We approach the group and get in line with them. Max is hugging Gwen's plush raccoon while Gwen hugs Ash, leaving Zack staring at his phone.

"Do you want to sit next to me or your sister?" I ask in hopes of getting his attention.

Zack sighs before pocketing his phone. "Both," he says with a smile. "I want to be squished between my two favorite people."

"Since when was I your favorite?" Chrissy asks while crossing her arms over her chest.

"Since you started dating my best friend. You're finally calm-ish," he teases.

Chrissy purses her lips.

"And I don't have to deal with your hyper ass as much

anymore, and don't get me started on cleaning up all the broken hearts you've left behind. I'm thrilled to finally catch a break. Thank you for your service, Rome Carter." Zack salutes me.

"I'm going to remember this," Chrissy quips. "Especially when you ask me to hook you up with one of my friends."

"You don't have any friends," he fires back.

"Hey!" Gwen calls.

"Besides Gwen," Zack adds.

As they bicker back and forth, what Zack said repeats in my mind.

"All the broken hearts you've left behind."

How many men did Chrissy leave? Did she break up with all of them? If so, what were the reasons?

Chrissy offers him a lopsided grin. "Just wait." She pokes his chest as we approach the front of the line.

"Yeah, yeah. Just let me have my way." Zack rolls his eyes.

No, don't think like that, I tell myself while wrapping my arm around Chrissy's waist and kissing the crown of her head.

She looks up at me and beams, her cheeks flushed from the heat and her brother.

Look at her. She's head over heels. She wouldn't hurt me like that. I trust her because she knows what I've been through. I need to relax.

"I adore you. All of you," she whispers as I trace my thumb over her jawline.

I kiss her forehead again and exhale. "I adore you too."

The gate opens, and the six of us take up two cars, Gwen between Ash and Max—who is still embracing the raccoon—and Zack in the middle of Chrissy and me. The rails are neon green, and the seats are deep and secure. The guards come down, and I secure it over my body, locking it in place. The ride's attendants come by to make sure everyone is locked in.

"Why did I agree to this?" Max groans and grips the sidebar until his knuckles turn white.

"Don't hug him so tight. You'll make his eyes pop out." Gwen is definitely more concerned over her stuffed animal than Max.

It makes the rest of us chuckle.

"I think I lied, Rome." Chrissy leans over and smiles widely. "Max might scream louder than me."

And she's right.

When we reach the top of the drop, Max curses, and after that, he's all screams and pleas for the ride to stop.

At the end of the ride, he drops his head and sighs, "That wasn't so bad."

We all hold back our laughter, and once we exit the roller coaster, we agree it's time for more snacks and to find a spot to watch the fireworks. With all the fried food we can get our hands on, we find a spot near a tree, close to the back, away from most of the crowds.

I'm picking at a sugar-dusted funnel cake, and my fingers are a mess of grease and thick sugar, but I don't care. Today is all about forgetting one's responsibilities, letting go, having fun, enjoying your loved ones, and celebrating America.

Chrissy leans against my shoulder and rests her hand on my thigh.

It's strange being open about our relationship after months of attempting to avoid our growing feelings. My eyes dart over to Zack, and the lingering suspicion that he's going to jump me or stab my eyes out for touching his sister creeps over me. Instead, he's sitting next to Gwen and Ash, engaged in deep conversation, not even looking our way.

"Your brother confuses me," I whisper against the top of her head.

Chapter Thirty-Seven

"You're telling me," she mumbles back with a hint of laughter.

Chrissy shifts so she's looking at me, a warm smile spreading across her lips. "I'm really happy. I want you to know that. You *make* me happy."

Reaching forward, I rest my hand against her sunburned cheek. "You and me, Wildflower. I wouldn't have it any other way."

Fireworks reflect in her eyes, exploding in her irises. The sudden burst of explosions doesn't shake us. With a shared look of love and admiration, I pull her back against me and look out across the field.

The reverberation of each firework echoes through the air, creating a symphony of crackles and pops. The once-tranquil night sky becomes a canvas of vibrant colors and patterns.

We're silent as we admire the show, no one daring to move or speak. Multiple fireworks erupt simultaneously, filling the sky with an exhilarating crescendo of light and sound. The crowd erupts in applause and cheers, their faces illuminated by the brilliance above. The air is alive with a sense of joy and awe as memories are created that will etch themselves into our lives.

When the final embers fade away, the tranquility resumes. No one moves; we're too busy basking in the afterglow. Chrissy wraps her arms around my waist and kisses the underside of my jaw. With a soft smile, I look across the way and catch Ash's approving expression.

With a smirk, he mouths, "I told you so."

And I've never been more pleased to have been proven wrong.

Chapter Thirty-Eight

Chrissy

Today is the first official check-in with Professor Clastis, and I'm a bundle of nerves. With my paper in hand and my head held high, I head toward her office. Even though all I really want to do is hide in Rome's bed, wrapped up in his arms.

This last week has been nothing short of bliss. Most days, Rome is busy with football, but we always end our nights together. I meet him at his apartment, and we hang out, fool around, eat food, talk, and fall asleep in each other's arms. I don't think I've ever been this happy or cared for. Rome makes me feel as if the stars are about to collide, summoning the end of the world as we know it. I have nothing to fear though. Let the stars collide, let the world end. As long as I have Rome, nothing else matters.

Every two weeks, Professor Clastis wants us to turn in a report of our findings and methods while complying with HIPPA, the act that protects a patient's identity. We must keep our mentee unnamed, so she doesn't know who we're partnered with, and because of the abundance of football players and students, identities are safe.

Technically, the relationship between Rome and I is inappropriate, given that I'm acting as his therapist. I should back down, ask for a reassignment, but I was never one to play by the rules. There are things about Rome I need and want to discover. We get deep, but it's surface-level deep. And let's not forget the shark in the water; he lied to me. He thinks I don't know about him still doing Malik's work. He's under the assumption that I believe he told Malik to fuck off. That's not the case though.

As much as I want to confront him about it, I want him to want to tell me. He needs to learn that I'm someone he can trust, someone he can go to in times of need. If I confront Rome about lying to me, he'll get defensive and take two steps back. This way, he'll learn what he needs. I just have to let him grow, even if it's painful to watch.

I round the corner, and her office door comes into view, always open. I'm not sure why I'm nervous. Professor Clastis and I have always had a good relationship. It might be knowing that she's going to ask me questions that has me nervous. I was never good at being drilled on things, no matter how confident I am.

My hands are shaking when I knock on her door.

She peers over her computer screen and smiles at me. "Ms. Willows, please, come in."

Her office is spotless. The wooden desk where her two computer screens are is clean from dust and clutter. Various certifications, awards, and academic degrees line the burgundy walls.

She rolls her chair near the edge of her desk, and I sit in the plush leather seat in front of her.

Her smile is flawless and bright. Her eyes are dark, but they sparkle with kindness and love. She cares for each and every one of her students. There's a reason she's the head of the Psychology and Behavioral Health Department at Castle Brook University. Her dark hair is shaved short, with wisps of curls, and her umber skin shows no sign of age. She's the definition of beauty and wisdom.

"How is the program treating you?" she asks, her voice like velvet.

"So far so good." Why do I sound out of breath?

"Good, and how is your mentee? Treating you and this program with respect, I hope."

"Oh, yes. He's open to the experience, and he's been nothing but respectful."

Until he throws me into his bed . . .

"Excellent. Have you noticed any signs of burnout or depression?"

With a subtle drop of my shoulders, I nod. "Burnout. He does a lot for the team. Most are tasks that aren't his responsibility, but he does them because the person in charge of them doesn't. I informed him of the symptoms, and he's aware of the condition, but he isn't willing to accept the fact that he's close."

"I see. Our job as behavioral health specialists is to inform them, show them what can happen and what is happening. We are to inspire change, and it seems like you're on your way there. But I encourage you to not let up. Check in on him every session. Ask him how his day-to-day life is, and what his current workload is like. If he seems tired, ask him what he intends to do to rest. Highlight the need for self-care and remind him that it's okay to lessen his load. Keep up the good work, and please let me know if there is anything I can do to help."

I meet her kind expression with one of my own as I hand her my paper.

As I head out, I stop and turn around. "Professor?"

Her eyes meet mine.

"His mother is the root cause of a lot of his trauma. He's told me about her, but I can't help but wonder if there's more to the story. He's lied to me already; how do you think I should proceed?"

"Parents are most are. May I ask what seems to bother him the most?"

"She left when he was eight. No explanation. His father doesn't know why she left either."

"Unfortunately, we can only work off what our patient is willing to provide. If your mentee doesn't know why her mother abandoned him, nor his father, the question may never be answered. I'm sure he has an abandonment fear. I would work on addressing that, have him talk through those moments and fears, and tell him that it's normal, but he shouldn't dwell on it. He can't let feelings such as those hold him back. Remember, don't push too hard. Once you lose a patient's trust, it's nearly impossible to get back."

"Thank you. I'll keep talking to him. I'll be sure not to push any boundaries." I turn to leave.

"Ms. Willows?"

I face her again even though my mind is swimming with tactics and theories on addressing situations like this.

"Keep up the great work. You're at the top of this program for a reason, don't forget that."

With a small smile and renewed motivation, I nod. "Thank you."

My next goal for the day is to go back to my dorm and call my parents. I haven't talked to them in a few days, and I miss hearing their voices.

Taking the path toward home, I see a familiar face, and she looks awfully relieved to see me.

"Chrissy, thank the stars I found you."

Her greeting has me wrinkling my brow. "Is everything okay, Raina?"

With a tired sigh, she runs her fingers through her dark hair. "Malik . . . he's a total ass. I thought I was making progress, but that guy is a fucking snake. He said something about Rome, and it's not sitting right with me."

"What did he say?"

"I know you two are friends, and I trust you care about him." She scans the area before taking a step closer and lowering her voice. "He talks shit every day. Tells me how Rome offered to take up extra tasks, stealing his spotlight and work. I don't know Rome, but I know you, and I know you don't surround yourself with people like that. Malik hinted about the team not taking him seriously. He thinks they prefer Rome over him—"

"They do," I respond without thinking.

"I know . . . it doesn't take a genius to figure out why. But listen, he's up to something. The way he talks about Rome, the way his body reacts . . . I don't trust him. It's in my report, and I'm going to talk to Professor Clastis about it, but you have to be aware. You have to tell Rome to be careful."

Dread and worry settle over me like an uncomfortable blanket, leaving me feeling beyond sick. The team isn't practicing today, but Rome is at the center. What does Malik gain from getting "revenge" against Rome? He would lose the person who does his work.

"Thank you, Raina. I have to go." I start down the path, heading straight to the football field.

"Please text me!"

"I will," I shout over my shoulder.

Would Malik try to hurt Rome or his reputation? No, he

wouldn't. He can't. Right? My pace increases as my thoughts continue down a darker path.

"Rome is okay," I tell myself, but it doesn't work.

The feeling in the pit of my stomach will only fade once I see him. So, I focus my sights on the stadium and walk as fast as I can.

Chapter Thirty-Nine

Rome

"Keep it up, one more rep," I encourage Levi as he works on finishing his bench presses.

His forehead is covered with perspiration. The AC in the gym is working overtime, but his body is working harder.

"I can't," he grits through his teeth, struggling to complete his lift.

"You can, come on!"

With a loud grunt, he raises the weights, and I help him place the bar in its stand.

"Fuck, I can't feel my arms."

"Good job." I grip his shoulder and give him a firm shake.

"Fuck you."

I chuckle at him. His arms are dangling toward the floor, his chest heaving, trying to catch his breath. His cheeks are red, and he's in need of a cool shower.

"You'll thank me when you wake up one morning with arms of steel."

"Yeah, yeah, whatever you say." He brushes me off weakly.

"Are we good for Friday? Is a day enough rest?"

"Yeah, Friday . . . Whatever you say."

I snicker again as I gather my gym bag. "Shower, eat, drink water, then rest. You hear me?"

"Yes, boss."

Leaving him to his temporary resting place, I head into the corridor and rest my back against the wall while reaching for my phone; seeing a message from Ash.

Hey man, busy tonight?

Not that I'm aware of. What's up?

Want to come over? Hang out with me, Zack, maybe Max? Gwen is working, and Zack said something about Chrissy talking to her parents, which tends to run all night.

Sure, sounds great, but be warned, I'm starving.

Per usual. Don't worry, friend. I have all the snacks! Just don't touch Max's yogurt!

Can't I just have one?! They're so good! You need to try one.

Fuck me, you can't say I didn't try. Don't tell him, but I'll try one too lol.

I'm typing out my next message, but the sound of the doors blasting open diverts my attention.

"Chrissy?"

"Hey, handsome." She sounds distracted as she scans the hall.

"What are you doing here? I thought Ash said you were going to call your parents?"

She looks disheveled; her cheeks are red like she ran here.

"Yeah, I am. Have you seen Malik?" Her question leaves me confused.

"Not today, why?"

"Just curious." She's watching our surroundings like a hawk.

"Are you feeling okay?" I reach for her, resting the back of my hand to check her temperature. "You need to cool off and drink some water."

"Yeah . . . I think I just need to get back to my dorm." She sounds distant, and her gaze has yet to land on me.

"I was going to go to Ash's, but how about you come back to my place? You can call your parents in my room. I'll cook us something to eat, and afterward, we can hang out. Blast the AC and watch all the TV we can handle."

With a small sigh, Chrissy finally looks at me. "That sounds wonderful."

"Okay, let's go—"

"Carter!" Coach's voice startles me.

"Yes, sir?" I ask while turning around.

"Can you step into my office? We have to talk."

My stomach plummets into the floor, leaving me, and my voice, an anxious mess. "Sure, I'll be right there."

I look back at Chrissy, and she offers me a gentle look. "I'll wait here. Don't worry, okay?"

I release a long exhale of nerves and nod. "I'll be right back."

I've only been called into Bradson's office to be lectured. I'm preparing myself for the scolding of a lifetime when he closes the door and gestures for me to sit in the chair across from his desk. We stare at one another for a moment, and I shift in the worn-down chair, my leg starting to jostle.

"Do you know why I called you in here?" he starts.

I shake my head. "No, sir."

"Think hard, Carter. Why are you sitting across from me right now?"

I open my mouth and then close it when he slides the plays I reviewed for Malik toward me. A shaky puff of air leaves me when he taps on the papers.

"Is this your handwriting?"

If I say yes, Malik will be outed for being a terrible captain, but he'll also make my life a living hell, and he'll take me down with him.

"No," I respond with as much confidence as I can infuse into my voice.

Coach offers me a pen and paper, and my insides contract.

"Prove it. Write your name."

"I can't do that."

"Why not?" he fires back.

"Because . . . it is my handwriting."

Coach sighs. Spinning around in his chair, he reaches for more folders and opens them to display more of my handwriting.

"I should have known. Honestly, Malik was never detail oriented. I mean, he didn't even have to do this. He came to me because he wanted to learn how to craft plays. Why pass them off to you and claim both the criticism and praise?"

"I'm not sure, sir." My tone turns quiet, and I sink into the chair.

I'm ashamed of what I've done, and Coach is disappointed. It's written all across his brow.

"I wouldn't have noticed if it wasn't for Levi Faulkner."

"Faulkner?"

"I didn't think I was obtuse, but I wasn't paying as close attention to the team as I thought I was. Faulkner and a few other players have recently come to me to discuss their concerns about Malik as captain. I've seen you helping the newbies in the gym, ensuring the guys are staying hydrated, pumping them up before practice and last season before games. These are things a captain is supposed to do . . . but here you are, doing it for him because he's slacking off. With your permission, I would like to hold a vote. You or Malik as the new captain."

"Me as captain?" I repeat, dumbfounded.

"I've been watching you. This is something you can handle, Carter, not because of the kind of player you are but because of who you are as a person. Plus, you've been doing it without the official title for who knows how long now. I won't move forward until you give me the okay."

A thousand little thought gremlins run through my mind. But the biggest one is screaming, *"He won't throw you the ball if you do this. Your future career will be nonexistent. You won't be able to help your dad. You'll be a failure."*

"I don't kn—"

"Think it over. I don't need an answer until the end of August. The sooner, the better, but this is a big decision. Just know that I'm here if you want to talk it over."

"Thanks, Coach," I mumble.

I don't remember getting up to leave or the firm pat on my shoulder as I left his office.

What I do remember is seeing Malik backing my girl against a row of lockers.

My fingernails dig into my palm, my jaw tightening to unbelievable levels. With one foot in front of the other, I'm about to rain hellfire down on him. He can torture me all he wants. If he thinks he can touch my girl, he's going to pay.

Chapter Forty

Chrissy

He's fine. He's safe. Granted, a little red and tired, but he's okay. Relief and a blast of cold air washed over me when I walked into the sports center. Rome's expression twisted in both confusion and delight when he saw me.

I could have gone back to my dorm after checking on him, but I want to be with him—in all manners. So, I'm left waiting in the corridor for him while he talks to his coach. I hope he's not in trouble. All that boy does is help his team and that douchebag of a captain. He's the last person who deserves an ear lashing.

I pull my phone out of my pocket and text my parents in our family group chat.

> I'm going to be a few minutes late, had to check on a friend.

> Mom: That's okay, honey! Dad and I are ready whenever you are.

> Zack: "Friend"? ;)

Son of a bitch . . . I should have known better.

I haven't told Mom or Dad about Rome yet. I planned on introducing them when they came out in August. What does this asswipe think he's doing?

> Yes, my friend. I have friends, unlike you.

> Zack: I have friends!

> Name one besides Gwen and Ash!

> Zack: Rome Carter ;)

Am I dumb?! I totally lined him up for that comeback.

> Dad: Why the winky face? Is there something you have to tell us, son?

> Mom: That would explain the lack of girlfriends . . .

> Zack: MOM! No, OMG . . .

A snort leaves my mouth as I giggle at the slew of messages flying across the screen.

> Dad: Zack, it's 2016, we'll love you no matter what.

> Zack: I'm not gay! Rome is Chrissy's boyfriend, but he was my best friend first.

> No, he's not!

Oh, this fucking jackass. I open the chat between the two of us and pound at my phone screen.

> Zackary Willows, you had no right!

Zack: They thought I was gay, I panicked!

There's nothing wrong with being gay! You son of a bitch. Now I have to talk to them about Rome. I wanted them to meet him for the first time in August.

Zack: I'm sorry . . . It's not like they don't know already. He's been in all of our group photos since May.

You owe me, you hear?

A text in the family group chat interrupts my so-called brother's badgering.

Mom: Rome Carter, as in THIS Rome Carter?!

A picture follows of Rome in his football uniform with the tagline All-Star Wide Receiver of Castle Brook University.

Yes, THAT Rome Carter . . .

Kill me now.

Dad: Have I told you recently that you're my favorite daughter?

I'm going to tell Gwen you said that.

Dad: No, don't!

I cackle at his panicked message.

Dad: I mean to say that you're my favorite biological daughter.

Uh-huh, sure.

Mom: When can we meet him?

In person, when you come out to visit. But you can talk to him during our video call later if you want.

Mom: Please!

I'm about to respond when I hear a shuffle of feet. I look up from my phone, and my smile fades into a sneer.

"Well, if it isn't my favorite blonde . . . How are you today? You're looking ravishing."

"Fuck off, Malik," I bite out as I look back down at my phone.

His hand wraps around the device, and he takes it from me before I can react.

"My eyes are up here, sweetheart."

"Sorry, haven't you heard? You're not supposed to look into Medusa's eyes." I glare at him as I reach for my phone.

"Ask nicely," he teases.

"Fuck off."

Malik holds my phone up in the air, like he wants me to jump for it. I'm not jumping for any man just like I refuse to smile for them.

"Fine, keep it. But my brother and his friends won't appreciate this. Rome certainly won't either."

"You think I care what Rome or your brother can do to me? I'd like to see them try." He hands me my phone back, and I wipe it off with a disgusted look.

"I could tell your professor, you know."

"Tell her what exactly?"

"That you're dating your mentee. I'm pretty sure it's against the rules."

"It's a program, Malik. It's not like he's my actual patient." I sigh in annoyance.

"Yes, but aren't we supposed to be treating it as a real-life scenario? I could go to her now . . . tell her to switch you with Raina. I wanted you first, and I can still get you." He takes a step forward, and I back away.

He doesn't stop until my back is pressed against the lockers, and I'm seething up at him.

"Back up, now," I hiss through my teeth.

"Make me," he drawls with a gross smile.

Rome appears out of the corner of my eye. His jaw is tight, his fist ready. If he hits Malik, he could be benched. If I hit Malik, well, I'll get what I've wanted since the moment I met him.

"I'm warning you." I give him one last chance.

Malik smirks down at me, and he licks his lower lip. He doesn't back away, so, per his request, I make him.

Adrenaline courses through my veins, my heart pounding it through my body.

Raising my hand, I allow my body to take control, and I slap him across the face. My palm and fingers sting from the contact, and a red mark forms on his cheek, almost in the shape of my hand.

I shake my hand off, and he winces while stepping away from me. No one warns you about the effects of slapping someone 'cause damn, this hurts.

"What the fuck was that for?" he grunts while massaging his cheek.

"For not backing up. Next time, give people their personal space, and they won't have to make you."

Malik scoffs through a chuckle before looking at me, and something sinister glimmers in his dark eyes. "That was hot. Do it again."

"Do we have a problem here?" Rome's voice is tight, stern, giving off "fuck with her and find out" vibes.

And I would be lying if I said it wasn't doing something to me.

"Rome, there you are," Malik casually says, almost like he's playing off what just happened.

Rome keeps his eyes on Malik as he swoops in beside me, placing his hand on my lower back. He looks down at me and leans toward my ear. "Are you okay?" he whispers.

I nod. "I'm okay."

"Were you just talking with Bradson?" Malik cuts in.

"I was, what of it?"

"I'm on my way to talk to him now. Any idea what he wants to see me about?"

"None. Now go before I give you a black eye to match that slap mark across your face."

Malik tongues his cheek while smirking and walking away. "See you two later!"

"Fucking dick," I mutter.

Rome pulls me into his chest, and my face presses into his pec, muffling my words as I ask, "What's wrong?"

"Can we get out of here? I'll tell you when we get back to my place."

Looking up at him, I nod and offer him a soft smile. "Let's go."

Back at his place, I'm quick to get comfortable. I kick my shoes off and plop face-first onto his bed.

Rome chuckles while he gets undressed, preparing to take a shower.

"Make sure you're decent when you get out!" I shout as he walks into the bathroom.

"Why?" Walking backward, he arches an eyebrow and smirks.

I flip over on my side and purse my lips. "Zack may have told my parents we're dating."

The last guy I introduced to Mom and Dad was back in freshman year. His name was Ryan Sliverskawitz. We dated for a few months, nothing grand in the scheme of things. I thought he was nice, and he is. Mom approved, and Dad played along. They met him during a trip out to visit Gwen, Zack, and me. A few weeks later, we broke up.

I don't introduce my parents to many of the guys I date solely because nothing ever lasts. This is different, though. Rome is different.

"They didn't already know?"

It's such a typical Rome answer that it makes me smile. "No, they didn't. I . . . I don't introduce them to the guys I date."

"How come?"

Would it be rude of me to ask him to put a shirt on for this conversation? His rippling abs and mountains of muscles make it difficult to concentrate and talk without sounding like a blabbering idiot.

"Most of my relationships don't pan out . . . take Miles, for example."

Rome rests his arm on the doorway, and my heart pitter-patters all the way toward my clit.

"I don't know what happened between you and Miles. Why did you break up, if I may ask?"

"It didn't feel right. I felt like I was forcing myself into trying to love him. I thought we ended things amicably, but I could be wrong."

"You and I both know love hurts. Things never end without some kind of pain. He'll be okay, he's Miles Summers." Rome gives me a warm smile, and I return the gesture.

"Anyway, I told Mom you might be able to say hi, but that's up to you."

"I would love to. I'll make sure I'm decent, don't worry."

"Thank you!" I say loud enough for him to hear me from the bathroom.

Steam billows out of the bathroom as I fiddle with my phone. If I were a good and innocent girl, I would wait patiently for him to return and call my parents, but I'm not in the right headspace, so I'll call them tomorrow.

As quietly as I can, I tiptoe to the bathroom and work on taking my clothes off.

The water splatters on the tile in the shower. The curtain is drawn closed, and the mirror is foggy. I remove my bra and stand facing the navy blue fabric separating Rome and me. With a step forward, I put on my game face. With another step forward, I hold back the giddy giggle that threatens to leave my lips.

When I draw the curtain back, Rome's eyes linger over my body, and his lips form a lopsided smile. "Took you long enough."

"Oh, I'm sorry. Should I come back later?" I tease.

Rome grabs my wrist and urges me into the shower. I stumble into his chest and giggle before he cuts me off by kissing me fiercely.

"Do I need to fuck the sass out of you?" he growls in my ear as his hand drops lower down my body.

"Possibly," I sigh and rest my forehead on his shoulder.

"I get the feeling you enjoy it a little too much," he chuckles.

"Fucking you?" I ask in amusement.

"No, me fucking the sass out of you."

"You're right." I smirk before kissing his pec.

His hand keeps dipping, and before I know it, his finger is

against my clit, unmoving. I grunt in frustration, sucking the spot above his nipple.

"Rome," I groan. "Please."

"So needy." He grazes his teeth over my ear, nibbling my earlobe.

I arch my back into him, trying to get closer. His cock is hard, pressing against my lower stomach. I rest my hand over his, and he starts to circle my clit using his pointer finger. I moan and smile in bliss. The built-up desire from earlier releases into my bloodstream, leaving me dizzy and wanting.

"That's really nice," I mumble out of breath, and his speed increases.

"Like that?" His breath is hot against my neck, and I hum.

"Yes, just like that."

My heart begins to pound in my chest, leaving me weak in the knees. I reach back and grasp his hard length, stroking him in time with movements.

"Fuck me," he growls.

And I so desperately want to fuck him.

I spin around and weave my hands around his neck, pulling him down into a kiss. Our touch is hot, needy, full of passion and love. I'll never get over his full lips and how they make my own tingle. His body underneath my palms makes every inch of my skin pebble. Rome makes me feel things I've never felt before, and I'll do everything in my power to not fuck this up.

"Rome, I need you," I plead as I suck on his lower lip. "Please, right now."

Not wasting another moment, Rome picks me up and presses my back against the wall. He slides me down just enough to line his cock up with my entrance, and with a bit of assistance, I guide him in.

I moan and press my fingertips into his shoulder blades as he fills me with his impressive length. My walls contract around him, attempting to accommodate him. The stretching was uncomfortable the first time I took him, but now I find it addicting, and I can't get enough.

Thankfully, I don't plan on letting Rome go, because I don't think I could ever go back to using condoms again. Rome is too . . . magnificent. I need to feel every pulse and twitch. I want to feel him and everything that he has.

My head hits the tile as I try to arch myself to accept more of his length. Rome thrusts into me, but he keeps losing his footing, and we end up laughing at our attempt at hot shower sex.

"This is better in the movies," I snicker.

"Alright, fuck the shower. Let's go, missy."

I giggle when Rome turns the shower off and picks me up in his arms. On the short walk to the bedroom, we kiss and laugh intermittently.

The frigid AC shocks my body, and when my back hits the mattress, I shiver. But Rome is quick as he presses himself back into my entrance, and my body is quick to accept each and every inch.

"Fuck." I wrap my legs around his waist.

"That's my girl. Spread those legs for me," Rome grunts.

His movement turns sloppy. He drives his cock into me, hitting my G-spot and leaving me a whimpering mess within seconds.

"Rome, yes, baby, right there."

"Look at you, soaking my cock like a good girl." He leans down and sucks on my peaked nipple.

I moan at the contact, filling the room with my song of pleasure.

"I'll never get tired of hearing that noise." He runs his tongue over my nipple, licking and sucking as he fucks me senseless.

Fire spreads through my lower stomach, settling in the

tension in my thighs and legs. I tighten my grip around him, and his balls slap against my ass, adding fuel to the fire. I grunt, and my head rolls back against the bed.

"Rome, please—"

"Need more?"

I nod; it's all I can do.

Grabbing my legs, he rests them on his shoulders, and he hammers into me. I scream and cry his name, the fire in my legs boils through my body, and I'm left a writhing mess.

"Motherfucker!" The tension frees itself, and my body spasms as I ride out the orgasm Rome brought me to.

I tilt my hips, grinding against his shaft to extend my euphoria.

Rome looks down, watching me work against his length. Before I can register what's happening, Rome flips us over, and I'm on top of him, his cock still inside me.

"Ride me. Be a good girl and ride me until we both come."

"I can't come again." My shoulders drop at the thought. I'm already so tired.

"You *can*, and you *will*." Rome rests his hands on my hips, urging me to start moving.

Not wanting to disappoint, I start moving my hips, riding him like he wants. My hands rest on his lower stomach as I discover the rhythm he wants. It's not long until his eyes are closed, his lips parted.

I lean down, press my bare chest against his, and kiss him sweetly while bouncing up and down on his length.

"Like this?" I whisper, and his grunt makes me smirk.

I go faster, hitting the spot of my own pleasure and relishing in the fact that I'm making him quiver underneath me. His hands travel up my back, but I take them in mine and pin them over his head. His eyes shoot open, and he grunts.

"You know I can free myself? You're just a tiny thing."

"I know, but you won't."

"Why won't I—fuck." He moans when I ride him faster.

"Because I'll stop if you do."

I love it when Rome takes control, but something about making him fall under *my* command gets me going. He could free himself from my grasp in the blink of an eye, but he won't. For one, he respects me, so he wouldn't do something I asked him not to. And two, he enjoys this. His expression is the only reassurance I need.

"Please don't stop," he moans, his voice hitching.

I glide up and down his cock while holding his hands in place.

"Fuck, I want to curl my hands in your hair so bad, fuck you until you scream again."

I giggle against his ear before sucking on it gently. "Are you going to come for me?"

He grunts, the muscles in his thighs firming against my own. My eyes glance over his jawline, down to his neck, which is turning a glorious shade of pink.

"Will you fill my pussy?"

"Yes," he groans, the vibration rumbling into my body.

"Good."

I free my grasp and let him take control. He grips my hips, and I move in time with his silent order, grinding faster, bouncing harder. My own body climbs to a new state of bliss. With a loud curse, I press my chest against his again and let him ram his cock into me.

"Right there, right there. Yes, yes! Fuck, Rome!" Stars fill my vision, and my lips form a pleased smile.

With a deep groan, Rome releases himself, and I come with him. His muscles flex underneath my body. His length twitches as he fills me with his cum, a new warmth I've grown quite fond of.

We're both gasping for air as I roll off his body and lie next to him, letting the AC cool me down.

"Fuck me," he mumbles, and I giggle in response.

"I second that."

"You, my beautiful wildflower, are too much for me."

"Me? No." I snicker, and he smiles widely.

"You're not all sunshine and rainbows. You . . . you really like getting railed."

I punch him but end up flinching, which only makes him chuckle.

"Why can't I ever learn?!" I call out and shake my hand off.

"Your poor hand has been through so much today." Rome takes my hand and kisses my knuckles one by one.

"You have no idea." I pout playfully, and he smiles.

"I really love you."

My eyes widen, and my heart soars out of my chest.

"You what?" I whisper, not believing what I just heard.

Like he didn't realize what he said, his eyes widen as they dart around my face.

"Shit, I'm sorry, I didn't mean—"

Placing a finger over his lips, I smile at him and look into his endless green eyes.

"I love you too, Rome Carter. I really, *really* do."

His cheeks flush, and his expression softens when I return the sentiment.

Inching closer, I kiss the tip of his nose. "I won't break your heart. It's safe with me, I promise."

With a subtle nod, Rome closes his eyes and pulls me close, wrapping his arms around me and holding onto me for dear life. "I know, baby girl. I know."

Chapter Forty-One

Rome

I didn't mean to say it. The words just came out. I knew once I said them, I couldn't take it back. I was trying to formulate the best response, make it seem like I was talking about something else, but I panicked. This is Chrissy though, and I should have known better. She said it back, and now, she's curled in my arms, sleeping peacefully.

I don't think I've ever been happier. The girl of my dreams is finally mine. I love her, and she loves me. What more could a guy want?

The hum of the air-conditioning fills the room. If it were just me, I would have the fan going as well, just for the white noise. Instead, I have Chrissy and her small intakes of air soothing me to sleep. When I close my eyes, worry doesn't fill my mind and settle in my bones. For once, it's love, and it starts to mend all the cracks that formed over the years.

The bed shifts when the sun rises. I groan sleepily, not ready to wake up. A pair of lips press into my temple, and her words float into my ear.

"Keep sleeping. I'll be right back."

I grumble an incoherent response, and Chrissy snickers.

She leaves the room, closing the door quietly behind her.

I reach for my phone to check the time and groan again. It's 8:00 a.m., and I've been slacking on my morning runs. My palms meet my eyes as I try to wake myself up. If it were up to me, I would sleep until noon, but Coach would have my ass if he knew I'd been skipping my workout routine.

So, I climb out of bed and change into a pair of black athletic shorts and a black sleeveless tank. Looking in the mirror, I ruffle my hair to make it seem like it's a casual look and not because I just climbed out of bed. When I step into the hall, I hear Chrissy talking quietly. I peer into the living room as I head into the kitchen, and I smile when I see she's talking with whom I assume to be her mother on a video call.

As they talk, I grab my shaker bottle and fill it with milk and a scoop of my favorite chocolate protein powder. As I shake it, I walk toward the blonde sitting on my couch, making sure I don't appear on her phone screen.

Her eyes light up when she sees me. I want to bend down and kiss her head, but I'm not sure if she's ready for her mother to see me. If she wants her mom to know that her daughter has been spending the night at a guy's house.

Chrissy holds the phone to her chest and lowers her voice. "Do you want to say hi?"

My stomach roils with nerves, but I nod and give her a genuine smile.

Raising the phone again, Chrissy looks at her mom and blushes. "Mom, ready to meet Rome?"

"Yes!" Her mom responds without hesitating, and my smile grows.

Chrissy scoots down the couch so I can sit next to her. I wave at the camera and grin at the woman who looks just like her daughter.

"Hi," I say, sounding shy.

"Oh my goodness, those cheeks!"

"Oh, here we go," Chrissy sighs.

"I just want to squeeze them!"

"Mom!" Chrissy scolds, and I chuckle in response.

"It's Faye, right? I'm Rome," I say through a hint of laughter.

"Oh, trust me. My husband and I know who you are—"

"Is that Rome?" a man calls off camera.

Faye looks off-screen and gestures for the man to make an appearance. The first thing I notice is how kind his eyes are. They're dark blue and smooth, almost appearing matte. He has a few deep-set wrinkles in his brow, most likely the result of raising a troublesome set of twins.

"You look different compared to the photos we've seen."

"Ethan," Faye mumbles and slaps his arm.

With a chuckle, I say, "I recently cut my hair. The tangles were a bit too much to manage."

"Oh, we know *all* about tangles," Ethan teases, and Chrissy clicks her tongue.

"These curls came from one of you. I don't want to hear it."

Faye's attention is locked on me while her husband and daughter go back and forth. We offer one another a smile, and a wave of pride crashes through me.

I'm not a bad guy. I'm not perfect, but I'm not bad. I have trauma, anxiety, and fear of losing people I love, and that fear overwhelms me most days. Chrissy is helping me heal from that part of my past though. Her love and empathy are the reason she's on my couch. She's shown me time and time again that I can trust her.

"Rome has to go on a run now." Chrissy interrupts my thoughts.

"Wait, I was hoping we could talk about football," Ethan counters.

"You two can talk about football all you want when you come visit in a few weeks." Chrissy purses her lips and then offers a small smile.

"Okay, fine. Nice to officially meet you, Rome. I look forward to getting to know you better." Ethan waves before stepping off the screen, leaving Faye behind.

"Be good, you two, and have fun. But not too much fun!"

"Bye, Mom," Chrissy giggles. "Love you!"

"Talk to you later." I grin at Faye as the call ends.

With her phone still in hand, Chrissy wraps her arms around my neck and embraces me. "Thank you."

"For what?" I choke out as she begins to squeeze the air from my lungs.

"For being you." She places several kisses on my cheek. "I really do love you."

With a warm and sincere smile, I place a loving kiss on her lips. "And I love you."

Sweat beads across my forehead, trickling into my eyes as I finish the last lap around the park by my apartment. It's the middle of July, and I can't wait for summer to be over. I'm more than ready for the autumn weather. Hoodies, hot chocolate, cool days, and even cooler evenings. My favorite thing about fall is when football starts. The atmosphere is brimming with excitement for the new season.

The stands in the stadium fill to capacity, and the buzz of anticipation always settles in my bones. I can do without the lingering heat during the beginning of the season, but once a few games are under our belts, the temperature will decrease, and that's when the real fun starts. Don't even get me started on playing in the snow. Nothing can top that.

When I reach the end of the block, I raise my arms and do some stretches as "Jungle" by X Ambassadors plays in my earphones. My phone vibrates against my arm. Once I finish my stretches, I free it from the strap and see a text from Malik.

I don't want to deal with this today. I was hoping to avoid this for as long as I possibly could.

> He took that task away from me. Do you know how crucial that was on my resume? It gave me a leg up, and you took it away!

> I didn't tell him! I don't know who did!

> Willing to bet you do, and you don't want to snitch. Fucking coward.

> I don't know, and even if I did, I wouldn't tell you. Call me a coward all you want, but deep down, you know they did the right thing.

> I warned you, Carter. You're nuts if you think I'm passing you the ball. Just wait for our first game at the end of August. You're fucked.

"Fuck!" I shout, not caring who is around.

If I could afford a new phone, I would slam this one to the pavement to hear the satisfying crack of the screen. I would watch the bits of plastic fly and disappear into the dry summer grass. But I can't afford a new phone, and if I want to keep my future intact, I have to kiss his ass.

> What can I do to fix this?

> What are you willing to give me?

> Anything.

> I want Chrissy Willows.

My eyes practically bug out of my skull. I tighten my grip on my phone. Is he fucking insane?! First of all, Chrissy is her own person. Why does he think he can use her as leverage? Why does he think she'd not only be okay with being used like that but that she wants anything to do with him? He's a snake and a camouflaged one at that. I wouldn't touch him with a hundred-foot pole with a cozy sock at the end of it. Yesterday, when he cornered her, I almost lost it. But Chrissy stood up for herself and some. That woman can handle herself, but that doesn't mean I won't do everything in my power to protect her.

Not going to happen.

Then you better freshen up on your American history . . .

Chapter Forty-Two

Chrissy

The door bursts open and then slams shut, startling me out of my skin. Turning around, I catch Rome storming off into his bedroom. I ready myself for the next door to slam, but it doesn't come.

I can't approach him now, even if I wanted to. One of the first things we're taught in psychology is to not confront someone while they're hot. They'll likely say something they don't mean because they aren't thinking rationally.

So, when I hear the shower turn on, I pray to the universe he cranked the temperature as cold as it can go so he can simmer down.

With slow and methodical steps, I walk into his bedroom. The first thing I see is his phone on his bed, and the lock screen is a picture of me. Tilting my head, I recognize where the picture was taken, and my heart melts.

I'm wearing his red hoodie, chewing on a straw from the frozen drink I got at the movie theater, and my face is scrunched at him. I don't remember him taking the photo, but

I'm glad he did. The next thing to pop up sets my once-melted heart ablaze.

Fucking Malik.

I can't see the message because his phone is locked, but my blood boils at the sight of his name. I'm not sure how Rome deals with that guy almost every day. I would have set him on fire by now.

I'm still not sure what happened yesterday. Rome hasn't told me about the conversation he had with his coach yet. I wonder if it has anything to do with what Raina told me. Malik was acting stranger than usual, but I can't say for certain. Nothing is clicking, and it's frustrating.

What makes matters worse is that Rome is still lying to me. He doesn't know that I know he's still helping Malik with the play reviews. He told me he was going to take a step back, but he didn't. That boy is going to push himself off the brink, and there's only so much I can do to help him, to cushion the fall.

I need to see this message . . . but it's against my code to break into someone's phone—unless your name is Gwen. I can't cross this line, especially because I'm his acting therapist. There's a reason you don't mix business and pleasure, and the fact that I want to protect him so fiercely is one of them.

Give him a chance.

With a long release of air, I step into the bathroom and rest my back against the sink. I listen to the sound of the running water hitting his body and flooding down the drain, contemplating making the first move.

"Do you want to talk about it?" I start, being as careful as I can.

No answer.

"I'm here for you. You know that, right?"

Nothing.

"Was it Malik?"

"Just leave it alone, Chrissy."

"What did he say? Please, I just want to help."

"As my girlfriend or as my psychologist?"

A sting lances my chest, radiating and spreading through the rest of my body.

"As your girlfriend who cares about you, who loves you."

Silence.

"Okay, we don't have to talk right now. But it would help you feel better. I can go back to my dorm and give you some space—"

"Coach told Malik he knows I've been reviewing and making the plays. He also knows I've been helping the rookies. Malik found out, and now he won't toss me the ball, which means my future as a football player has ended before it even began." Rome pulls back the shower curtain, and I meet his tired gaze.

"There has to be a way—"

He cuts me off before I can continue. "There isn't. It's this or . . ."

"Or what?"

He looks at me, unmoving.

"Or what, Rome?"

"It's out of the question. He's a prick and an entitled one at that. He's not going to get what he wants from me. End of story."

"What does he want?" My voice turns pleading and desperate.

His gaze darkens, almost like he's gauging whether or not I can handle the truth.

"Tell me," I insist.

"You."

My brow furrows.

"He wants you."

"I'm not yours to give away. I'm not some sort of prize to win."

"I know, and that's why I said it's out of the question." He pushes the curtain closed, but I'm not done talking to him face-to-face.

Gripping the shower curtain, I pull it back just enough so I can see him. "He won't throw you the ball unless he gets me? What does that even mean?"

"I don't know. I didn't press further because it's *not* going to happen." Rome's tone is tight and stern. He's not going to budge.

"What if he only wants me to be his mentor? I can swap with Raina—"

"No, Chrissy," Rome orders.

"I won't have you jeopardize your future for me," I respond with the same resolve. "Not now, not ever."

"I said no. End of discussion. I won't give him what he wants. You said so yourself, you're not a prize to be won."

We stare at one another, neither of us willing to submit, to admit we're right or wrong. Rome and I are alike in many ways, and our stubbornness is at the top of the list.

"You can't tell me what to do," I retort.

"If you go to him, I will know, and I'll never forgive you."

"Even if it's to secure your future?"

"You said you wouldn't leave me. I fell in love with you because you swore you wouldn't break my heart. If you do this, I'll see it as nothing more than an act of betrayal, and I won't forgive you."

"You really don't listen to me during our one-on-one sessions, do you?" I don't wait for a response to continue. "You're burned out. You take on way too much for that team, and you don't get the credit for it. I'm willing to bet how the coach discovered you've been stepping in, and I'll place good money on a bet saying that he wants to make you captain. But you won't do it. Want to know why?" I pause, taking a deep breath before I continue. "You're afraid."

His expression twists, but I don't stop.

"Malik Chen won't toss you the ball if you steal his title and spotlight. He won't toss you the ball if he doesn't get the girl he wants. Either way, you don't get the fucking ball. You've told me time and time again you want to be drafted into the Philadelphia Eagles because not only is it your dream, but it will allow you to be closer to home. And you're willing to throw that all away just to prove something to Malik. Well, Rome Carter, I don't fly that way. Call it whatever you want, but what I'm going to do is certainly *not* betrayal. For once, let me help you."

Our eyes stay locked. Rome doesn't waver, and neither do I.

"I can't do that." His tone is low and dark.

And I leave on that note.

"Professor Clastis?" I call as I knock on her office door.

"Ms. Willows, please come in." She waves me forward.

I take a seat with a polite smile, even though the last thing I want to be doing is smiling right now.

"There's something I have to discuss with you," I begin.

Do I want to do this?

No.

Do I have a choice?

Yes.

I'm doing this for Rome.

"I made a mistake. I broke the first rule in the 'what not to do with your patients' handbook. You see, my mentee and I are good friends, but over these last few weeks our relationship . . . deepened. I can't give him the care he needs because I can't separate the lines between professionalism and my relationship with him. I broke a rule, and I'll understand if you dismiss me from the program. I just can't move forward with this on my conscience."

It's not a lie either. Deep down, I knew that moving forward in this program with Rome was a bad idea. Either way, I don't want to lose him. But it feels like I have him as my patient or my boyfriend. It can't be both. Doing this will clear the weight off my shoulders, and it will protect Rome's future. Fuck Malik Chen, I'm my own woman. I can play hardball too.

"If you'll still have me, I spoke with Raina Bennett, and she is willing to trade partners with me. We'll catch each other up and include it in our next paper, and if you're not happy with the results, I will step down. I just want to do what's right."

Again, not a lie. I don't want to evaluate Malik, but I'll do what's right for Rome, even if it means putting my happiness on the line. I can handle Malik, even though Rome doesn't think I can. I handled him in the store, and I managed him in the hall. I've proven that I can stand up for myself. I don't need Rome, or any man, to do that for me.

Professor Clastis sighs, her lips tilting into a small grin. "Thank you for coming to me about this, Ms. Willows. I'm glad to hear that you know a line was crossed. And because of your upstanding and academically impressive record, I will grant you this one time pass. You may switch with Ms. Raina Bennett. But I do expect a full report by the end of next week. Is that understood?"

"Yes, ma'am. I'll have it ready for you."

"Then you best get to it."

My chest feels lighter, and my heart isn't pounding against my eardrums. Rome is going to despise me for this, he said so himself. But I can't stand by and allow him to give up. Relationships are a team effort, and I'm only doing what I believe is best for him.

I take my phone out and read Raina's message, then copy and paste a certain asshat's number into my phone and text him.

You got what you wanted. Meet me tomorrow at the cat café. If I hear that you didn't pass the ball to Rome, I will end this partnership before it even starts. Understood?

Yes, clear as day ;)

Chapter Forty-Three

Rome

Chrissy and I haven't spoken in two days. A brutal combination of emotions is warring inside me. I'm angry at Malik for suggesting such a ridiculous idea, and I'm upset at Chrissy for getting upset at me. I was doing the right thing. I was protecting her. If she were to go to Malik, he would know she's where I'm vulnerable. He can use her to get to me. He can use me all he wants, but he can't touch her. She's off limits.

I have a one-on-one with her this afternoon after practice. I'm sure we can clear all this up and get back on track. My heart aches as I walk toward the stadium. I constantly check my phone to see if she messaged or called me. Not that I would miss it; my hand is practically glued to my phone, waiting for her to make the first move.

Dropping my bag on the floor in the locker room, I look at my phone one last time before giving up. I take a seat on the worn wooden bench and text the one person who will know what's going on with Chrissy.

Hey Gwen, have you heard from Chrissy recently?

I spoke with her this morning before she went to talk to her professor.

Which professor?

Clastis, I believe that was her name.

Did she say why she was going to talk to her?

She said she would tell me today during my shift at the café. Will I see you then? I wanted to talk to you about something anyway.

Yes, I'll see you there. Thank you.

Chrissy, what the hell did you do?

My question was answered the second Malik threw me the ball, and I wanted nothing more than to wipe that smug look off his face and for practice to be over. I didn't give anyone the time of day once Coach dismissed us. I got showered and changed in a hurry, ignoring Malik's faux positive energy. Faulkner knew something was up right away; he's new, but he's not an idiot. He didn't press me, though, which earned him future brownie points.

After running to my car, I buckle myself in and drive to Tea and Kittens. As I park the car along the curb, I consider taking a moment to compose myself, but fuck that.

Careful not to scare the cats, I enter the café, but I don't see her. She said she was going to meet me, where is she?

"Gwen?" I call out, and something in the back room tumbles to the ground.

A bang of metal clatters on the floor, jarring the room full of cats and kittens.

"Shit," a familiar voice grunts. "Sorry, be out in a sec!"

I pace the room, looking out the window every now and then for a certain blonde to dance through the door. Instead, Gwen appears from the back room, holding a particular white cat in her arms.

"Thank goodness you're here." Gwen sighs in relief.

"Is everything okay?"

Gwen looks like she's been through hell and back. Her hair is tied back, but flyaways are sticking up in all directions. Her white shirt is drenched in what I hope is water, and a new kitten just flung itself at her shoes. Korra chirps when she sees me, her lime eyes almost sparkling in reaction.

"I know you're looking for Chrissy, but I have to ask you the biggest favor."

"Okay . . ."

"Would you consider fostering or adopting Korra? I know it's a lot to ask. You're rarely home, and you're busy with school and football. But when I tell you that this cat doesn't calm down unless you're here, I mean it. I mean, look at her—"

Gwen holds Korra out toward me. The cat tilts her head, and she meows while reaching out.

I take her in my arms, and her body slumps against mine as she rubs her face on my collarbone.

"Not even two minutes ago, she chased me into the back, and I spilled my water bottle all over me. The moment she heard your voice, she relaxed. Ryan and I will do anything. We'll give you all the supplies you'll need. Give it a few days to a week, and if it's not working, we'll take her back. I just . . . I don't want to see her go to another shelter. She didn't do well in the last one she was at, hence why she's here."

Gwen is on the verge of tears. She cares so much about these animals. It's no wonder Ash was drawn to her; her energy is warm and loving, just like Chrissy's.

"I don't know how to take care of a cat," I say quietly.

"I can teach you. A week, that's all I'm asking."

Running my fingers through Korra's velvet white fur, the tension in my muscles eases, and the weight on my shoulders starts to lessen. Maybe it's not a bad idea. I mean, it's seven days, right?

"Okay," I say with a smile.

"Really?" Gwen squeals.

"Really. I'll give it a shot."

"Thank you!" Gwen looks like she wants to jump in my arms, but she doesn't want to disturb Korra, who has fallen asleep cradled against my chest. "You're going to do amazing. I just know it."

With a small nod, I continue petting the cat as Gwen gathers the supplies. I walk over to a chair and sit down, being cautious not to wake the furball in my arms.

"Why do I get the feeling you're going to be a diva?" I whisper on the top of her head.

With a long puff of air out of her nose, she yawns and snuggles closer. Yeah, she's going to walk all over me. And I'm going to let her.

My phone vibrates in my pocket, and I almost leap out of the chair. With the amount of care I'm taking with Korra, you would think I was holding a newborn baby. But something tells me she deserves it. She seems like she's had a rough go of things.

I free my phone from my shorts pocket and see a number pop up that I'm not familiar with.

Hey Rome, this is Raina. You met me in the conference room on the first day. Are you at the cat café?

I am. Why?

Chrissy and I will be there shortly.

Why is Raina accompanying Chrissy to our session? Why hasn't Chrissy texted or called me? Nothing is making sense, and it's causing a pit the size of a meteor to form in my stomach.

Gwen finished gathering the items and brought them to me. An assortment of cat food, toys, a cat bed, and a box of litter are ready for me. With Korra still snuggled against my chest, I fill out the paperwork in order to take her home. I don't know if I want to adopt her or not, pretty sure I'm not going to have a say in the matter. But Gwen has been completing the foster form just in case.

The bell above the café door chimes, and I feel her presence before I see her. She's warm like sunshine, but something is off. I don't have to turn around to guess that her nose is crinkled upward and that her brow is wrinkled. Chrissy is preparing herself to face the storm, and I wish I could say that storm wasn't me.

"Rome?" Raina asks as she comes into my line of sight.

Glancing up at her, I give her a small smirk and nod. "That's me. Are you going to say hi as well, Chrissy?"

Chapter Forty-Three

And there's the eye roll. I can feel it like a soldering iron.

"You don't have to be so snarky about it." She sighs, and my heart shatters into a million tiny pieces.

Her eyes are tired, subtle, deep bags resting underneath them. Her hair is pulled back and free from frizz. Even her complexion is off; her normally rosy cheeks are nowhere to be found. What happened within these last two days? Do I look the same way she does? Because I can safely say I've missed her.

"Care to explain why Malik threw the ball to me during practice today?" But that doesn't mean she didn't cross a line.

"Raina and I are switching partners. You will be working with her, and I will be mentoring Malik Chen" is all she says.

With an irritated click of my tongue, I drop the pen I was holding and look at her head-on. "I told you it was out of the question."

"And I told you I wasn't going to let you ruin your future for me. It's an easy solution—"

"You fed the snake, and now he won't stop. He knows you're my weakness, you just gave him fuel. You think this will be his first demand? You're wrong—"

"Rome, let's just take a moment," Raina interjects.

"No, I won't take a moment. Chrissy, there was more than one reason why his demand was out of the question. And you just gave him *everything* he wanted."

Raina's shoulders drop in defeat. She's been working with Malik, so I'm sure she knows what he's capable of.

"I'm doing this for you—"

"I didn't ask you to!" My voice raises, and Korra stirs in my arms and leaps onto the floor.

"I'm doing this on my own volition. I'm doing this to secure your future. I will do *anything* for you because I *love* you. Why can't you understand that?"

"Because you love falling in love!" I shout and slam my hand on the table. "How many hearts have you broken? How many times have you fallen only to run away? Love isn't enough, Chrissy. It doesn't stop people from leaving others behind. You don't love me; you just don't want to be alone."

The words sting when they leave my mouth, but it feels good. They've been corrosive in my throat for far longer than I realized. And now that they're free, I don't bother sugarcoating it.

Chrissy stares at me like she's trying to dissect my brain. Her cheeks are bright red, and she presses her lips together while taking a step back. Raina observes us, probably wondering if we need couple's therapy.

It was bound to happen. Chrissy and I are both energetic, stand-by-our-beliefs, hardheaded people. An argument was unavoidable, whether we wanted it or not.

"Don't say things you don't mean, Rome," Chrissy tells me, sounding a little too calm. "I know things too, and I'd rather not have this conversation here."

"Then why have you been avoiding me?"

"I could ask you the same question. The phone works both ways."

Silent tension fills the space. I never want to disrespect Chrissy, even if she is pissing me off.

"Fine, we can talk about this later," I say as I stand.

"Okay." Her tone turns meek, and I know I'm the bad guy in her eyes—as she is in mine.

"There you are," Gwen chirps as she pops back into the room, completely unaware of the situation. "Chrissy, you're not going to believe what Rome just did."

"Oh?" She crosses her arms over her chest and quirks a brow in my direction.

She's holding back. That girl wants to slam my face into the ground and smear it with gravel.

"He's going to foster Korra!"

Chrissy side-eyes me, curiosity settling in her expression. "Really?"

"Yeah, I was about to take her home. Will you join me? So we can talk."

Chrissy huffs and nods. "Okay, let's go."

Chapter Forty-Four

Chrissy

This was not where I expected the day to go. I didn't plan on being here, at Rome's place. Not only am I here, I'm here with him and his new cat, the one who drives the café up a wall. Don't get me wrong, I *wanted* to be here today, but I had a feeling that Rome wasn't going to be happy with me once he found out what I did. And I was right, so I'm really unsure why I'm sitting in his living room while he tries to coax Korra out of her carrier.

I should have talked to Rome myself; bringing Raina was a bad idea. I just wanted to introduce them, but I should have done that at another time. I know Raina and Rome are going to get along. Perhaps he won't lie to her, and she can help him confront his battles head-on.

His back is to me, and my heart is breaking for him. Everything he went through with his parents, growing up alone with no siblings and only a few friends. He didn't date much out of fear, and he grew used to being alone. All Rome wants is companionship and love, which I know I can provide him.

Love like Gwen and Ash and my parents have is rare . . .

Rome said so himself, I don't want to be alone. It's not true though. I know who I am, and while I'm a fucking mess, I know, deep down, I only want a grand love that's worth fighting for.

Rome is upset, and it's up to me to maintain my composure even though his words leave my chest aching. My psychology courses prepared me for moments such as this, so it's time to put them to use.

"Chrissy." Rome pulls me from my thoughts.

"Rome." His anger is gone, but my feelings are still hurt, and it's apparent in my tone.

His shoulders drop, and he looks down at his folded hands. "I know you were trying to do what you thought was best, but I do feel like you went behind my back. I know Malik, and this isn't going to end well. For either of us."

"It sounds like you don't trust us."

"I don't trust him," he responds solemnly. "I don't trust that we'll survive Malik Chen."

"Your lack of faith is disturbing . . . God dammit Ash." I slap my forehead and groan.

With a small chuckle, Rome looks up and meets my eyes. "His Star Wars references will always haunt you. Trust me."

"I don't want to fight. I can handle Malik. I've done it before. You will always believe you're doing the right thing, just like I will. But I'm standing firm. I won't budge. I won't let you ruin your future because of some asshole quarterback."

"I can be a history teacher—"

"Not yet," I say with a tight voice. "You can teach history when you're ready to stop playing football. Right now, you're not ready. Don't try to convince me when you can't even convince yourself."

Rome sighs, and that's how I know I'm right.

"You're good. You're an all-star for a reason. And what's

even better? You love what you do. You pour passion into it. You care for your teammates. Hell, even after you promised me you would step back from some of the responsibilities that jackass thrust on you, you didn't—"

He cuts me off with a disappointed look. "You knew about that?"

"Of course I knew about that. You're a terrible liar," I say with a soft smile. "I've known for a few weeks now, and you have yet to tell me what your coach wanted to talk to you about."

Rome looks at me for a moment. Out of the corner of my eye, I spot Korra crawling out of her plastic carrier, but I don't say anything. One, I don't want to distract Rome. And two, I don't want to spook her.

"He, um, he wants to cast a vote for the captain title. A few of the players went to him, and he noticed the plays weren't being done by Malik. He's noticed that I've stepped up, and he wants the team to pick between Malik and me. But—"

"Malik won't throw you the ball if you take his title," I say, releasing an exasperated groan. "Fucking bitch waffle."

Rome holds back a chuckle as I rake my hands across through my hair.

"He got what he wants, but I don't even know if you doing this will guarantee that he'll toss me the ball. I won't know for sure until the season opener at the end of August."

"What do we do until then?" I ask, feeling guilty but standing by my decision.

"We have four weeks. If you want to stay assigned to Malik, I won't stop you, but I'm not happy about it. I think we should bide our time."

"I think we need a plan."

"A master plan?" Rome smirks, and I giggle.

"Exactly. Plan A is to ensure everything I do keeps your

position and future secure. Plan B, if Malik goes against his word to me, you'll talk to the head coach and find a reason to either bench him or kick him off the team."

"Or have him replaced." Rome lights up as his smile grows.

"Who is his alternate?" My heart starts to flutter, hope reawakening in my body.

"Levi Faulkner."

"The freshman? I met him at the party, I remember. He was sweet."

"He has a massive crush on you. Malik is not an upstanding student or citizen. Karma won't be upset with us for carrying out some revenge on her behalf. And Levi is good. I can start going at him harder, teaching him more plays and amping up his workout routine. He won't think twice about it."

"Precisely." I smile at Rome, confidence surging through my veins.

"I can do that. I can definitely do that."

Korra continues to stalk forward, but I keep my mouth shut.

"What you said earlier . . . about me not wanting to be alone—"

"I was upset," Rome starts, but I interject.

"Strong feelings cause people to speak the truth, and you're right. I don't want to be alone. But there's more to it." Tears start to fill my eyes in response to what I'm about to say. "I thought I would never find a real love. I see what everyone around me has, and I get jealous. The nicknames people used to call me in middle and high school re-emerge, and I'm left feeling numb. I thought I was doomed to be a serial dater. Until you . . ."

Rome observes me, and the tears in my eyes free themselves, slipping down my cheek and staining my face.

"I was looking for a mythical being. I was so sure I would never find someone who would adore me like my father adores my mother. I'm scared of being alone, yet I resigned myself to the fact that I'm destined to be alone. I thought I was cursed."

I sniffle as my vision blurs. My palms meet my eyes, and I try to wipe away the tears, but they don't stop. Something nudges against my leg, and Rome chuckles.

"I'm glad you find my destiny amusing." I hiccup through my tears.

"No, Chrissy, I don't find your sadness amusing. I find you rather cute and endearing, and so does Korra."

Looking down, I find the white puff of fur staring up at me. Being careful, I offer her my finger, and she sniffs it. I ready myself for her to bite me because that's all Pickles does when he sees me. Instead, she rubs her nose along my finger, allowing me to scratch her cheek.

"You're not cursed, Wildflower. Want to know how I know?" Rome asks quietly.

Korra jumps onto the couch and sits on my lap, cuddling against my stomach.

"Gwen told me that cats can tell whether or not someone is a good person. Korra is a little crazy, but if you were cursed, she wouldn't be giving you the time of day. And I know you're a wonderful woman. I knew when you and Gwen were spying on us in the pavilion, before the Halloween party, before we talked to one another in the library. You reflect everything good in this world. I will protect you, even if it means putting my future at risk. You deserve love, and you are worthy. I love you, Chrissy Willows. We may not have a love like Gwen and Ash or your parents, but I know we're meant for one another. I was *made* to love you, and I'll do everything in my power to remind you of that—forever."

"Dammit, Rome." I cry harder as Korra starts to purr. "I was supposed to be comforting you. This wasn't supposed to happen." I look at Rome and smile through my tears. I taste the saltiness as they land on my lips.

Rome thinks I'm worthy, and I know he is deserving of everything wonderful in this world. He's lied to me before, but he wouldn't lie about this. Rome is an upstanding man. If he thinks I deserve love, then it must be true. All my life, I've struggled with self-image and self-worth, and as I got older, I worried that a forever kind of love wasn't in the cards for me. It will take time to internalize and accept these new truths. Change doesn't happen overnight. But with Rome, I know I can work on myself and these new thoughts and avoid self-sabotaging what we have. Loving Rome will help me discover myself.

"You know I love you, right?" I say through my tears. "And I won't leave you, ever."

Reaching forward, Rome takes my hand and squeezes it. "I know now. And I need to trust you. You only want the best for me, just like I want for you."

"We're a team," I say with a loving smile.

"We are, my love. And I'm sorry."

Korra moves from my lap to Rome's, nudging into his hand and commanding more scratches. She's a daddy's girl for sure, and Rome is such a cat dad.

"I'm sorry I lied to you. I'm sorry I made you cry. I'm sorry I didn't trust you. You didn't betray me. I was being an asshole. I prepared myself for the worst because it's what I'm used to. After all we've been through, I should know better, but I'm a fool. I'll do better. I promise."

"We're both messes, Rome." I inch toward him. Our knees touch, and I rest my palm on his cheek, cooling his hot skin. "Let's be messes together."

"I'd love nothing more than that," he says with a genuine smile.

"These next few weeks are going to be difficult, but we're a team. You, me, and Korra."

Korra looks at me again, her lime eyes sparkling with happiness.

"What's our first step, boss?" Rome asks, and I can't help but feel content.

"You're going to work with Raina. Let her help you. Tell her everything about your mom, and work on facing that trauma. I will earn Malik's trust, and in the meantime, you'll help Levi. If Malik doesn't keep his word, we'll do everything we can to have Levi replace Malik. But Rome . . . you need to talk to your coach. The best thing for your team is *you* being captain. We have a plan, trust in it. Trust in *us*."

Rome smiles at me, and it makes my heart sing. "I'll talk to him soon. The vote will be scheduled, and if it goes the way I think it will, I'll be named captain."

"Are you excited?" I trace small shapes onto the backside of his hand, trying to comfort him.

"I'm not sure I'll be any good at it."

"You've been doing it this entire time. I told you during our first one-on-one. Don't change anything you're doing, and you'll be great. I believe in you." I squeeze his hand and lean forward to place a kiss on his cheek.

"Thank you, sunshine, for everything."

I wrap my arms around him and embrace him tightly, nuzzling into the crook of his neck and sighing peacefully.

"I've always said that I'll never find a love that was written in the stars. But, Rome, I think I'm finding it with you," I admit under my breath.

"You are my star. I would burn the world to protect you. I swear to you that I will protect and love you far longer than time will allow us."

The tears return, and I cuddle into him, dampening his skin. I ball his shirt in my fist and refuse to let go.

Rome Carter . . . you were the last person I was expecting, but you're everything I could ever want. You'll burn the world for me, but I'd let the world end for you.

Chapter Forty-Five

Rome

Gwen told me it might take Korra a couple of days to acclimate to her new environment. Cats are finicky creatures, and they'll come to you when they're ready. Well, Korra was ready within two hours of being home, but I wasn't. This cat isn't young. Gwen thinks she's about four or five, but that doesn't stop her from sniffing every corner and climbing onto every ledge.

Chrissy went back to her dorm. Things are better between us, but our feelings are still fragile. Some time apart won't hurt us in the long run. Besides, I have a cat that needs my constant attention. I'm afraid if I look away for one second, she'll bolt and knock something over or, worse, hurt herself.

After a few hours, I gave up. I retreated to my bedroom in hopes she'd follow me. I don't know why Korra likes me. During my first one-on-one with Chrissy, Korra locked her sights on me and almost claimed me as hers. I wouldn't say she prefers one sex over the other. She tortured Gwen just as much as she did Ryan. Korra showed Chrissy some attention but then grew tired and cuddled close to me. Do I smell weird or something? Maybe it's all that salmon I used to eat in high school . . . It's finally catching up to me.

The box fan in my room is running along with my air conditioner. I became used to having Chrissy sleeping beside me. I miss her quiet snoring and the shift in the bed. I forgot how loud my thoughts were until now, and all they're doing is reminding me how lonely I am.

When was the last time I talked to my father? Christmas, maybe? I can't say for certain. We used to check in with one another every day, but that stopped last year. If I'm honest with myself, I think I'm avoiding him. Not because I don't love him, that's not it at all. It's because there's nothing I can do for him right now. I don't have the means to care for him, to help save him from himself. That man needs loads of therapy, and even if you have health insurance, those bills pile up. I want to ensure he lives the rest of his life in comfort or at least be able to quit one of the many jobs he had to take on to support us. If I ignore him, his problems don't exist, even if it's only temporary.

I think about Dad meeting Chrissy; he'd like her, but that's not a concern. She would charm him with her smile and win him over with her warmth.

I reach for my phone and decide to be the man Chrissy thinks I am.

> Hey, Dad, just letting you know I'm still alive. Text me so I know you're alive as well. I miss you.

I wait a moment to see if he responds. It doesn't come as a surprise when he doesn't. So, I drop my phone and get comfortable on my side of the bed, pretending Chrissy is lying next to me. I close my eyes and focus on the sound of the fan's blades rotating, the hum of the AC, and the unfamiliar pitter-patter of a white cat walking down the hall. When the noise stops, I peek my left eye open and find a fluff of white fur staring me down.

"Korra." She tilts her head to the side. "Have you made yourself at home? Because you and I both know this is going to be a foster failure. Even if I wanted to return you, I couldn't. You won't let me."

Korra releases a tiny huff and struts toward me.

"I wouldn't ever want to return you though."

I raise my hand and offer her my finger. She bypasses it and climbs onto my chest to observe me.

"What was your life like before the café?" I ask like she's going to respond. "Gwen said you've been to a few shelters. It sounds like you never found your home, your person." Being as careful as I can, I start to scratch behind her ear. "Am I your person?"

She melts against my hand, pressing her head into my palm and plopping onto her stomach. Her purring vibrates my ribcage, and the melody fills the room, seemingly louder than the box fan.

"I hope I am," I say as I kiss the top of her head. "Because you're home now."

"Rome is officially a foster failure. Cough it up," Gwen says as she holds out her hand toward Blake.

"You two bet on me?" I ask as Blake hands Gwen a five.

"What? I didn't expect you to adopt a cat, a fluffy white one, at that." Blake shrugs before pushing his glasses up the bridge of his nose.

"She's more than a fluffy white cat . . ." I mumble under my breath.

"Oh, right, sorry. She's your pretty princess," Gwen teases.

The one time I called Korra my pretty princess in front of Chrissy was a big mistake, and I will never live it down. It's not my fault the cat is cute with her bright green eyes and soft fur. Plus, she adores me, which only adds to it.

"Is Chrissy meeting you today for your one-on-one?" Blake asks as he ties his apron around his waist.

I forgot he works here with his partner, Ryan. I wonder if the guys know he hangs out with kittens on a daily basis.

"No, I've been reassigned to Raina Bennett."

"Makes sense. You shouldn't date your therapist in real life, and you definitely shouldn't fuck them—"

"Blake!" Ryan scolds from the back.

"What?! Tell me I'm wrong," Blake shouts, holding back a laugh. "Anyway, I've heard Raina is really nice. She would have helped Malik if he gave her the chance."

"Yeah . . ."

Chrissy is meeting with Malik for the first time today. I'm trying my best not to dwell on it. We've been okay with one another. The tension from the previous fight is still lingering, and it's painfully obvious. She hasn't been around as often as she used to, and when we are together, she looks at me like I'm an injured puppy, either waiting to be loved on or on the verge of biting her. I'm hoping to cut the tension today, and it starts with talking to my new mentor.

A few kittens run toward the door when it opens, but Raina is quick to block their attempted escape. She keeps an eye on them as she walks toward me, and they watch her eagerly, like they're waiting for something.

"We'll stage a coup later," she whispers with a hint of a laugh. "Hi, Rome."

"Hi, Raina."

She sits across from me, preparing her notebook like Chrissy used to. I already miss that girl's note-taking and the nose wiggle she used to do while she was studying me.

"I'm sorry about last time." I offer her a sad smile. "I wasn't myself that day. I'm not normally so—"

"Abrasive?" she asks with a smirk.

"Yeah . . . it wasn't my best day."

"I understand, don't worry. I took no offense."

I release a tiny puff of air through my nose when she looks at me.

Her eyes are hazel with a dark green ring around the irises. She has long, dark auburn hair and a beauty mark on the edge of her nose. I don't know much about her other than that Chrissy likes her.

"Chrissy caught me up on where you two left off. Are you ready to get started?"

I nod while playing with my thumbs under the table.

"What has happened since your last check-in?"

When was our last one-on-one? I feel like it's been an eternity.

"If I remember correctly, the last official check-in was before the Fourth of July, and I've been lying to Chrissy."

"How so?"

"She thinks I'm on the verge of burnout. I told her what I do for the team, along with my own routines, classes, and social life. I've been taking on additional tasks to help Malik, but he took advantage of my kindness. She suggested I give him some of the tasks back, and I didn't, even though I said I would."

Raina writes all this down, keeping her eyes locked on me. "Why did you lie to her?"

"I—" I stumble over my words.

Why did I lie to her? I'm not prone to lying. I'm an open book. So, why did I lie to the one person who has done nothing but reassure me, who has tried her best to help me? Chrissy was only looking out for me, but if she hadn't known that I hadn't kept my word, what would she have done?

"I didn't want to disappoint her," I say under my breath. "I was afraid she would leave if I did, and I would be left alone."

Raina's gaze softens, and her lips trickle into a small smile. "Like when your mother left?"

All I can do is nod.

"Do you think she left because you disappointed her?"

"I don't know," I mumble as I fight the tears in my eyes.

"I'm sure Chrissy has told you this, but I will say it again. It's not *your* fault."

"Then why?" I ask through my tears.

Raina drops her shoulders as she sighs. "You may never get your answer, Rome. Accepting that fact will take time. It's important to remember that you did nothing wrong. You were a child, and that child is still within you."

The thought of eight-year-old me makes me cry harder, and I'd give anything to give him a hug.

"You parented yourself, didn't you?" Raina asks carefully.

"What do you mean?" I ask as I grab a napkin to wipe my nose.

"When our parents don't live up to our expectations, we often seek things our inner child wants or needs. Comfort, love, security, reassurance, protection. It seems to me that you had to provide those things for yourself, and you still are. But you have friends who love you, a girlfriend who will do anything for you. You're a good person, and you offer a lot of people some of the things you provide yourself. Hence why you won't give up some of your tasks for the team." Raina smirks knowingly, and I chuckle through my tears.

"That makes sense."

Her eyes dart over my shoulder, and her smile widens. "You have a rather antsy-looking barista looking at you."

"That's Gwen," I say with a light laugh. "I'm fine, Gwen."

"I'm sorry, but I really want to give you a hug. I hate seeing you cry."

"You can hug him." Raina chuckles and beckons her over.

Not a second later, Gwen wraps her arms around me and hugs me with all her might.

"Therapy is so hard. You're doing such a good job." Gwen sounds like she's on the verge of crying herself, pride soaking through her tone.

"Thank you." I sniffle and hug her back.

Gwen pats my back and pulls away, wiping a tear away from her cheeks.

"How's Korra?"

"A downright princess," I chuckle, and she laughs.

"Sounds about right."

She turns to look at Raina, and her smile grows. "Nice to meet you, I'm Gwen." She extends her hand toward Raina, who happily takes it.

"Nice to meet you too, I'm Raina. Chrissy has told me so much about you."

"Really?" Gwen asks, sounding shocked.

"Your ginger ale trick for nerves? It's a miracle."

"Ginger ale is magic."

"It really is!" Raina exclaims, matching Gwen's excitement.

Chapter Forty-Five

As they go back and forth, their grins grow with the unfolding conversation.

Taking the moment to gather myself, I rest my hand over my heart, and little Rome from years ago materializes in my mind. He's been through so much, always trying to keep a smile on his face, even when all he wants to do is cry. I've kept that facade for years, but the act has started to break. It's time I focus on what I need, and it starts with taking what I deserve.

Chapter Forty-Six

Chrissy

I'm not looking forward to this. I think I'd rather trim Zack's toenails. But, alas, I am sitting in a crowded coffee shop, waiting for his royal pain in the ass, Malik Chen. I would have preferred the cat café, but I was afraid Gwen would act like an overbearing mother hen. I needed somewhere public to be on the safe side. I don't think he'll try anything, but the fact that he "wants me" is more than unnerving.

My leg jostles anxiously as I stare at the door. Malik strolls through the door, and a scoff I meant to keep inside rumbles in my throat. He's about to reach for his phone instead of scanning the room for me, so I speak up.

"Over here."

He sees me, and I wave him over.

"There you are." He smiles, flashing his perfect white teeth at me.

"Here I am," I say as I try not to roll my eyes.

With my notebook already out, I click my pen repeatedly as he gets settled.

I went over Raina's notes the past couple of days, and I've concluded that Malik has been playing her. Which she was aware of. He feigns remorse and guilt but quickly returns to his usual ways. He's a pro at manipulation and gaslighting, and he knows it.

"How has your day been?" I decide to start just so we can get this over with.

"Better now," he says in what I'm sure he thinks is his most charming voice.

I look at him for a moment, unsure how to react. The professional in me tells me to smile and pass it off, while the woman in me screams and cringes. Mama never taught me to be a doormat. She taught me to stand my ground with a smile on my face.

"Charming," I say with a fake toothy grin, giving in to the smart-ass within me. "So, let's get this over—started. The last topic you and Raina covered was taking personal responsibili-ty." *How quaint.* "What have you done since that conversation to take responsibility?"

"Well, you were there the day the coach wanted to talk to me. Remember?"

"Yes, I was."

"Since that conversation, I started to really look at myself. I wasn't doing my job as team captain. Rome was picking up my slack, and I let him. I won't be doing that anymore."

"Mm-hmm, and how will you do that?" I ask while main-taining eye contact to see if I can catch him in a lie.

"I'll be creating and reviewing the plays myself again. I will also be stepping in during workouts to help the rookies." His tone is even, his eyes are steady, and his fingers are still.

This guy is good, but I'm not a dummy.

"That's great to hear. I'm sure Rome will appreciate it." I put on my chipper voice, even though it hurts.

"He'll have more time for you." And he fucking winks at me.

Gag.

"Lucky me." I don't bother hiding the disgust that laces my words.

"A lot of girls would kill to be in your position, you know."

And here we go.

"Yeah? Why is that?" I get ready to jot down as many notes as I can.

"For starters, I'm a fine piece of art. I mean, look at these bad boys." Malik flexes his forearms, and the vein in my forehead throbs.

"I'm melting in my seat," I say, unamused.

"And I'm the captain and quarterback for a top-ranking college football team, bound for greatness and a top draft pick."

Could someone be any more into themselves? What a self-centered prick! Malik could get a hard-on from his own reflection.

"You intrigue me," he admits, and it gets my mind running.

"How so?"

"From the moment I met you, you weren't impressed like the other girls."

"I'm pretty sure Raina wasn't impressed either," I retort.

"True, but you . . . There's something about you. I can't put my finger on it. Ever since the party—"

That fucking pool party. If I knew wearing that bikini for Rome would garner Malik's attention, I would have worn a potato sack instead. And he better not lay his fingers anywhere near me if he wants to keep his hand.

"I'm not a puzzle to be solved. I'm here to help you and teach you about mental health. Is that understood?"

Malik throws me a lopsided grin, and I know he definitely does not understand.

Chapter Forty-Six

"Yes, ma'am."

The meeting ended after that, and I couldn't thank the stars enough. I'm not sure what to do with myself. If it was a normal day, I would go to Rome's apartment, but things haven't been right since the argument. I could go to Gwen's, but I'm not sure I'm in the right headspace for that either. With a dejected sigh, I start back toward campus.

The sun begins to set, casting a warm, golden hue across the horizon. The sky reminds me of pink cotton candy, with wispy clouds and hints of blue from the lingering afternoon sky. The air has a gentle breeze that carries the scent of freshly cut grass. More people trickle outside, and lamp posts automatically turn on as the evening sets in. Castle Brook looms in the distance, the castle-like structure looking magical and astonishing.

A pit forms in my chest, the hollow feeling radiating to my stomach. I miss him more than words can express.

Pushing that thought to the back of my mind, I focus on the walk back home. Fireflies light up the grass, and it brings a smile to my face.

Memories of Zack, Gwen, and me catching them in our

front yard surface. We used to stay out past nine, catching those bugs, only to release them all at the same time, just to watch the light show they would create. We would often end those long summer nights with s'mores or Italian ice. I miss being a kid. Why was I excited to grow up? I'm always under some sort of stress, and my free time is vanishing. I would pay good money to be a kid again, even if it's just for a day.

"Bubbles?"

My sneakers scuff on the concrete outside my dorm hall. I spin around and face an amused Rome.

"You were in deep thought, weren't you?" he asks with a smirk.

"Yes, sorry," I say with a breathless chuckle.

My eyes dart over him, landing on the bag he's holding in his hand. "What are you doing here?"

He holds the plastic bag up and closes the distance between us. "I thought we could have a sleepover."

The thought brings a toothy smile to my face. "Really? What about Korra?"

"She'll be fine. I set her up in a fluffy bed and left the TV on."

I snicker at the thought of that white cat lying in her cat bed watching TV, but what makes it even better is the fact that Rome did all that for her.

"I wouldn't have pegged you as a cat dad," I tease.

"What can I say? I'm full of surprises." He shrugs, and we smile at one another.

Moments pass, and neither of us says anything or moves a muscle. My heart swells with his proximity, and I'd give anything to hug him and never let go.

"Are you going to invite me inside?" He leans in and brushes a stray curl behind my ear.

I blush at the contact. You would think we were back to friends who had a crush on one another.

With a slight chuckle, I nod toward the door. "Let's go. I hope you have some sweets in there."

"Of course I do. Who do you think I am?"

I peer over my shoulder just as he reaches in front of me to open the door. His eyes are red, and his nose sounds stuffy. He was crying earlier today, and now the urge to hug him overpowers me.

Without another thought, I wrap my arms around him. I rest my head on his chest and listen to his heartbeat. The rhythmic thumping increases, and his ocean cologne surrounds me. Rome rests his chin on the top of my head, and I nuzzle closer.

"I want us to be us again," I whisper against his chest.

"Why do you think I'm here?"

I look up at him and meet his twinkling green eyes.

"I'm glad you're here."

Rome lets out a peaceful sigh and kisses my forehead. "Me too."

Chapter Forty-Seven

Rome

I knew I had to see her after my little breakthrough with Raina today. Gwen suggested a self-care night, and it was brilliant. I ran to the store to buy all the supplies and found myself waiting outside her dorm building with no time to spare.

Chrissy leads me up the stairs to the third floor. We walk down the hall in silence, but I already feel the tension between us fading. I rest my hand on her lower back as she unlocks her door, soaking in the sensation of having her by my side again. It hasn't been long since we last saw each other, but with the tension, it wasn't right. Now, I feel us clicking back into place.

She opens her door, and the room is lit with a warm light she must have left on before leaving today. When I step inside, she closes the door and I take my shoes off.

"So, what do you think?" she asks, and I take in the sight.

Her room is as I imagined it would be, maybe just a tad cleaner. Her bed is pushed into the corner, and it has a white cotton comforter and matching white pillows with a couple of light pink ones for accent. Fairy lights are strung along the wall with multiple pictures of her and her friends. A plant sits in the corner, and it looks well watered and alive. I'd be willing to bet good money that it's fake. The entire space smells like fresh strawberries with a hint of vanilla bean. I immediately feel at home.

"It's very you," I say.

"What does that mean?"

"It means I love it."

The rest of Chrissy's tension melts away as her expression lightens and her shoulders drop. I offer her my bag and smile widely when she grabs it with nothing but excitement. She places the bag on her bed and starts to go through it.

"You want to do face masks with me?" she asks in disbelief. "*And* watch a princess movie?"

"Duh," I chuckle.

"This is great, thank you!" Chrissy leaps in my arms and wraps her legs around my waist, hugging me like her life depends on it.

"I'm sorry for everything. For how I reacted, for not trusting you."

She nods against my shoulder and kisses my cheek. "I'm sorry too. Let's work on us and forget all about that dickhead."

I snicker when she pulls back to look at me. "Deal."

With our face masks in hand, Chrissy strolls into her bathroom, and I follow her. She props herself up on the bathroom counter and tears open the first package. I stand in front of her, looking at the colorful sticky notes on the mirror.

"Everything okay?" I nod toward the mirror, and she looks over her shoulder.

"Oh, those are self-affirmations."

"Do you say these a lot?" My eyes land on the note that says, "Your hair is beautiful." And my heart snaps in two.

"Most mornings. I used to get teased in school. Mom made these for me, and we recited them every morning."

I twirl one of her curls around my finger. "Do you still believe you're not beautiful?"

She's silent for a moment, but her response is louder than any words can be. "Sometimes."

With a soft smile, I kiss her forehead. "You are far more beautiful than you'll ever believe. I'll remind you every day."

With a smile of her own, she holds out her finger, which is dipped in the gray clay face mask.

"Do I get to do you afterward?" I smirk when I realize what I said.

"Yes," she laughs. "Where would the fun be in that if I did it myself?"

I position myself between her legs, and she begins to paint my face with the mask. It's cool to the touch, with the smell of witch hazel and something I can't quite identify.

Chrissy is having the time of her life, like I handed a toddler finger paints for the first time. She lathers on the clay, making sure not a speck of skin is untouched.

When she's done, she admires me like a painting, and when she's satisfied, she hands me the next package and ties her hair back. "My turn."

I take the package and open it with a soft smile.

Looking at Chrissy, I dip my finger in the mask. "Ready, princess?"

Chrissy closes her eyes and snickers. "Paint me like one of your French girls."

"Oh, you know about them?"

She opens her eyes, and I plop the mask on the tip of her nose, matching her laughter and wide grin.

"Rome Carter!" she squeals.

"I couldn't help it," I laugh while smearing the mask over her face. "Now relax. This is supposed to be calming."

With a few mumbled remarks, Chrissy closes her eyes

again and lets me finish applying the clay mask to her gorgeous face. When I'm done, she hops off the counter, and we look at one another in the mirror.

"We look fabulous."

"Hottest couple on campus," she deadpans.

Our composure cracks within seconds, and we start laughing.

I wrap my arms around her waist and haul her back into her room.

Once I place her on her bed, she grabs her phone and opens the camera. "Pretty please?"

"How can I say no to that face?"

We take a series of selfies, and it's not long before the mask dries, and we wash it off, leaving us feeling refreshed with smooth skin. I turn the lights out, and she gets comfortable in bed. I didn't bring a change of clothes, but thankfully I'm not wearing jeans today.

I watch her as she starts to play the movie I picked up for us to watch. With snacks in hand, she rests her head on my chest, and I wrap my arm around her. She sighs more than once, but none of them sound irritated, more like peaceful and content. As the movie plays, I run my fingers through her curls and close my eyes.

A lot has happened, and I haven't had the time to process it. Chrissy and I had our first big disagreement, Malik is threatening my chance at being drafted, Dad hasn't messaged me back, classes resume soon, and the first game of the season is a month away. If I could freeze time, I would. I want to stay in this moment forever. No outside influences or drama. Just us watching a movie about a princess, a man from the streets, and a genie.

"I think this may be my favorite movie." Chrissy cuts through my thoughts.

"Not *Rapunzel?*" I ask with a raised eyebrow.

"No, this is my favorite."

"Why is that?"

"They knew they loved one another and were willing to sacrifice part of themselves for the other. This is forbidden love at its finest."

I trail my fingers from her hair to her bare arm, tracing random shapes. "And they got their happy ending."

"They did," she agrees.

A moment passes before she shifts. She scoots back and looks at me with a wistful look. "Do you think we'll find our happy ending? Or is that only for fairy tales?"

With a gentle smile, I run my thumb over her jawline. Her skin turns pink under my touch, so I repeat the motion.

"I'm not sure if I believe in happy endings. Not because I don't want to, but because they're unrealistic. We'll face challenges; the universe will always throw obstacles at us because she wants to see us grow. Humans are meant to change and adapt. What would be the point of continuing if we all had a happy ending? I think you and I are stronger than a happy ending. We'll have our moments where we can't stand one another, moments when we're sad, but we'll have so many moments when we're happy and in love. And I'm going to remember each and every one of them because my time with you is nothing short of bliss."

And I mean it. I want it all with Chrissy. The messy, the chaotic, the funny, and the happy. I don't see myself ever growing tired of her. There is a before her, but there isn't an after. There can't be. I refuse to consider it.

She looks at me, her eyes shimmering as tears fill them. When they fall from her eyes, I catch them with my thumb and wipe them away.

"That's all I want." Her voice cracks. "You're all I want."

I weave my hand in her hair and rest my forehead on hers. "Even though I can be a prick?"

She chuckles and meets my gaze with nothing but love. "You're not a prick, Rome. You just don't know when to listen to me, but that will come with time. You'll learn that I'm always right."

I'm already learning this important lesson. If I'd listened to her from the beginning, if I had given Malik some of his tasks back, would we be here today? Or would I feel so tired and at a loss? Would Chrissy be in the center of our feud? I can't say for certain, but I can say that I'm learning.

"And that you make masterful plans," I say with a smirk, which earns me one in return.

"My plans are foolproof, and you know it."

"Sure, let's go with that."

She punches my arm playfully and is quick to flinch in response.

"I'm going to need to fatten you up," she teases, and I laugh.

"I don't doubt that you will. Especially if you stock our future fridge with that fancy Max yogurt."

"Deal," she responds with a wide smile.

The thought of us sharing a home one day makes my heart swell. I pull her in and kiss her like I haven't touched her in years.

"I love you," I whisper against her lips.

"And I love you." She returns the sentiment, cementing my place in her life.

She collapses back against my chest, and we finish the movie. Chrissy is quick to fall asleep, and I'm about to close my eyes when my phone vibrates on the end table. Careful not to wake her, I reach for my phone and flip it over, surprised to see a text from my dad.

> Sorry for not responding. I'm glad you're doing okay, can't wait to watch the first game of the season.

When I see his text, a weight is lifted from my shoulders. He's alive, he's okay, and for now, that's all that matters.

> Glad to hear you're okay. Maybe I can see you soon?

> Dad: That would be great. If you let me know when I'll try to take time off work.

I smile to myself. He's never visited me on campus, and an idea pops into my head.

> Maybe you can come to one of my games? Or if we make the cup?

> Yes! Keep me in the loop, but know I'll be watching from home in the meantime.

We've gotten close in the past, but now I have a new form of motivation pushing me. If the team makes it into the cup, Dad will come to a game, which means he will get to meet Chrissy and the crew.

> Listen, there's something I want to say, really quick.

> Is everything okay?

I've been working on myself and on being a better father. It's time you knew that I'm thankful for you. You stepped up and did the job of two parents, and it couldn't have been easy. Thank you for always being there for me. I love you, son.

I have to reread his words before they finally sink in. I swallow hard and type out a response.

I love you too, Dad.

I can't manage much more of a reply than that. Emotions clog my throat, and my heart hammers in my chest. I close my eyes feeling happy and hopeful for the first time in a long time.

Chapter Forty-Eight

Chrissy

I've managed to survive two more meetings with Malik, making today the last one. Thank the fucking universe. Gwen insisted I have the final meeting at the café because afterward, our little family is going to see a movie.

I'm in my normal booth, sipping Gwen's specialty drink, iced chai, and picking at a blueberry muffin when the table wobbles, disrupting my peace.

"Malik," I say without looking up from my notebook.

"Not Malik."

Lifting my gaze, I smile without a second thought and almost leap across the table. "Aren't you a sight for sore eyes?"

"Thought you might have missed me," Rome teases.

"I always miss you."

"Even though you woke up in my bed this morning?"

"What can I say? I'm a clingy bitch."

"It's true," Gwen calls from across the room, making Rome chuckle.

"I thought you weren't coming until later," I say as I try to fight back my own laughter.

"Practice ended early. I thought I'd treat myself to a snack before we go to the movies and eat more junk food."

"Solid reasoning, but you have to behave yourself," I tell him, noticing Malik outside.

"I will, don't worry," Rome responds as the door opens.

"I mean it." I point my pen at him, and he stands with his arms raised.

"I will. I will. I'll be right over here playing with the cats and eating muffins. Right, Gwen?"

"Aw, and we can talk all about our feelings," Gwen says, and Rome and I smile widely.

"There's my girl." Malik greets me loud enough for Rome to hear.

I side-eye him, giving him a "move and suffer" look. I can handle myself. Momma didn't raise a coward.

"Sit," I instruct him, and he obeys.

I flip through my notes before starting a new page. Since this is our last meeting, my goal is to figure out if he learned anything over the last couple of months. My money is on no.

"So, is there anything you want to discuss before we part ways?" I ask him with a fake, wide grin.

His eyes dart to Rome, then back to me, and I prepare myself for the worst. "What do you see in him that you don't see in me?"

"Our meetings aren't about my personal life, Malik. They're about teaching you about mental health," I respond professionally.

"What if I told you my self-esteem is low and I genuinely want to know what I can do to work on myself?" His cocky smile doesn't sell his proposition, but I give in anyway.

"You don't have self-esteem issues, but let's pretend you do. If you think you're unattractive, I would suggest self-affirmations. Look in the mirror and repeat phrases that will make you feel good about yourself. For example, 'I am strong. I am good. I am worthy. I am enough.' Then I would ask where your issue stems from. Is it a belief that you're not good looking, or is it something else?"

"Let's say the girl I'm interested in doesn't think I'm good enough." His flirtatious tone makes my skin crawl.

"Did she say that, or are you making an assumption?" I fire back.

"She didn't say it, but she definitely believes it."

"Hmm. I would suggest you look inward. What qualities do you think you possess that would make her feel that way? Or is she just not into you, and she's trying to really drive her point home so you'll leave her alone?" I ask with a quirked brow.

"I think she's playing hard to get."

"Of course you do," I sigh as I jot down more notes. "I'm going to be honest. You have made zero improvement since the start of this program, and while it doesn't surprise me, it does disappoint me. We should always be working on ourselves. No one is perfect, *especially* not you, Malik Chen." I close my notebook and stand from the booth. "I wish I could say it was a pleasure, but it wasn't."

As I reach for my bag, he wraps his hand around my wrist and pulls me into him. Forcing me against his chest, he looks down at me.

"Tell me you don't feel it," he whispers before moving in to kiss me.

Feet shuffle, and I know Rome is making a charge to save me, but I'm not a damsel in distress or a prize to be won.

Pressing my hands against his chest, I push Malik hard, making him stumble backward.

"What don't you fucking get?!" I shout at him as Rome comes to an abrupt stop. "You aren't Rome. You'll never *be* Rome. Not to your team and certainly not with me. If you ever touch me again, I will kick you in the balls so hard you'll taste them in your mouth! Do you understand me?" My throat is raw from raising my voice. I don't often yell, but when I do, I mean it.

I pin Malik with a glare.

He stares at me, unsure what to do next. His eyes are blank, no fear, just confusion. Like I had the audacity to push him away.

"I said, do you understand?"

Without responding, Malik turns on his heels and walks out the door, leaving me stuck between fury and vulnerability.

Chapter Forty-Nine

Rome

I wasn't watching them the entire time. I promised Chrissy I wouldn't and that I would behave. It was only when he put his hands on her that I moved, ready to shove him through the window and pummel his face in. She didn't want him to kiss her, and why would she? He's gross, and his intentions are slimy.

Like the coward he is, he scrambled out the door, leaving the three of us in shock.

Malik tried to kiss my girl. *My* girl. In front of me. He didn't care. He wanted her, and he's not learning his fucking lesson. He'll never get my wildflower. She doesn't want him. He isn't worthy of someone like her.

"Are you okay?" I ask quietly, unsure where her mind is at.

When she nods subtly, I reach for her.

"Can I hug you?"

"Please," she mumbles, her voice cracking as her chest heaves.

Without wasting another moment, I wrap my arms around

her, holding her tightly against my chest. She continues to work on catching her breath.

Gwen appears, and I meet her worried expression and give her a nod, telling her that she's okay. She presses her lips together before walking over to the front door and deadbolting it.

"You're okay," I whisper as I kiss the top of Chrissy's curls. "You're safe."

Her arms find their way around my waist, and she embraces me back.

"I won't let anyone hurt you or touch you."

She nods and nuzzles closer. I run my hands up and down her back in an attempt to soothe her.

"It's you and me, right?"

With another nod, she looks up at me and releases a shaky breath. "Right."

"That's my girl."

I kiss her forehead as a car parks outside the café. Max, Ash, and Zack are here.

"Your brother is here. Do you want me to get him?"

She grips me tighter, not budging from her spot.

"Don't go. Not yet."

"Okay."

Gwen returns with a bottle of water, and she approaches us with a careful look on her face.

"Hey, girly. Why don't we head back to the Waylens' instead of going out? Or we can reschedule for another night?"

"It's okay. I want to go. I won't let that asshole ruin the evening." With one last sigh, her shoulders drop, but she doesn't leave the comfort of my arms.

"Are you sure?" Gwen asks with a soft tone.

"Positive."

Chrissy takes the water as I grab her things. The three of us head outside, where Zack jumps out of the car and tackles Gwen with a bear hug.

"There's my two favorite girls!" When he pulls away, he sees Chrissy, and his expression drops. "What happened?"

"Can you ride with us? I'll tell you on the way," Chrissy responds.

Zack looks at me before looking back at his sister. "Okay, let's go."

During the ride, Chrissy tells Zack all about Malik. The two of them are in the back, leaving me alone in the front seat. In the rearview mirror, I watch Zack's fists clench and unclench. He's officially joined the Malik Is a Prick club, and I'm starting to think we need jackets to establish our membership.

When we get to the theater, Chrissy leans against me for support, and Zack gives me an approving look. He knows I won't let anything happen to her. She's safe with me, and she'll never have to deal with Malik again.

"He's not going to toss the ball to you, is he?" Chrissy whispers as we stand in line for our snacks.

"Let's not worry about that now, okay?" I smile down at her, not letting an ounce of worry show.

"Okay . . ."

I already know Malik won't throw me the ball during opening day, but I'll cross that bridge when I get there. We have a backup plan. And while I have no idea how we'll get Levi to replace Malik, we will because Chrissy and I will overcome anything that stands in our way.

Even Malik Chen.

Chapter Fifty

Chrissy

The final paper for the mentorship program is written and ready to hand in. The fall classes have begun, and the first game of the season is tonight. Rome has been at practice most days, leaving me spending my days at the Waylens' or in my dorm.

My paper consisted of information on Malik Chen, leaving him unnamed and unidentifiable. Being as professional as possible, I roasted him to pieces.

Class A narcissist.

Sociopathic tendencies.

Lacks guilt.

Believes he is above the rules.

Doesn't take no for an answer.

Unwilling to change.

I ended the paper by stating what I would do in a real patient-to-therapist setting: continue to work with them to the best of my ability. We'll know by the end of this week whether we earned the extra credit. At this point, I'll take anything.

When I get back to my dorm, a package is waiting outside

my door. I stop in my tracks to look at it. This could be one of two things: Malik has gone full psycho and gifted me his left hand, or it could be something completely innocent.

I eye the package as I approach it, waiting for it to start ticking. When nothing happens, I bend down to open the box. My shoulders drop when I don't see a bloody body part waiting for me. I reach in to grab the jersey Rome left me, and I hold it to my chest to hug it. Number 35, Carter. The only thing that could make this gift better is if it smelled like him. Or *better* yet, if Rome was wearing it.

With my new jersey in hand, I enter my dorm to get changed. The sun is setting, but the buzz in the air is palpable. Everyone, even our non-sporty fan group, is ready for the first game of the season. Everyone said they would meet me outside because they were afraid someone would get lost if we met inside the stadium. *Cough, cough, Gwen, cough, cough.*

I put on some jeans and slip the jersey on. My reflection in the mirror makes me smile, and my heart fills with pride. This is my boyfriend's number, his last name is on my back, and hopefully, if Malik plays nice, he'll dominate the field tonight.

Leaving my hair down, I slip on a pair of tennis shoes and head outside. No one is waiting for me when I exit the building. So, I reach for my phone to text the group chat.

> Where are you bitches?

> Gwen: We're walking now. We managed to kidnap Max.

> What?!

> Max: She dangled Rome in front of me . . . What can I say? I'm a sucker for that boy.

> Ash: Proud dad moment. Brings tears right to my eyes.

"Hi, Chrissy!" Zack shouts and waves with both of his arms farther down the path.

Putting my phone away, I walk toward our group and barrel into my brother. "I missed you," I tease.

"Get off me, woman. I don't know where you've been."

I gasp loudly, grabbing my chest and feigning shock. "My feelings have been hurt. I hope you're proud of yourself. Ash, hold me."

I fall into his arms and thank the stars that he caught me.

"Sometimes I wonder where I would be today if I hadn't taken biochem last fall," Ash says with a playful sigh.

"You'd be bored and lonely," Gwen says in a singsong voice.

Max snorts as the rest of us chuckle.

"She has a point," Ash says as he wraps his other arm around Gwen, holding us like he did at Horror Fest last year.

"Let's go. We don't want Rome to think we forgot about him." Max ushers us forward, and we fall in step.

The football stadium is alive, unlike the last few times I've been here over the summer. Students and college football fans are all dressed in red and black, ready to cheer on the Castle Brook Dragons. I didn't keep up with sports my last four years here, but Rome tells me that every year they get close to winning the cup. He hopes they win this season, not only to help his drafting prospects but for the team and a final farewell.

I have no doubt they'll make it. My only concern is Malik Chen. No one knows what he'll do tonight. If I didn't push him away the last time I saw him, he might have kept his word in passing Rome the ball. Malik is a wild card, though, so who knows what will happen.

With a release of air, I move over to Gwen and take her hand in mine. She squeezes it, and the show of support has me righting my posture. I don't know why nerves are twisting in my stomach. It could be that football is a dangerous sport, and with one wrong move, Rome could end up with a concussion. Or maybe it's that I don't trust Malik to not hurt Rome himself. Or perhaps it has everything to do with the fact that I'm about to see Rome in his full uniform. Either way, I'm sure tonight is going to be eventful.

Rome got us front-row seats near the middle of the field, behind the players' benches. Chatter and music float through the warm air, and excitement settles in my core as we all get comfortable in our spots. Gwen bounces in her seat as the boys talk about something I can't quite understand.

Reaching for me, she takes my hand and offers me a wide smile. "Ready?" she asks.

I open my mouth to respond but am cut off by the booming voice of the announcer on the loudspeakers.

"Castle Brook Dragons! Are you ready?!"

Everyone hoots and hollers in response.

"Let's usher in the 2016-2017 season and give our team the welcome they deserve!"

Music begins to play again, and in the far left corner of the field, the team runs out, the cheering reaching a crescendo. I can't make out anyone's faces because they're all wearing their helmets, but when I see number 35, my heart rate increases and a smile plants itself on my face.

Here goes nothing. *Go kick some ass, Rome, and don't let Malik get to you.*

Chapter Fifty-One

Rome

"Gather up!" Coach Bradson yells over the team's nervous and excited chatter.

We huddle around Coach, who stands on a wooden bench so everyone can see him. He takes a moment to scan the locker room, making eye contact with as many players as he can. When his gaze lands on me, he gives me a firm nod, and I return the gesture.

"This is what we've been preparing for. I'm not expecting perfection tonight, but that doesn't mean I don't want each and every one of you to give it your all. Remember our practices and plays. Remember to rely on your team and ask questions if you have them. It's the first game of the season, which means there are scouts from the NFL. Don't let it get to your heads. Do you hear me, seniors?"

"Yes, sir!" we all respond in unison.

"We'll gather here at halftime. Malik! Get up here and talk to your team." The disdain in his tone is evident.

I wonder if the other guys notice it like I do.

Malik takes Coach's spot. With a cocky smirk, he looks out

into the crowd and starts to try and amp us up for the game. "Alright, guys, we're playing against the Arcadian Owls. For those who were on the team last season, you know we lost against them in the final cup. I don't know about you, but I'm craving that sweet taste of revenge!"

A few yeses and yeahs fill the room in response.

"I want us to kick ass! We'll prove to those assholes who rules the Northeast! Let's make this game the start of a winning season!"

Everyone chants and agrees, grinning all around me, and if Malik and I were on good terms, his speech would have amped me up as well. Instead, a different feeling settles inside me, and I let it fuel me.

Give him hell.

The tunnel is dimly lit. The buzz from the crowd puts my head where it needs to be. I'm near the front with the other seniors. Malik is at the charge, per usual. The music lowers, and the announcer begins to rile the crowd.

Malik turns his head, meeting my gaze as I bring my helmet up to my head. We stare at one another, the tension that has been building between us apparent. With a look full of nothing but fury, I secure my helmet over my head and refuse to give him the reaction he's looking for.

Go ahead, Malik. See what happens if you don't throw me the ball. You want to win this game so bad? Prove it.

The announcer's voice breaks through our stare off, and Malik secures his helmet over his head. "Let's usher in the 2016-2017 season and give our team the welcome they deserve!"

Cheers follow suit, and when the music returns, we start onto the field for the first official time.

My last first time.

I was always a wide receiver. It started when I was a kid. I was quick and rarely dropped a pass. I made the junior varsity team in ninth grade and moved to varsity the following year. I poured myself into this sport. When Mom left, Dad was gone as well. Yes, he was there physically, but emotionally, he was a husk. All I had was football, and it never let me down.

When I run onto the field, I absorb the energy from the crowd. A proud smile splits my face. Dad is watching from home, and my girl is here, along with the rest of the crew. Newfound determination sets in, and I'm more than ready to leave my mark on my final season as a Castle Brook Dragon.

When I near the players' bench, I take my helmet off and scan the crowd. The familiar feel of the grass under my cleats grounds me. I can't help but smile at the fans who cheer and clap for me, but they're not who I'm looking for.

A tug pulls on my heart, pleading for me to look to my right. With a slight turn, I meet my girl's dazzling blue eyes and beaming smile. She left her curls down, and they're as wild and gorgeous as ever. And she's wearing the jersey I left for her. Seeing her in my number makes my heart swell with love and pride. I can't wait to hold her in my arms and kiss her.

But first, we need to win this game.

Everything I've done has led up to this moment. Scouts are in the stands, the cameras are rolling, and my teammates are anxious in more ways than one. I spot Blake sitting next to Levi, and with a final wink toward Chrissy, I turn around and make my way over to them.

They're whispering when I approach them. Levi looks like he's about to projectile vomit across the field. First-game jitters are real, even if you aren't playing. Anything can happen, and Coach can call on you at any time.

"You okay, Levi?" I ask.

All he can do is nod.

"You know how it is," Blake offers with a warm smile, and I smile back at him, knowing exactly what he's talking about.

"Faulkner." I squat in front of him, earning his attention. "Breathe with me." I take in a long breath and watch him do the same. Holding it for a moment, I start to release it slowly, making sure to expel every ounce of air I just took in. "Again," I instruct, and he follows suit.

Once we've taken a few deep breaths, I meet his dark brown eyes and place my hand on his shoulder. "You're on the team for a reason. You're a damn good quarterback. Coach knows it, the assistant coaches know it. Not a lot of freshmen are alternate quarterbacks, remember that. You might not even play today. Just focus on observing." I give him a firm shake.

"Okay," he mumbles with a nod. "You're right, thank you."

Coach starts to bark orders. Blake and I look at one another and smile.

"Ready for our last first game?" I ask.

"Let's make it count."

The team gets into position, and I ready myself to burst down the field and drive the ball as far as I can. I don't bother looking toward Malik. He begins to shout numbers, signaling which play he wants us to execute.

Silence fills the air, and my muscles are taut. With a quick snap, Malik has the ball, and I book it. My legs devour the yards, navigating through the defense like they don't exist. The crowd's cheering becomes a distant hum as my heartbeat echoes in my ears. I'm open, and I turn to see what the holdup is.

With the ball still in Malik's hand, I catch the moment he sees me, but he turns his attention to the other wide receiver, Michaels, who is completely covered. He chucks the ball, not caring about the opening. Time slows as the ball flies through the air, losing momentum within seconds. Michaels propels himself in the air, and while he manages to catch it, he's tackled the moment his feet meet the ground. Michaels never stood a chance.

Malik, you fucking moron.

Coach is pissed. He's already shouting at Malik, questioning his rationale. Time doesn't allow Bradson to pull Malik to the side. With the clock running, we get back into position and repeat the motions.

And each time, Malik never tosses the ball my way.

"Chen?! What the fuck is wrong with you?!" Coach shouts, his face red.

Malik doesn't respond. Instead, he tosses his helmet into a locker. The bang rings in my ears, and some guys flinch at the sudden noise.

"You won't get your revenge if you don't get your shit together," Coach continues, not caring that Malik is ignoring him. "Go ahead, pretend like you can't hear me. I don't want to hear it when I bench your ass and put a freshman in your position."

"You wouldn't dare!" Malik hisses, spit flying from his mouth.

"Oh, he speaks? Talk to me like that again, boy."

They continue shouting at one another, and I peel my attention away from them, noticing that most of the guys are looking at me. They're discouraged. We're losing, twenty-one to seven, and with Malik being, well, a stupid prick, hope is diminishing for a first-game win. A certain someone is going to hate me for this, but fuck it.

"Listen up!" I shout over the argument in the back, earning everyone's attention. "We've been working toward this moment. All the drills in the summer heat, every ounce of sweat and cursing we've poured into this—it's led us to this moment. These last sixty minutes will define our season. Take a moment and look around you. We are more than a team, we're a family. We're messy and complicated. But we're always a tight-knit foundation of support. I've considered you guys my second home. We're stronger than those Owls. We're Dragons, for god's sake!"

"Yes, we fucking are!" Blake shouts, and the rest of the team echoes him.

"Who are we?!" I ask, my voice straining.

"Dragons!"

"Motherfucking Dragons! No regrets! No holding back! Let's get out there and kick some ass!"

A chorus of determination and renewed hope brings a wide grin to my face. The room transformed from building hostility to fierce readiness with one goal in mind: Win.

"Let's fucking go!" I finish my speech, and we start to file back out.

When I take a step forward, a hand grips my shoulder and pulls me back. I turn around to meet Coach Bradson.

"And that is why you need to be captain."

Coach benched Malik, replacing him with Levi without so much as a second thought. Levi was nervous, but he put his trust in his team, and we won by the skin of our teeth. The crowd roared for me every time I landed in the end zone, scoring us touchdowns. And I smiled each time for more than one reason. I imagined what Dad must be doing, watching his son dominate the field. I swore I could hear Chrissy over the crowd, screaming my name with pride. And then I imagined Malik's face. He was right, revenge does taste sweet.

When we reach the locker room, the energy is an addicting mixture of delight and hunger for more.

Malik is silently fuming, and Coach is watching me, waiting for my approval to move forward. Malik's proven to me and this team that he's selfish and only cares about himself and his own future. It's time I take a stand. It's time I claim what is rightfully mine.

If things go well, I'll be captain by the next game. But that doesn't erase my concern over Malik. As much as I don't want to, it's time I tell Coach what has been going on. I decide to do this for my team, not for me, because their futures are on the line as well. And I'll do anything for my family.

Chapter Fifty-Two

Chrissy

Surprise, surprise. Malik Chen fucked up. He almost cost his team the game because of his hard head. While I have no clue what happened in the locker room during halftime, when the team returned to the field, Malik was on the bench. The game was close, but the Dragons won twenty-eight to twenty-one.

Rome is a god on the field. Football is a mystery to me, so the guys had to explain things to Gwen and me more than once. While Gwen caught on, I was still puzzled. All I knew was that Rome caught every pass. He's a powerhouse, and that's why he was deemed an all-star.

When the game ended, the team celebrated, and everyone in the stands cheered and shouted random players' names. Max was the loudest over the crowd, screaming "Carter" with all his might. Now, I'm a loud girl, but even I couldn't match his volume.

It's nice seeing Lawyer Man out and about. Anytime I see him, he's always tired or taking a nap with Pickles. There's a reason we try to drag him out with us; our little work-obsessed lawyer needs a taste of fun, and he's finally getting it.

The crowd begins to thin out, but I keep my eyes on the field, or rather, on number 35. His black jersey clings to his padding, and his legs and ass are toned underneath his black . . . what are football pants called? Are they simply called pants? Or are they leggings? Football leggings? I glance at Zack, debating whether I should ask him. But I get the feeling they are most definitely not called football leggings. I'll ask the internet when I get home.

However, I don't need the internet to tell me that Rome looks hot. I know he's all sweaty and covered in grime right now, but if he were right in front of me, I don't think I would be able to control myself.

Before he runs off the field with his team back to the locker room, he waves and throws me a lopsided smile. I offer him the same gesture in return, ignoring Gwen as she coos at me.

"I can't stand how adorable you two are!" She shakes my arm as she turns away.

"We're not cute." I laugh shyly. "Not like you and Ash."

"Oh, please. Ash and I aren't cute, not like you and Rome. Ugh, my heart has melted for you. I love that you finally found the love you've been looking for."

I watch as Rome runs down the field, jumping onto another player's back and rubbing his fist in his hair. If I had to guess, it's Blake. The old Rome is coming back, but he's also changed. This Rome knows his worth. He knows that he does everything he can for the people he cares about. Unlike the past, he's now willing to stand up for himself.

Coach Bradson isn't stupid. He saw Malik almost throw the game. He'll do the right thing. He won't let his quarterback walk all over him. I don't know Levi well, but Rome likes him, and that's enough for me.

Gwen takes my hand, and we start to make our way back onto campus grounds. As we walk, I put my trust in my clumsy best friend and reach for my phone to text Rome.

You were fantastic! Meet us in the parking lot when you finish getting changed :)

Chapter Fifty-Three

Rome

I take a quick shower and change into a clean jersey and sweatpants. I want to speak with Coach before he gives the team his game recap speech. A few guys pat my back as I run past them. When I reach Bradson's office, I almost bump into him as he steps out.

"Carter? What's the rush?" he asks while he grabs his chest.

"It's time we have a talk."

With a stiff nod, he gestures for me to step into his office. I sit in the chair across from his desk, and he closes the door. I wait for him to get settled before I start what is going to be an uncomfortable conversation.

"I'll keep it quick. I know the guys are waiting to be dismissed." I start from the beginning. How Malik had a strange interest in Chrissy, how he treated Raina and the mentor program. None of that matters in the long run, but they are necessary details. "As you know, I've been picking up his slack. I was going to stop, but he threatened to not throw me the ball during the games, which you saw tonight. I gave in to his demands. I kept up with the plays and training the newbies. But when he threw my girlfriend's name in the mix, he went too far. After she denied his advances numerous times, he tried to kiss her, and while I know this has nothing to do with football, I want you to understand why Malik and I aren't seeing eye to eye. He was willing to throw the game just because of our tension. I don't care what he does to me, but he's screwing this team over. I won't stand for it."

Coach observes me, the wrinkles on the corners of his eyes crinkling as he thinks. He purses his lips, and his shoulders drop as he places his hands on his desk.

"I didn't know about your girlfriend. I apologize on his behalf for his actions. I told Chen that if he wanted to keep his captain title, he must take back the tasks he passed on to you. I assume that has not happened?"

I shake my head.

"With how the game went today, I worry he will act selfishly just to piss you off. I'll talk to him again and give him one final chance. If he fucks up again, I'm benching him. We'll see how he handles having a freshman replace him. Maybe then he'll learn how to act as a team player."

"Thank you, Coach."

"Does this mean you're ready for the vote to be held? If things go as I suspect they will, you'll be captain within the next ten minutes."

My chest tightens, and my lungs hold onto all the oxygen inside them. I've been acting as unofficial captain for two years now. Would anything change if I become the official captain of this team? I can't say for certain. What I can say is that this team needs a leader, and for some reason, their eyes are landing on me.

"Yes, I'm ready." When I say the words, my shoulders relax and I begin to breathe normally again.

Here goes nothing.

"Gather up!" Coach demands as he walks into the locker room.

The team is excited and more than ready to get out of here to celebrate our first win of the season.

My sights land on Blake and Levi as I move through the players to stand beside them.

"You okay, buddy?" Blake asks as he pushes his glasses up the bridge of his nose.

"You'll know in a moment," I manage to say before Coach starts to talk again.

"I know you're all itching to get out of here, so I'll make this fast. I was expecting more from my senior players this game. When I mentioned not expecting perfection, I was talking to the rookies. You let me down, and now I have to take action. It has come to my attention that our current captain isn't maintaining his duties; more than a couple of you have reported this. After speaking with the other coaches and the other candidate, it's time to cast a vote."

Murmurs fill the room, and a few eyes land on me.

Levi nudges my arm, so I turn to look at him. "You deserve this."

"Malik and Rome, step forward."

Blake squeezes my shoulder before I walk toward Coach. The guys part as I walk through them, and more than a couple whispers of good luck welcome me. I face Coach and Malik. Malik's face is red, and his jaw is clenched. Worry doesn't overcome me like I was prepared for. Instead, fierce determination courses through my veins. I'm doing the right thing. I need to remember that.

"If you wish to keep Malik as your captain, raise your hand now."

A couple loyal seniors raise their hands, but it's only ten of them.

Malik clicks his tongue and scoffs.

"If you want Rome Carter as captain, raise your hand now."

I had a feeling it would turn out this way, but I wasn't ready for the overwhelming support. When the rest of the team raises their hands, my heart flutters in my chest and chills spread over my arms.

"Congratulations, Rome Carter, you are the new captain of the Castle Brook Dragons football team," Coach announces before clapping his hands.

Malik curses under his breath and storms away, not caring that he looks like a sore loser.

I let out a shaky breath and smile as the guys applaud and call out for me. I'm not perfect. I'm a mess and have more trauma than I first realized. Humans are messy, though, and there's nothing wrong with being a mess. I'll give this my all, and I won't let this team down. They deserve the best, and that's what they'll get.

Twenty minutes pass before I get back to my locker. When I see the message from Chrissy, I have to stop myself from running out of the room, down the hall, and outside the stadium. Keeping my cool, I stroll outside and shove my hands in my pockets, but I stop when my phone begins to vibrate. I take it out, and a surge of excitement flutters in my chest. I find a secluded part of the hall and answer it.

"Hey, Dad," I say as I answer the phone.

"Before we go any further, I have to say this—"

The eagerness that brewed in my chest melts into little anxious butterflies. A shaky breath escapes me as I wait for what's to follow.

"I'm so proud of you, son."

My shoulders drop, and a relieved chuckle escapes my lips, leaving me smiling like a kid.

"I watched the entire game. You owned that field, Rome."

"Thanks, Dad." I press my palm into my eye to stop the tears from forming. "They made me captain."

"Are you serious? Holy shit!" The pride in his voice is evident, and no matter how hard I try to stop them, the tears break free.

"You're the first person I told," I choke out.

"Well, I'm deeply honored. You deserve it, son. You deserve a lot more than I ever provided you." His voice cracks. "Listen, I found a job that provides good health insurance. I'm finally getting the care I need."

"That's great."

"Care that you said time and time again I needed to get. You were always there, even when you shouldn't have been. You know me, I hate talking about my feelings, but this is important. I was wrong to fault you for what happened. It's not your fault she left."

It's not your fault she left.

Tears stream down my face, and I'm left trying to control them so I'm not a blubbering mess in the middle of the hall. For so long, I've waited for something, *anything*, to provide closure on that chapter of my life, and Dad just gave it to me.

"We'll never know why she did it, but I'm tired of dwelling in the past."

"Me too," I say before I sniffle.

"I want to be there for you, Rome. I want to make up for all the time we lost while I was stuck in my head. It was wrong of me to place it all on you. You were just a kid."

"It's okay—"

"I'm not asking for forgiveness. This is something I have to prove to you, and I want to start by being there for you. But only if you want me to be."

"I do. I *really* do."

"Thank you. I'll make you proud. I promise. Now, get out there and celebrate your win. I love you, son."

"I love you too, Dad."

I took a moment to compose myself and dry my tears before peeling myself off the wall.

Finding the crew is easy because not only are they loud, they stand out among the lingering fans because they're my family. I could spot them from miles away if I had to.

I take a few steps forward, and Chrissy lifts her head, meeting my gaze. Not wasting a moment, she leaps off the ledge she was sitting on and runs toward me. I remove my hands from my pockets before she crashes into my chest, jumping into my arms and embracing me with all her strength.

"There's my girl," I mumble.

She nuzzles into my neck. I close my eyes and breathe in her delicious scent. After a few kisses against my throat that leave my stomach in butterflies, she pulls back and smiles warmly.

"What's wrong?" she asks while trailing her fingertips under my eyes.

"I'll tell you later. For now, want to hear some good news?" I ask as I admire her expression.

"Spill it." She snickers and leans in closer.

I lean in also, pretending like this is a big secret. "You're looking at the new captain of the Castle Brook football team."

"Fucking finally!" she squeals and goes back to hugging me, almost squeezing the life out of me. "I'm so proud of you," she whispers in my ear before kissing my cheek. "So, so proud of you."

That's really all I've ever wanted. I wanted Chrissy for so long. For months, the thought of having someone like her was merely a dream. I didn't think I was worthy, but she helped rewire my brain and showed me the truth.

I squeeze her back, hoping she knows just how important she is to me.

"Are you going to hog him all night?" Max whines from somewhere nearby.

I open my eyes and smile when I find our little family approaching us. Gwen has her hands clasped, and she's jumping up and down, clearly trying to contain herself. Ash and Zack just smile at me. I'm surprised to see Max. I knew the others were coming, but I thought Max had to work.

"Good to see you, Lawyer Man," I say.

"Dude, you were amazing! Mom and Dad won't stop blowing up my phone. They wanted me to tell you that you're pro material. They can't wait to meet you tomorrow," Zack tells me.

"I appreciate that, and I look forward to meeting them."

"Chrissy, you have to share Rome," Max says before smirking.

"No, I don't! He's *my* boyfriend."

I chuckle as she clings to me, balling my jersey in her hand.

"He eats *my* yogurt!"

"Slander!" Chrissy defends.

"You two are ridiculous," I laugh before setting Chrissy down on her feet.

"Fine, I'll share him . . . for now." Chrissy leans into me and gently pulls on my lower lip with her mouth, hinting I need to bring her somewhere secluded ASAP.

Max is the first to pull me into a congratulatory hug, followed by an eager Gwen, Ash, and Zack. I let them know that I'm the new captain, and Gwen hugs me like I suspect a mother might.

"He's allowed to eat all the yogurt he wants, you hear me, Max?"

"Yes, Mom," Max sighs while playfully rolling his eyes.

Chrissy tugs on my arm, signaling it's time to go. I'm about to find an excuse to leave, but a familiar voice interrupts me.

"There he is! Plus my two favorite girls," Raina calls out as she nears us. "Rome, you kicked ass, per usual."

I smile at her as Chrissy leans against my arm.

"Hey, girly, how are you managing this semester so far?" Chrissy asks.

"So far so good. You know Professor Clastis." she laughs.

"Loves piling on the work the moment we walk through the door." Chrissy chuckles.

"Hi, Gwen!" Raina waves at Gwen, and I catch the moment Raina's eyes land on someone else.

Peeking over my shoulder, I spot who she's looking at, and I don't stop the grin from spreading across my lips.

I don't know Raina as well as Chrissy knows her. We had a few sessions together, but she was only ever professional. But from what Chrissy tells me, Raina is like an extroverted version of Gwen, but throw in some sass and spice. When I look at her, I see the perfect mixture of Chrissy and Gwen. So I hold in my laugh when Zack catches her gaze.

Raina raises her hand and waves at the group, but mainly at Zack. "Hey, everyone, I'm Raina Bennett."

Zack doesn't respond, his eyes focusing as he takes her in.

A smirk forms across my lips because I'm sure I had the same look on my face when I first truly noticed Chrissy.

Chapter Fifty-Four

Chrissy

I'm a ball of raging hormones. Thankfully, I'm on birth control because I would let this man get me pregnant tonight. I tuned out when Raina appeared. Everyone was introduced, but not too long after, we all went our separate ways. With Rome's hand in mine, we walk toward his car in silence. I just need to hold it in until we get to his room. I can do that. I'm a big girl.

"Ready to go home, sunshine?" he asks with a grin.

And I internally combust.

"Mm-hmm," I hum through my closed lips.

"What's wrong? Cat got your tongue?" He unlocks his car, opening the passenger side door for me.

I attempt to take my seat, but he wraps his arm around my waist, and I stop in my tracks.

"Talk to me, Wildflower." His voice is low and demanding.

It sends shivers along my spine.

"We need to get home," I whisper while I look up at him.

"Why?" he teases.

"You know why."

"I want you to say it." He takes a step closer, pressing the backs of my legs against the car.

"I need you to fuck me."

With a low chuckle, he releases his grip, and his smile turns mischievous. "Well then, let's go."

He can't get the keys in the lock fast enough. My hands are roaming underneath his jersey. My palms meet his sculpted abs, and warmth floods my clit as my hands dip down to untie the knot on his sweatpants' drawstring.

With a click, he twists the doorknob, and it opens. Before I can react, he spins around to scoop me in his arms. Our lips meet, and he carries me inside. My back meets the door as my feet are set back on the ground, and he locks the door without breaking contact.

A low growl leaves his mouth as he squeezes my ass, urging me forward. We stumble through the living room, walking to his room.

The way Rome kisses me tells me how much he loves me. Not only does he have my heart, but I have his. His touch reminds me that I'm beautiful and that he cherishes every inch of my body. My self-esteem has grown since he entered my life.

I'm no longer constantly fussing over my hair or makeup. Rome doesn't care if I wake up looking like I surfed through a tornado. He only cares that I'm there with him, and that fact is helping me realize that the love I've been looking for is right in front of me.

I trip over something on the ground, and I start to fall back. But Rome is quick to catch me by tightening his grip around my arms.

"What the—"

Korra meows and bats at my ankles, reminding me that Rome has a companion in his home who thinks she's a princess.

"Sorry, she's been sleeping in the middle of the hallway recently," Rome chuckles.

"Because the five beds you bought her weren't enough?" I sass.

"Are you jealous?" he asks with a cocky look on his face.

Korra throws herself at his legs before walking into the kitchen, presumably to eat.

"No."

"Don't lie to me," he whispers and takes a step forward, making me take a step back.

"I'm not jealous of your cat," I chuckle, but I might be a teensy bit jealous.

"That's okay. I'll remind you why you're my number one girl."

Rome picks me up, and I squeal in response. We barrel into his room, and he closes the door so a certain white cat doesn't interrupt us.

I part his lips with my tongue, and I moan when his tongue meets mine. Rome grunts, and before I can register where I am, he drops me on his bed.

"Ahh!" I scream and giggle as he settles between my legs.

"You're so fucking gorgeous," he murmurs against my lips, toying with them.

I tug on the collar of his jersey, more than ready to throw it across the room so I can feel him against me.

"As much as I enjoy seeing you in your gear, you look better without it on," I say before leaning up to tug his lower lip into my mouth, gently sucking on it.

"You look way too good in my jersey," he chuckles. "But I'd have to agree."

He plants his knees on the bed, resting on either side of my body. Crisscrossing his arms, he removes his jersey, and my clit throbs as I watch him. His core is tight and layered with muscles. Moving my gaze down, I sigh in pleasure at the sight of the deep V before his groin.

I push myself off the bed and kiss his chest, sucking just enough to leave marks on his skin. With rasps and moans of his own, Rome pushes me back on the bed and smiles down at me while working the jersey I'm wearing over my body.

"Let's make this fair, shall we?"

I lift myself so he can take off my shirt. He throws it across the room, leaving me in just my black bra and jeans. My breathing falters when his eyes travel down my body. He feathers his thumb over my lower stomach and unbuttons my pants, revealing the hem of my matching black underwear.

He looks back up at me, and I smile softly. My back arches off the bed while he pulls my pants off. Standing in front of me, he removes his sweats and boxers slowly, like he knows I'm watching him strip.

"Take those off," he orders while nodding toward my underwear.

Securing my fingers on the edge of my panties, I tug them down and let them drop to the floor.

Chapter Fifty-Four

"That too." He nods at my bra, and I'm quick to free my breasts.

I lie before him naked, my chest heaving, waiting for Rome to make the first move.

"Open your legs." His green eyes light up as he throws commands at me.

I allow my legs to drop to the sides, revealing myself to him. Rome smiles and licks his lips before looking at me.

"Do I get to see this after every game?"

"Only if you win," I say with a mischievous grin.

"And what if I lose?" he asks while tugging on my ankle, bringing me closer to the edge of the bed.

"You'll get special treatment."

Rome hums as his lips meet the inside of my right thigh.

"Better than this?" he asks as his lips travel closer to my core.

"Possibly," I say breathlessly.

"Hmm, sounds tempting . . ."

"Don't lose just to find out— oh fuck!" I cry out.

He devours me with his mouth, and the sensation of his tongue licking my pussy forces me to move closer to him. Rome chuckles in response, the vibrations traveling through my body.

"I fucking love how your body reacts to me," he whispers against me with a dark smile.

Chills and goose bumps envelop me as he runs his tongue over my skin, kissing and sucking on my clit at random intervals. I ball his sheets in my fists as he brings me closer and closer to climax.

"Fuck, that's so good," I moan.

He increases his pace; the lapping of his tongue is like music to my ears. My back arches off the bed, and I shudder when his finger plays with my entrance.

"Rome, I'm going to come," I warn him.

He grunts and shoves his face closer, shaking his head before whispering, "Not yet."

I groan in frustration when he slows his pace. His tongue is still over me, but it's not moving. With a final kiss, Rome pulls away and starts to stroke himself.

"This is what you want?" he asks with a moan.

"Please."

He continues to touch himself, firming his erection. "Prove it to me," he says while biting his lower lip.

I'm quick to respond, earning a deep chuckle from him. I settle on my stomach, arching my back with a knowing smirk on my face. My hand replaces his, stroking him before kissing the tip of his cock.

"Mmm." A moan leaves my lips when I taste his pre-cum.

"Like that baby?" He uses his hand to form a makeshift updo with my hair, giving him a clear view to watch me work his cock in my mouth.

I look up at him and nod before wrapping my mouth around his tip, kissing and moaning.

"Fuck, yes. That's so good."

The last time I did this was in the dark. I wonder if he's enjoying the change of scenery right now. I move farther down, taking more of him in my mouth. When I reach the halfway point, I close my mouth and pull back while sucking.

Rome curses and tightens his hand in my hair, gently tugging. "That's my good girl."

I work my way back down his length, but stop before I gag. When I move back, Rome grunts and tries to bring me back. I stop at the tip, sucking and running my tongue around it.

"I can't take it anymore." He pushes me back on the bed and places himself between my legs again.

Clashing his lips against mine in a searing kiss, he presses his cock against my pussy and stretches his way inside me.

I gasp and dig my fingernails into his back while he settles inside me. My walls contract around him, hugging his girth and accepting his length. His balls are against my ass cheeks, adding to the sensations while he thrusts in and out of me.

"Rome!"

He buries his head in the crook of my neck and nibbles my earlobe while he loses control.

"I fucking love you. You know that, right?" he whispers in my ear.

I nod while the tension in my lower stomach builds. "Yes," I rasp. "I love you too."

With a deep grunt, Rome rams inside me, hitting my G-spot. Stars fill my eyes, and heat rushes over my body. My legs start to spasm because he doesn't stop.

"Oh my god, Rome!"

With my exclamation, he presses and holds himself against me, and I come around him. My joints turn into jelly, and my vision blurs and hazes. I move my hips against him as I ride out my orgasm. I'm gasping for air when the feeling subsides.

Rome starts to resume his motions, but when he mutters a curse against my ear, his cock flexes inside me, filling me with his cum.

"Fuck me," he moans while working on catching his breath. "I'll never get tired of that," he admits while falling onto his back beside me.

I chuckle and look over at him. "Me either."

We stare at one another, nothing but love and admiration filling our gaze. I reach out and brush a stray hair from his forehead. My finger lingers over him for a moment, remembering the time I used to crave this motion.

"It's you, Rome," I whisper so quietly I wonder if he can hear me.

"What's me?" he asks with a soft smile.

All this time, I've been searching for this feeling that hugs my heart. Not once did I think I would find a love such as this. Why would I be worthy of a love that transcends the stars? Why would I be worthy of a soulmate? Looking at Rome, the answer is simple. I'm worthy because we're all worthy. Everyone deserves love, even douchebags like Malik Chen. Love is precious, and the universe is the only being that knows when you're ready for it.

"I thought I was cursed before you. I was searching for this feeling." I place my hand over my heart. "You make me feel so many things. Some feelings I didn't think I deserved. But you . . . you showed me I do deserve them. You're the love I've been looking for." Tears fill my eyes at the admission.

Rome looks at me, and I mean, really looks at me. He inches closer, brushing his thumb over my tears to wipe them away.

"You always saw something inside me, back to our first conversation in the library. You saw me, every ounce of darkness. You didn't run when it came to light. You faced it, and you helped me accept it. I'm working on being a better person for myself, thanks to you. You showed me what it feels like to be loved, to not be alone. You're my wildflower, my sunshine, and I can't live without you." His eyes fill with tears, and I smile at him before placing a soft kiss on his lips.

He wraps his arms around me and holds me close. This is one of those moments that will live in our memories. We'll think back to the day we lay in his bed after he won the first game of his senior year, how we made love and cuddled one another. I'll remember the moment I came to the realization that I'm more than I think I am. And I'll definitely remember the moment when I realized I wasn't doomed to be cursed forever.

We have two more semesters before we graduate, many

more games, and the draft that will determine his future. But together, we can get through anything. We've proven that to ourselves over these last few months.

When Rome looks at me, we smile at one another, the love pooling from our expressions. I've only ever wanted this. I was a fool to try to ignore it at first.

"Promise me something?" he breaks the silence.

I raise my eyebrow in response.

"Will you wear my hoodie until we're old and gray?"

I chuckle and smile as widely as I can. "Far longer than that, my love. Far longer than that."

Epilogue Part One

Rome

Three Months Later

Sweat beads across my forehead. We're racing against the clock. With the ball in our hands, we have ten more yards to go. If we get this touchdown, we win the game, and we'll make it into the Division Championship.

Everyone is in the stands today. Not just the usual suspects, but my father and Chrissy's parents. Eyes are on Levi Faulkner, who has taken the field for more than half the games because Malik was being a prick. Levi's name is often chanted in the stands. He's making a name for himself, which doesn't happen often in someone's first year.

Numbers start to be thrown out, and I smile to myself at the play he has in mind. It's one of my own, and if we get it right, red and black confetti will rain on the field. The December air bites at my face, my breath visible as time seems to slow.

Snow starts to flurry from the sky, and the ground beneath my feet has begun to freeze. My breathing becomes the only sound in my ears. Glancing over at Levi, the ball is thrown, and I burst into action.

Our defense is tight; they manage to keep the Northland Jaguars off me.

They close in on Levi, and I curse under my breath when he throws the ball toward the end zone. I'm nowhere near where I need to be. With a leap of faith, I launch myself in the air and reach for the ball, hoping it lands in my chest.

When I land, the clock runs out. It's only when the announcer's voice blares overhead that I realize what happened.

"The Castle Brook Dragons have scored! Number 35, Carter, has secured the game!"

Black and red strips of paper fly in the air, mixing in with the snow flurries. My head collapses against the ground as I cradle the ball, savoring this moment.

"Let's go!" my teammates shout as they hoist me up.

When I'm on my feet, I hold the ball in the air, and the crowd goes wild. Blake charges at me, crashing into my chest and pulling me into a hug while patting my back.

"You fucking son of a bitch! We're going to the championship!" he shouts over the cheering crowd.

Levi removes his helmet and jogs toward us.

"Faulkner, get your ass over here!" I say with a broad smile.

His dimples pop on his cheeks, and sweat shines on his complexion. I toss my helmet on the ground and pull him into me. I don't care that the cameras are on us. I pat his back repeatedly and smile at him.

"I told you. I fucking told you that you could do it!"

He pats my back in return and nods. "Thank you."

We pull away, and I hold his face before slapping his cheek. "Go find your mom."

With a sniffle, he heads into the crowd to search for his

parents. Blake and Ryan find one another, and I grin when the camera zooms in on them kissing.

"Carter!" a reporter calls for me.

I don't see my girl yet, so I decide to give the media the attention they're always craving.

"How does it feel to win the playoff game and to make it into the championships?" she asks while holding the mic out for me.

"It's beyond exhilarating. I've been working toward this moment for three years. I'm really proud of this team."

"Was it a shock when Coach Bradson made you captain?"

I chuckle at the question. "Yes and no. It feels great he trusts me to carry this team. It's more than an honor. I can't wait to bring us further and see where the rest of the season takes us."

Wild blonde curls appear in the corner of my eye. The reporter tries to ask another question, but I politely cut her off. "Please excuse me. I'm going to go celebrate with my girl."

With a kind smile, she nods, and I turn away to face the girl who outshines the lights in the stadium.

We start toward one another. She gains momentum and crashes into my arms. I swing her around, and her feet lift in the air, causing her to giggle.

"You did it!" she cheers.

Placing her back on the ground, I kiss her. The flurries melt against my cheeks, and a few pieces of confetti land in her hair.

"There he is!" My dad's voice cuts through the crowd.

Chrissy steps back and lets my dad give me a firm hug. He slaps my back, his black and gray stubble grazing against my cheek.

"I'm so proud of you," he whispers, emotion cracking his voice.

I fight my own tears when he pulls back. Nothing but pride settles on his face, shining in his eyes.

Behind him, Gwen, Ash, Max, Zack, Faye, and Ethan Willows smile at me. A rush of belonging surges through me. Chrissy wraps her hand around mine and places a kiss on my cheek.

I don't need my mom here. Even if she came back, I'm not sure I would want her in my life. These are the people I want to surround myself with. Even though we're chaotic and messy, we're a family.

And this is my home.

Epilogue Part Two
Chrissy

Standing on the field, watching the red and black confetti rain down on us along with the snow, I don't feel cold. All the warmth I need is radiating from Rome's smile. I watch as he observes our little family, his eyes sparkling when they land back on me.

Rome met my parents back in August, and it was perfect. Dad puts me in for the running as Rome's biggest fan. Rome's dad is exactly as I pictured he would be, maybe more loving than Rome described. The way he looks at his son makes my heart sing. Rome doesn't have his mom, but he has a dad who loves and adores him with every fiber of his being. All Rome wants to do is provide for his dad, and ease his aching bones. I'm glad he was able to afford to take time off work to come here.

"So, can I say 'I told you so' yet?" Gwen asks while nudging my arm.

"What do you mean?" I ask without looking away from a beaming Rome.

"I told you time and time again that Rome was more than

you wanted him to be. It's written all over your face." She squeezes my cheeks like Mom would, and I laugh.

"Yeah, yeah, you were right, okay?"

"Thank you very much. Remember me when you become a rich football player's wife. Don't go replacing me," she teases.

"Please, I wouldn't dream of it."

Ash steps up and props his elbow on Gwen's head, making her chuckle.

"Cough it up, girly." He holds out his hand.

"What do you want?" I ask with a playful eye roll.

"You owe me five bucks," he tells me.

"Since when?"

"Since that bet we made in my bedroom. Remember?"

"We never made a bet," I say with a smile.

"It was an implied bet. I told you that you two would end up together. Look at you now."

Rome pulls me into his chest, placing a kiss on the top of my head.

"Make him pay, he'll be making the big bucks soon." I direct Ash toward Rome, who only smiles in response.

"If he's paying up, he owes me buckets of that damn yogurt!" Max cuts in, and we all laugh.

"Who knew being in this family was so damn expensive," Rome remarks with an amused expression.

"I'll chip in as well. Now that I know what I want to do after I graduate."

"You made a decision?" Rome asks while looking down at me.

"I have, and I have you to thank for it."

I always wanted to help people, but I didn't know who or where I would do that. After working with Rome, I know for certain that I don't want to work with football players. My direction in life is leading me elsewhere.

"I'm going to work with teenagers and young adults. Those with self-image issues. I can relate to them, and I think I can make a positive impact."

Rome cups my face and rests his forehead against mine. With a loving smile, he says, "No matter where you go, your light will shine. You make a positive impact everywhere you go. Never forget that, Wildflower."

Without another thought, I kiss him, pouring my love and passion for him into my touch. He picks me up and spins me around. I chuckle, and we both smile against one another's lips. The confetti stops raining down onto the field, but the snow doesn't stop.

Rome and I hold each other's gaze, and as if the universe wanted to prove me wrong again, Rome asks me something that leaves me speechless.

"After we graduate, and if I get drafted by the Philadelphia Eagles, will you come with me? You, me, and Korra. Maybe the others will follow. We'll be closer to our parents, and we'll be together. What do you think?"

Butterflies swirl in my stomach. If I was trying to play it cool, well, let's just say there's a reason I don't play poker.

"Seriously?" I ask with the biggest smile I've ever had spread across my face.

"Yes—"

"Yes! A thousand times, yes!" I kiss him repeatedly, laughing when I feel his own smile against my lips.

I don't know where the future will take us. The others may not follow, but I know we won't drift apart. One thing is for sure, though, Rome and I will be together.

In the end, that's all I've ever wanted.

Zack

One Week After The Game

I tend to find myself in places where there are unique cats. For example, Pickles nearly chewed my finger off in the cat café, and now he lives at the Waylens' house. We tolerate one another. He no longer barrels toward me when I walk through their front door, which is a plus.

Korra is different; she's super affectionate. Rome and Ash are playing video games, and I'm patiently waiting to play against the winner. The second I sat down, Rome's cat jumped next to me and cuddled on my lap. I wouldn't say I'm a cat person, but she just won my heart.

"Dinner will be ready in five!" Gwen calls from the kitchen.

The aroma of her famous homemade baked ziti wafts through Rome's apartment, and my stomach growls in response.

"Zack, can you do me a favor?" my sister asks from the kitchen.

"What's up!" I shout back.

A knock sounds from the front door, but the guys don't seem to care.

"Can you get that, please?" Chrissy asks.

"I can't. Korra has claimed my lap, and therefore, I have cat paralysis."

"There's no such thing," she fires back.

"No, he's right. Cat paralysis is real," Rome chimes in, not removing his attention from the TV screen.

The knock sounds again, and my sister sighs and mumbles something about men being a pain in her ass.

"Sorry, apparently the guys lost the ability in their legs." Chrissy greets the person on the other side of the door.

With a small chuckle, my attention is pulled toward where my sister and her friend now stand.

Raina Bennett.

I first saw her outside the stadium. Her smile caught my attention, and then it moved to her hazel eyes and long dark hair. She's been hanging around Chrissy and Gwen more often, but I haven't seen her since the playoff game.

She looks over at me, pursing her lips in amusement.

"Cat paralysis?" she asks.

"Told you it was real," I tease my sister, who rolls her eyes at me.

"Gwen and I are almost done. You can hang out with us or—"

"Are you guys playing that new zombie game?" Raina asks, cutting my sister off.

With a lopsided grin, Chrissy shrugs her shoulders and heads back into the kitchen.

"Want to play a round? I'm about to kick Ash's ass." Rome chuckles, nudging his shoulder.

"Shush, I'm focusing . . . fuck!"

"Gwen's a much better teammate," Rome laughs before offering her the controller.

Ash stands when she takes it, dropping the other remote beside me.

Raina and I look at one another. My heart flutters when she grins, and my palms start to sweat when I pick up the controller.

"Want to be my player one?" I ask her.

She walks over to me and takes a seat. Our knees brush, and I gulp in response.

"I would love to."

Afterword

Thank you for reading Forever Cursed. I hope you enjoyed hanging out with the Forever crew as much as I enjoyed writing this story.

I didn't realize how much I missed this little family until I wrote Chrissy's first chapter. To me, these characters aren't a figment of my imagination. They are real and control their own stories. Does that make me crazy? At this point... I accept it.

Chrissy and Rome both have their struggles in this book, and that's what makes me more real to me. Like everyone else, Chrissy has self-image issues. It gets to her head sometimes, but she doesn't let it hold her back.

And Rome, can I dub him book boyfriend of the summer? I struggled with his story at first, but once he was ready to tell it, I simply relayed it on paper. Burnout is real, and it affects everyone differently. Make sure you take time for yourself.

You are worth it.

Acknowledgments

I wouldn't be doing this without my husband, Anthony. You never cease to amaze me with your support. Thank you for being patient with me, especially when my imposter gremlin rears its head.

A big thank you to my Alpha/Beta/ARC team. I owe the development of this story to you. Your support and excitement means the world to me.

My Distracted Inkings, I'm beyond proud to be part of this community, and I cannot wait for our future.

The ladies of the Writer's Guild, I would be lost without our friendship. Thank you for being amazing.

And last but certainly not least, my readers. Where do I even begin? When I started writing, I didn't expect to garner a following, but here we are. Thank you for giving me a chance, and I hope you enjoy the stories that are in my head.

About the Author

Amber Paige is an indie author focusing on fluffy, HEA's, and spicy novels. She's a big mood reader and writer, but once something captures her attention, she hyper-focuses on it. She mainly writes fiction, romance, and fantasy but isn't afraid to drive into another genre if it calls to her. She writes from her laptop, either in bed or on the couch, with a cat by her side. When she's not overanalyzing commas or letting her imposter syndrome get the best of her, you can find her playing video games, watching too much TV, reading, writing, or hanging out with her husband and three cats.

Official Website

The Forever Series

Stay tuned for Zack's book in the winter of 2025, and the series' conclusion in 2026. The final book will look into the crew's future and lives. I can't wait to write their stories and share them with everyone!

Also by Amber Paige

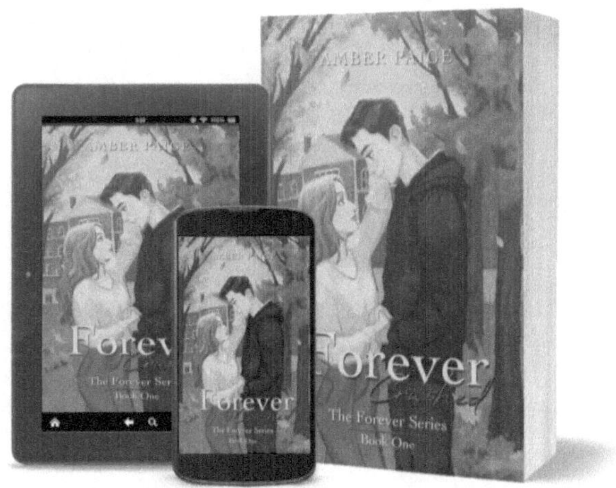

Long- term crushes are hard...

Gwen Roman has spent most of her life being overlooked. It never really bothered her all that much. Until she sees Ash Waylen, the guy she's had a crush on since the tenth grade. The moment he acknowledges her presence and says her name, that damn crush weaves its way back into her heart. So much for a stellar GPA this semester.

After his girlfriend shattered his trust and broke his heart, Ash Waylen plans to spend his junior year of college nursing his wounds and avoiding the opposite sex. The last thing he expects is to run into Gwen Roman and have her tugging on heartstrings he thought his ex-girlfriend took when he broke up with her.

Gwen was always the shy girl who followed Chrissy and Zack Willows around in high school, her head always buried in a book. She never caught his attention before, but this time, it's different.

In an act of self-preservation, Ash averts his gaze knowing only trouble will follow him if he pursues the one thing he wants.

While Ash tries to resist temptation, Gwen might just throw caution to the wind and go after what she wants for the first time in her life.

Also by Amber Paige

Perfection is key.

That's how Ayra Brightheart made it to Fraydora Academy. It didn't matter that her parents left her at the academy's doorstep when she was a baby; she had to earn her way in. Years of studying, late nights, taunting from her classmates, memorizing spells and recipes secured her spot.

And now, her final test awaits.

Every year, Fraydora Academy for Witches competes against Traquore Academy for Wizards in a series of games. Whoever wins earns themselves and their school high prestige.

Ayra has worked tirelessly throughout her years at Fraydora for a chance to participate in the games, and when she finds out she made the cut, she's ready to win, but the last person she expected to meet was Ryne Gwydion.

Ryne is a carefree, fun seeking, kindhearted ray of sunshine. He's the kind of wizard she should stay away from because he could derail her end goal, but the games have a different plan in mind.

The council is ready for the realm to change. They're tired of the growing tension between witches and wizards, so they take matters into their own hands. Changing the games— and this pair— entirely.

Let the games begin.